DOMINOES

Dominoes

PHOEBE McINTOSH

Chatto & Windus
LONDON

1 3 5 7 9 10 8 6 4 2

Chatto & Windus, an imprint of Vintage, is part of the Penguin Random House group of companies whose addresses can be found at global.penguinrandomhouse.com

Penguin
Random House
UK

First published by Chatto & Windus in 2024

penguin.co.uk/vintage

Typeset in 13.5/16pt Garamond MT Std by Jouve (UK), Milton Keynes
Printed and bound in Great Britain by Clays Ltd, Elcograf S.p.A.

The authorised representative in the EEA is Penguin Random House Ireland,
Morrison Chambers, 32 Nassau Street, Dublin D02 YH68

A CIP catalogue record for this book is available from the British Library

HB ISBN 9781784744892
TPB ISBN 9781784744908

Penguin Random House is committed to a sustainable future
for our business, our readers and our planet. This book is made
from Forest Stewardship Council® certified paper.

MIX
Paper | Supporting
responsible forestry
FSC® C018179

For Etta

It was a crisp evening in Angel. The kind where the sky is that deep, dark blue, clear and limitless. The kind you never get. The kind where anything is possible.

From the doorstep of the Regency town house, we could hear the party already in full force. I let Sera ring the bell. I stood with my arms folded, giving her a look out of the corner of my eye. It was yet another way for me to show her that I didn't want to be there, that I wished I'd gone straight home after work.

'Half an hour, tops, then I'm out,' I said.

Through the living-room window, I caught snippets of chatter and wondered if I could make it home in time to order sushi from the new place I'd found. That, and only that, would redeem the night.

'Twenty minutes,' Sera promised me. She was lying, which she knew I knew. She also knew I wasn't in the mood to pass the time with a group of strangers whose default topic of conversation would be either work or how they spent their time when not at work in order to forget about work. She knew because I'd told her three times: once in the staffroom when she'd asked me to go with her in the first place, again in a voice message, and for a third time on the way there.

'Watch me though. Twenty minutes gonna be too much for dese people!' She spoke in the voice we both had a habit of slipping back into when it was just the two of us. The one we'd used during our rude-girl phase as fourteen-year-olds. Sera began to dance to the beat, winding her waist like she wasn't really on a doorstep in the middle of a residential street at all but on a stage being watched by adoring fans, proving to me she was in the mood and there was nothing anyone could do about it. She stopped abruptly when the door was answered by a random reveller who let us in without bothering to ask who we were. Sera kissed her teeth and closed the door behind us, muttering that this was London and people shouldn't just be letting anyone and everyone in like that. As soon as we were inside, I could see her pulling a large bottle of rum out of her tiny bag like she was Mary Poppins. Then she morphed seamlessly into her alter ego, Rum-Punch-Stiltskin, a name I'd christened her with in a haze of daiquiris, Jean Harlows and mojitos on our graduation trip to Ibiza where I'd spent most of the week trying to forget that I'd only managed to achieve a 2:1 while Sera had got a first.

Turning round to look at me from the end of the corridor in that cavernous house, she gave me the same mischievous lip curl she'd been giving me since we were kids, and hollered, 'You know you love me, Lay Lay!' before being sucked into the vortex of a party she never had any intention of leaving. *Fuck*, I thought, wondering how many people were staring at me at that exact moment, on my lonesome. I seriously considered heading straight back out through the front door leaving Sera to it. I could probably even get away with blaming it on Leon breaking things off with me abruptly three days ago, despite, in truth, not being that bothered. After six dates and zero sexual chemistry, plus quite a lot of thought on my part about the many changes I'd make to his personality, whatever we were doing had barely got off the ground.

I scanned the rooms leading off the hallway trying to decide where to hide and scroll. I chose to bypass the living room full of people shouting into each other's faces over the playlist and opted for the more sedate open-plan kitchen with its expensive-looking bifold doors leading out into a garden featuring strung lights with exposed elements, a fire pit, an underwhelming water feature and a willow tree, wondering who in the hell could afford a house share as swanky as this one.

I made myself a drink, purposefully ignoring house-party etiquette by finishing off the Bombay Sapphire and claiming the last remaining chilled can of Fever Tree tonic without replacing them with anything because I'd arrived empty-handed. I inspected the nibbles on offer but then remembered to save room for my late-night sushi feast which I intended to eat in my kimono in front of *Valeria*, the Spanish version of *Sex and the City* I'd discovered on Netflix. I felt almost nauseous knowing there were unseen episodes I could be watching and maki rolls I could be eating, instead of standing on my own in a stranger's kitchen trying not to catch other strangers' eyes and thinking about how I could begin reclaiming my time as soon as humanly possible.

I nestled my lower back against the edge of the island. No sooner had I positioned myself with just the right amount of nonchalance in the angle of my lean, my elbow both propping me up and facilitating my browse, than I was interrupted. He was someone I'd describe with a phrase I reserve for only exceptional-looking individuals and use indiscriminately for men and women: he was quite, quite beautiful. Obviously tipsy but no less attractive for it. There was something stylish about him too. Not smart or particularly well groomed – but there was an effortlessness about the way he looked, the way he carried himself, that struck me as the epitome of good styling in a man. He wore a striped crew-neck jumper which he'd ruched up at the sleeves to reveal toned forearms, a Casio watch circa 1987 and a freckle on his left wrist. He was only a few inches taller than me – I'd put him at about five eight. The care and attention he'd paid to his clothes hadn't quite made it down to his feet. His Diadora trainers were so battered it looked like he'd lived in them for years. His hair was mousy brown, longish on top, shorter on the sides, but not so short that I couldn't make out a few silvery tones beginning to creep through before their time.

He asked me if I minded. I didn't know what he meant at first but then he pointed to a bottle of Grey Goose like it was mine so I shrugged and told him to go ahead. I could feel him looking at me as he chose a mixer, as he poured them one by one and replaced the caps on both bottles. And I could still feel his gaze – not creepy, just noticeable – after someone else at the party, who clearly wanted him to join her out in the garden for a cigarette, had come and gone, giving up on him and leaving him there staring at me staring at my phone. I took a sip from my emptying glass. He raised his in my direction, performing a sort of air toast which felt old-fashioned and an inappropriate thing to do at that kind of gathering, so far from a bar or dining table.

'Courtesy of the birthday girl,' he said. 'Cheers.'

'Yeah. To What's-Her-Name.' I mimicked his extended arm, miming the toast and stopping short of any meeting of actual glassware. I noticed him smirking but assumed it had nothing to do with me.

'What's-Her-Name,' he agreed.

We stood in silence playing footsie with our eyes for a few moments then I reached for my phone again. But before I could load BBC News, he asked, 'What's yours?'

'My drink?'

'Your name.'

I chose to reveal no more than the first syllable, telling him, 'Lay. Yeah, Lay's fine,' thinking that it would send the message that I wasn't really in the mood for making small talk, even if he was fit AF.

'Fine if it's your name, yeah,' he said, and I instantly felt stupid for not just saying *Layla. My name is Layla. Like the song.* So, while I tried to think of a way to rectify the situation, I smiled a smile I saw go right through him, as though it were a bright light hitting his retina at the optician's.

'Well, if you must know, my name is Layla McKinnon.' And then I waited. Half wondering if he'd be impressed when really I just sounded like I was at school calling the register.

'Really? That's my name.'

'Layla? Fuck off.'

'No. I'm obviously not called Layla. I meant McKinnon. I'm Andy. McKinnon.'

I suddenly felt the innermost part of my left ear begin to tingle, a sensation which spread along my jawline and into my lips. I didn't know what it meant but hoped it wasn't the warning signs I used to get before a migraine.

Part of me wanted to tell him to fuck off again. It would have been easy enough to have pretended to need the loo, to have walked off, leaving him standing there, to have forgotten about him and the encounter altogether. It'd just be one of the weird things that happened at a party I could barely remember. But at the same time, I felt temporarily immobilised. As though what was happening between us was a marker of some kind, something I might look back on and recognise as a moment of change. An awkward silence began to creep in and the only way I could think to put a stop to it was to knock back the rest of my drink and tell him I needed to look for my friend, the one I'd arrived with, who was the person who actually knew someone who knew What's-Her-Name, as she'd probably be wondering where I was, even though she'd abandoned me at the door and was dead to me.

'Stay for another drink,' he said.

'I think you've had enough,' I shot back without missing a beat.

6

He laughed and put down his glass. 'C'mon,' he pleaded. 'We can compare family trees. Make sure we're not long-lost cousins or anything.'

'You say that like it would be a bad thing.'

'It would be. Devastating.'

'Devastating? Really?'

Running the tip of my tongue along the bottom of my teeth, I felt the left corner of my mouth rise. This felt like a flirty thing to do, so I held it there for a moment before adding, 'How do you know I'm not here with my boyfriend?'

'Are you?' he said, calling my bluff.

'No.'

'Have you got one? Husband?'

'Straight to the point then.'

'Well, I haven't. A wife, I mean. Or girlfriend. Dog. Anything.'

'That's good. I'm not into animals.' It wasn't true but I wanted to fill the space with something before putting him out of his misery. 'I'm not currently in a relationship, no. There.'

He looked at me as if I'd just handed him a gift of some kind, as though I had made his week or possibly his year. And that look, despite the attraction of getting back to the sex lives of Valeria and the other Madrileñas, was enough to make me want to stay. I decided to let him succeed in his mission to make everything I said a conversation starter until I couldn't remember how long it had been since I last checked my phone and I'd used up all the spirits around us by making cocktails ranging from the extraordinary to the disgusting. I spotted Sera some time later, over Andy's shoulder, at the centre of a conversation with people I didn't recognise. I couldn't hear what she was saying but I knew it would probably be related to one of three topics: her recent obsession with the FIRE movement (and what she'd do if she could retire in ten years' time at the age of forty), American politics, or her new guilty pleasure Netflix binge, *Love Is Blind.* I turned back to Andy and found him looking at me so attentively I wondered if I was sporting a milk moustache from the White Russian I'd just downed. I rubbed my upper lip and tilted my head down more self-consciously than I wanted to, brushing a loose strand of hair back behind one ear. But then I thought better of it and lifted my eyes to meet his gaze. Maybe, just maybe, I thought, he couldn't take his eyes off me because there was something he liked about me. Something strange or rare that intrigued him. But then he had to go and ruin it all.

'What part of Scotland is your dad from?'

I'm usually prepared for dad questions, but that one hit me square in the chest. Ordinarily, I would mumble something about how I didn't have one – a dad – how it had always been just Mum and me without elaborating further. It was the truth after all. I didn't have one. I suppose, if pressed on the subject, I could admit that my mum had met a man in a nightclub in the early nineties, but he hadn't wanted to keep in touch or go through the grind of the whole parenting thing, so I preferred not to think of him as my dad, or to think of him at all really.

'That's a bit presumptuous,' I said.

'Sorry. Is he – Don't you – Did he –'

'No biggie. Just, no dad.'

'Shit. Sorry,' he said again.

'It's okay. He's not dead or anything. Well, he might be. I wouldn't know. Never met the guy. McKinnon is my mum's surname, from my grandad. That's where she got it. As opposed to being married to anyone with that name, if that makes sense.' I looked at the ground so he couldn't see my cheeks flushing.

But like a dog with a bone, he said, 'So whereabouts in Scotland is your grandad from then?' Now my cheeks were aflame.

'The Jamaican part,' I said plainly, and stared at him.

'You've lost me.'

So, I broke it down as simply as I could. 'The part that enjoyed sugar and rum and lots of overseas travel for a couple of hundred years. That part.'

'Ah. Oh. Shit.'

I could see then that Andy wished a hole would open and swallow him up. Perhaps cruelly, I was a little amused by this reaction, but I was also finding his awkwardness attractive. It was probably a bit inappropriate to bring up such a heavy subject within only a few minutes of meeting someone who was simply trying to make polite conversation.

He filled the silence as quickly as he could by saying, 'Sorry, do you mind if we just un-meet so I can go back in time and erase the last three minutes?' He said it so effusively it seemed like a genuine prospect.

'Sure. Never happened.'

'Cheers. And just for the record, the only time I've ever been to Scotland was for D of E, so, yeah. That whole – thing – nothing to do with me.' He said it jokingly, holding his hands up in the air.

'Noted,' I said. I didn't want him to give himself a hernia with all the effort he was putting into thinking of the perfect thing to say to make everything less awkward, so I changed the subject completely.

'So, who dragged you along to this thing then?'

'What's-Her-Name.'

'Oh no,' was all I could say, feeling a tightening in the pit of my stomach.

'Afraid so. My sister. Better known as Alex.'

We were even then. We drifted outside and stood by the fire. Beyond it, the shapes of other people began to soften around the edges, their movements slow down a little. The lights seemed brighter and the moon a little higher in the sky. Everything felt like it was expanding. *You're in trouble now, Layla. Good luck and Godspeed.*

We talked and joked about this and that and nothing and everything, for what seemed like hours. Essentially, however, we were just two strangers who had clearly had too much to drink, wondering how long we had to keep talking before we could have sex. Just when I thought we might have another round of drinks, instead he kissed me. The softest kiss. It was like I was a bubble, and if he pressed too hard, I'd pop or float away. After that, I made up my mind that spending the rest of the party kissing would probably be a better use of our time.

'Pretty sure we're not related,' I said, more to myself than him.

'Pretty sure you're right about that,' he said, as he held his face close to mine and peppered his sentence with kisses as though it were the only way to make it comprehensible and grammatically correct.

'That's good.'

'Yes. That's something.'

'Yes,' I echoed, nodding with my eyes closed. Then after pausing for the exact amount of time needed for a lingering 'yes' to make the palms of his hands feel noticeably warmer, I sweetened it with, 'Could be.' And this time, I kissed him. I wasn't sure if he realised it, but he had me then. I think that was the moment I decided to love him and not to stop. Bank that, I thought. Bank that whole moment and never forget it.

But that was before. Before our meet cute turned out to be not so cute. Before the documentary, before everything with Sera.

Before history caught up with me.

I

29 days until the wedding

'Miss, ain't you getting married in the holidays?'

I knew exactly who was talking behind my back. I didn't need to turn round to confirm it. It was Mahad. It was always Mahad. It was the final class of the final day of term, we were minutes from the bell ringing and being able to spill out into the warmth of the July afternoon to do as we pleased and Mahad, stirrer-in-chief, had chosen this moment as his opportunity to get his wooden spoon out. I made sure that I was facing the board so that the gradually growing pinkness in my cheeks could build and fade without being seen.

'Yes,' I said. 'Thank you for making it common knowledge if it wasn't already.'

'Congratulations for then, Miss,' said Chloe from a desk by the windows which overlooked the staff car park. I could already hear some of my colleagues pulling out of their spaces, emptying them until next term. Lucky fuckers.

'Thank you, Chloe,' I said expressionlessly, trying to nip the personal chat in the bud as quickly as I could. I hoped the Mahads in the room were taking note and turned back to the board. Striking the right balance between 'do-not-fuck-with-me' and chillest Spanish teacher at the school was something I fretted over, often in the middle of the night. I knew how easily I could become the one being threatened with physical violence or being told to 'suck your mother and die', or any of the other occupational hazards we had agreed to at the end of our PGCEs or the start of our Teach First placements.

'To your brother, Miss?' said Mahad.

'Sorry?'

'Ain't you getting married to your brother or your cousin or somethin'?' he said, snickering and twirling his pen between his fingers as he watched and waited for a reaction. The kid had what he wanted. The attention of the whole classroom. It was his dream and my worst nightmare. Until then, the lesson had been going pretty well. I say lesson. No teacher was mad enough to actually try to teach their students anything the day before the summer holidays. All I'd planned was an end-of-term vocab quiz – the fun kind, with prizes. They'd grumbled about it at first but soon they were laughing, whooping and cheering in their teams whenever a correct answer put them in the lead. I half wished I'd dismissed them all as soon as it was over and ended the year on a high.

'I think that one's a bit tired, Mahad. Maybe you can work on some new material over the summer?'

'I think a lot of us still find it pretty funny, Miss, actually.'

'Fine. Why don't you consider it a little favour that I'll

be marrying someone with the same surname so you won't have to get your head around a new one and you can focus all that brainpower on your coursework?' I hoped that would be the end of the matter. It seemed to be. The classroom went quiet. Pens scratched paper. I could hear breath rising and falling behind me in waves while I again turned my back and let a moment of calm wash over me.

I knew the bell would ring at any moment so I asked if anyone had any questions they felt a burning desire to ask before they were free of school for the next six weeks. Just as I was beginning to regret my phrasing, Mahad was speaking again.

'Miss McKinnon?' he said, smirking. I stared at the little *puta* without blinking, intrigued to hear what he was going to come up with next. 'Are you an albino?'

Stifled laughter and audible intakes of breath could be heard, mainly among Mahad's usual wingmen. But I'd had my looks commented on enough in my twenty-nine years – and I mean, the whole twenty-nine, my mum filling me in on the ones I would've been too young to remember, like the time her long-standing GP encouraged her to double-check with the hospital that she'd been given the right baby to take home – to take it in my stride. So, I treated this episode like any other.

'No, Mahad. I'm not. But thank you for asking,' I said coolly and began to pack up.

The bell rang, but for a few seconds no one moved. I wasn't sure what they were waiting for, but it felt like everyone was staring at me.

Unbidden, a montage played in my head of all the times my class had tried to push the teacher over the edge when I was at school. When Georgia Stewart wrote Mrs Frobisher was a Nazi in indelible ink on the board before a maths lesson; when Simmi Ahmed hid a mini keyboard in one of the desks and set it to play the most irritating jingle on repeat and no one telling Miss Strachan where it was. And the time Tania Ambrose spat in Mrs Kemper's coffee when she'd stepped out to get more worksheets. Instead of Tania silently enjoying the moment when the teacher took an unsuspecting gulp, she decided to tell her about the disgusting thing she had done in front of the whole class, so that she would always know she had drunk one of her students' saliva. Mrs Kemper wept real tears then and there. I had always promised myself I would never be that kind of teacher.

Finally, someone got up and a wave of movement rippled through the room as books were gathered up, phones were checked and people filed out. I could hear Mahad's voice getting closer and closer, louder and louder, as he made his way to the door describing a new pair of Adidas trainers he'd ordered. Suddenly, his conversation broke off and for a split second I thought he might apologise. But just in case he didn't I glowered at him and said, 'School's out, Mahad. Enjoy your summer.'

She's not even listening to me, I thought. She was scrolling through news headlines on her phone. I peered over to see what she was so engrossed in. Something about

Dallas. Another police shooting. 'Just another black life that doesn't matter,' I heard Sera mutter.

Working at the same place as your lifelong best friend had many benefits. We could always rant and rave without any filters when it came to workplace politics. There had been school trips abroad we'd both volunteered to chaperone together and we would often leave each other little snacks or Pukka tea bags in new and interesting flavours with Post-its attached in the staffroom. Seeing a little yellow square with 'S x' scribbled in the corner somewhere around the kitchenette on otherwise uneventful Tuesdays and the odd over-eventful Thursday never failed to make me smile. Post-lesson funks could be dispelled within minutes of the bell when we reunited to share battle stories. But today, Sera's reaction to what I had to say was lacking its usual levels of scrutiny or, in fact, any actual interest whatsoever.

'How are things looking with the hen?' I said, doing my best to make it sound non-accusatory. 'You've got everyone's numbers, right?'

She looked down at the lever arch file in front of her, pretending she hadn't been reading the news at all but was deeply invested in where the papers and dividers should go. Sera was my chief bridesmaid. It had been a given since we were kids that we would take on any and all roles of major significance for each other, but I'd still taken her out for dinner and given her a gift-wrapped keepsake to formally anoint her. I knew better than to overload her with the types of demands other brides were getting named and shamed for on Reddit, but nudging her about my hen wasn't something I thought I'd have to do. All I wanted was a relaxed, hassle-free overnight trip away somewhere for the bridesmaids, a few of the girls from school and my mum and, whatever it involved, I wanted to pay my own way. I'd told her I didn't mind it being fairly close to the wedding, but there was close and then there was 'let's do this before I actually get married'.

'Planning stages,' she muttered.

'Okay. Cryptic,' I said, putting on a laugh, wanting to shake her out of her bad mood. 'Have you saved the date with everyone? Do you want me to get the others to give you a hand? Andy's sister has got a lot on with rehearsals for a play or something, but Poonam and Siobhan wouldn't mind. And if there's anything you want me to do . . .' I reeled off questions and suggestions like an overexcited child demanding to be updated on preparations for their birthday party.

'I've got things going on, Lay. I'll get to it.' She was giving off a frosty vibe, colder than I'd ever felt from her before. It was even several degrees below the time I vomited in her bed and remade it again leaving her to find it and clean it up after a gathering in Year 11. I'd witnessed others on the receiving end of one of these Sera moods but had never had a helping of it myself. And even though I knew it was probably not about me, it made me feel like a stranger and I wanted to swill, gargle and spit so that the taste of it would go away.

'Caleb?' I said and waited. Asking if things with her boyfriend were going downhill again was high-risk, but I hoped it would come across as thoughtful rather than judgemental. She'd been with Caleb longer than I'd been with Andy and at no point had there been any hint that he was any more committed to her than he had been at the beginning of their relationship. They didn't live together. She was desperate for him to leave a T-shirt, a toothbrush, a DNA specimen of some kind at her flat so that it at least felt like one day things would develop and they would become people who couldn't live without each other. To me, it seemed like he'd do anything to spend as little time there as possible. He wined and dined her, took her on expensive holidays and bought her pointless yet eye-catching gifts but ultimately he remained remote, one foot in the door of their relationship and one just outside. Can't-trust-him-Caleb, I called him. Not to his face, obviously. Or hers for that matter.

'That waste of a manfriend? No. Just stuff.' She looked back at her file.

'Do you want to come to my fitting before we head to the drinks later? You can talk stuff while I do my meringue impression.'

'Can't.'

'Could?' I pinged back. I couldn't remember who had invented our little game of conducting conversations – sometimes proper, full-length ones – with only one choice word allowed from each of us. It was like a secret language. We were so tight, knew each other so well that sometimes one word was all it took to understand each other completely. We could hear the subtext, fill in the gaps, and amuse ourselves. And it was just for us.

'Can't,' she said, in a tone that suggested she wasn't playing any more.

I wondered if she just had a case of the end-of-term blues. Not exactly a feeling of melancholy about leaving the kids for the summer, and not because she'd miss seeing their faces every day, their progress, their small-scale dramas. A different kind of blues. The feeling that arrives when you finally run out of mental energy. There was always an air of utter exhaustion in the staffroom during the last few days of term, as if we'd all been dragging our heavy minds through each and every school week, and our regular 1 a.m. finishes from marking were about to break us. Sera bit and released her lower lip in a repetitive motion which I had never noticed before. But it told me she was stressed, and Sera was never stressed. The Sera I knew steamrolled through life's shitty bits at pace and looked good in the process. In that moment, she looked insecure and pained.

She wouldn't make eye contact which only amplified the disappointment in her voice when she said, 'Maybe next year I'll try not to spend months of my time going for a promotion I was never going to get and we'll see how I am then.' It was almost a throwaway remark, but one she definitely wanted me to hear, to make me feel bad for not asking about the Head of Year post she'd applied for. A number of internal roles had come up over the past few months, but the one Sera had gone for had been repeatedly pushed down the list. She had finally had the interview that morning. But instead of remembering and asking how it had gone, I had quizzed her about my stupid hen do, like the diva bride I thought I wasn't.

'Shit, Sera. You didn't get it? Did she say why?' I moved to sit next to her on the two-seater sofa and placed a hand on one of her shoulders. She promptly shuffled along, removing herself from my touch.

'Not in so many words,' she said, in very few of her own.

'What do you mean?'

'It's not exactly something you have to worry about. Maybe you should apply.'

I paused for a moment, baffled at how difficult the conversation was becoming. 'I feel like I'm missing something here.'

'Like I said, it's not something you have to worry about. Anyway, aren't you going to be late for your meringue?'

It felt like invasion of the body snatchers. This person looked like Sera but was not Sera somehow. The 'something' she was telling me I didn't have to worry about seemed like a thing I ought to be let in on so that I could judge for myself if worry were required. Staff flitted around the room, occasionally erupting in bursts of excited laughter, unable to contain their joy that the summer was finally here. I wished Siobhan, my other school-based bridesmaid, would make an appearance, restart the hen do conversation, or get Sera talking to test whether I was the one pissing her off or if it was the world in general, but she'd finished early. Imagining her already propping up the bar, I hated her a little bit.

'I'll just see you at drinks then?' I said. Sera shifted in her seat, hoisting her bag up from the floor and searching for something. I waited for her answer. She'd never missed end-of-term drinks before. Usually she even had some role in organising them. I figured it was highly likely that the Head would be there, but highly unlikely that Sera would want to give her any more of her time, become embroiled in any further discussion about the job she didn't get, or be in close confines with the person who'd actually got it and have to pretend she was pleased for them.

'Might,' she replied.

I let my eyes linger on her for a moment as I mouthed inaudibly the word *won't*, because I knew I definitely wouldn't be seeing her at the pub. She buried her head back in her file. The whole seating arrangement suddenly felt wrong, like there had only ever been room enough for one on the sofa, so I moved to perch on the armrest instead. I hoped she didn't think her mood would fly as an excuse to miss our regular Saturday brunch in the morning, and the other surprise I had in store for her. As sulky as I could have been about the hen party, all I really wanted to do was hold space for my friend, quietly, if that was what she needed. I thought about sacking off the drinks and just turning up at her flat later on, unannounced, which we both had a habit of doing. It had become an important part of our relationship: the unspoken permission to just arrive and burden the other person in a way that was not a burden at all, because of who was doing it. We'd drop everything and welcome each other with wine or tea or comfort food from the nearest yard shop, and the requisite belly laughs — the crusty kind, we called them, the kind of laugh we felt too embarrassed to do in front of anyone else. We went to each other for whatever we needed and I loved that we had this way of being with each other that was reserved only for those moments. Usually anyway. Today was a blip. I knew that after brunch she'd be spending the rest of the weekend with her mum, which I hoped would soothe her and get her back to herself.

I waded through the atmosphere and out of the staff-room, taking a quick look back at my oldest friend who barely noticed I was no longer standing next to her.

2

Before

'Not D&I dude, please!' Sera said at brunch. I'd started our Saturday ritual off sheepishly with 'Soooo, you know that guy from the party . . .' before turning crimson and giggling on the other side of the table like a giddy school-girl. I wasn't a huge fan of Sera's nickname for Andy and hoped it wouldn't stick. It had only come about because of how the night had ended, but being reminded of it now made me cringe a little.

Sera and Andy had had only the briefest of encoun-ters as we'd all said our goodbyes – me, Andy, Alex, Sera and Yasmin, who was the lynchpin between us all. She'd recently joined Heartview, and her and Sera had become pally fast, or, at least, it felt fast to me. Yasmin had been friends with Alex since they'd been at drama school together, and had insisted Sera come to the party. Some-how, and for some unknown reason, Andy had found the time to shoehorn into his farewell the fact that he was on the Diversity and Inclusion Panel at the con-struction consultancy he worked for in Development Monitoring – which sounded as cushy as it did confus-ing and I couldn't work out what he actually spent his days doing. The impromptu revelation that he was doing his bit to diversify the landscape of cost consultants and project surveyors at his firm could easily have been blamed on the alcohol, which had been flowing freely for several hours. But it was met with slightly puzzled looks from the three people of colour who stood in front of him who were wondering why it was relevant at that moment in time and whether he wanted a medal. Even though it had been awkward, I had forgotten all about it. It certainly hadn't been my lasting memory of our time together that evening.

Andy and I had been exchanging texts rapidly for the entire week. My stomach had flipped so many times with each ping of my phone that I'd become a nervous wreck. I realised then that instead of being in the moment with Sera, I was actually visualising Andy's face. In particular the flecks of yellow amid the grey-blue of his eyes. I'd congratulated myself on noticing them that night at the party, replaying the moment he'd come in for that first kiss a hundred times since. But now I wanted to gauge Sera's opinion on the highly romantic gesture Andy had made in his last text to make sure that it was indeed highly romantic and not something I should be running a mile from.

'He's taking half-term off work.'

'Why?'

'To . . . hang out. Spend the week with me.'

'And you said yes to that?'

'Is it weird? I'd told myself it was sweet but it's just weird, isn't it? I knew it.'

'No, I guess it's cute in an over-the-top, eager kind of way.'

'Do you think I should tell him I'm busy? I know we were thinking of going somewhere last minute. Do you still want to do that? I could just tell him I'm away.'

'I can't any more. Caleb and I might start viewing places that week. Not that he's booked any time off work for it yet, but he said he would.'

'Finally! A shopping trip, but this time for a flat. That's exciting, Sez.' I wanted to raise a glass but I didn't want to appear more enthusiastic than she was in that moment, so I tried to contain myself.

'We'll see,' she said, looking down at her nails briefly.

'Soooo?'

'What?' she said, genuinely having lost the thread of our conversation.

'What should I do? About Andy? Half-term?'

'Oh yeah. I suppose. If you want to but . . .'

'What? What is it?' I inched closer to her, on tenter-hooks waiting to hear her verdict on the guy I was falling for. It mattered to me, what Sera thought, about everything.

'Nothing. He just seemed a bit, I don't know . . . Too short, for one thing.'

'Shut up,' I threw back playfully. 'He's really hot.'

'He's a 7.'

'Sera!'

'Okay, okay, 8 but he knows it, which brings him back down to 7, if you even go in for that kind of thing, I mean,' she said, trying not to smile but failing. 'No, but seriously though, Lay, he's fine to practise on, but don't stay with him too long, yeah? And definitely no kids. If those kids have kids with white people too, your curls, your grandad's nose – all those beautiful things about you – will get bred out and no one will ever know your family was black.'

There was silence after she said that. It felt like we were both waiting for the other to laugh first, but also like she wanted me to know that if either of us did so, it would just be a sound we were making and wouldn't be because she had been joking. No, there was a serious-ness to the assertion, the premonition, the forewarning or whatever it was, that lingered in the empty space above the table. The thought of the skin colour of future generations of my family resting with me alone, and the idea that the blackness in us could simply fade out the further you got through a family photo album, filled me with intense sorrow.

'Not seriously though, right?' I said, expecting her to say *Of course not, girl. You do you.*

'Why don't you ever date black guys?' she asked point-blank.

'Hello? Leon?' I countered quickly.

'He was mixed.'

'No he wasn't. He was light-skinned but his parents were both black. I think. I'm pretty sure that's what he said. I never actually got the chance to meet them, did I? Anyway, why are we even talking about this?' I said, con-fused about how and when we had found ourselves on this tangent. 'I've been out with lots of black guys.'

'Two? Three maybe. And that was when we were teenagers. I'm just wondering why there haven't been more. Y'know, now we're grown and you're looking for someone to *be* with?'

'I'm not consciously *not* dating black guys. I'm just, I, er – er –'

'Okay, okay. It's cool. Don't hurt yourself. I was just curious.'

'Oh,' was all I could say, turning my attention to the menu. I wasn't really reading it, just staring at the mass of letters and numbers and pound signs while my mind lagged behind.

'So, how come you never date white guys?' I said. It was a question I had never asked her before, but since we were on the subject.

'Date? Pah. What's that?' she scoffed, full of sarcasm. 'I feel like I've been with Caleb for soooo long I don't even remember what that word means. And I won't be going back out there again. No way. Back into that cesspool of singleness. No offence. All dating apps and dick pics and awkward first dates. Not to mention all the shit, guess-work sex. Fuck no.' She had deflected the question masterfully and I couldn't help laughing along. She was right. Most of the time, it was hell out there. It made me want to dive into whatever was happening with Andy like my life depended on it.

'Go ahead,' she said finally. 'Do the half-term thing. Why not? See what happens. But don't be code-shifting around him. I hate it when you do that with white people. Just do you.'

Do I do that? I thought to myself. Code-shift? I could feel myself squinting, trying to pinpoint times I might have. Precise instances Sera might be alluding to, but none sprang to mind. And if I did, didn't everyone? At least to some extent. As people, we were thrust into so many different scenarios and environments. Surely we had to morph, adapt as required. Some situations demanded that of you. Whether it was donning protective armour to get through a family occasion, speaking your mind at a work event or the opposite – biting your tongue. Even just laughing at your boss's unfunny jokes. It was a survival technique.

While it wasn't a glowing review of Andy from Sera, I reassured myself that what she knew of him had only been gathered in the mere minutes it had taken for our Uber to arrive. My gut was saying *Fuck it. Jump at the crazy, romantic half-term offer this man is making. Do something different. Let go of having to plan everything all the time, Layla, and leap.* Besides, I could always just tell him I'd come down with something after the first day if I needed an out, especially with that bug going around that everyone seemed to be talking about.

For Sera, half-term ended up not being full of flat viewings. But for me, it was full of Andy.

We wandered and moseyed and walked and flaneured. We held hands. We talked about the TV shows we used to watch when we were ten (Andy: *Scrubs*. Me: *Sabrina the Teenage Witch*) and the ones we were bingeing on now (Andy: *Succession*. Me: *Insecure*). We told each other what we wanted to be when we grew up (Andy: pet detective. Me: astronomer). We confessed to what we were most afraid of (Andy: biting into mouldy fruit. Me: dying in a plane crash). We slurped ramen noodles in a little cafe I would never be able to find my way back to that looked unremarkable from the outside but made you want to move to Tokyo once you were in there eating the food. We took photos together in a vintage booth we came across in Soho and showed each other snaps of our families, friends and long-since dead pets in our camera rolls. We climbed up the tower at Westminster Cathedral for a majestic view of London for £3 when everyone else was paying £30 to go up the Shard. All the while I was getting to know his traits, his little quirks and foibles. Like his Earnest Eyebrows – a nickname I ended up giving a particular look of his which made him laugh hysterically rather than take offence. He never seemed to know he was doing it which made it all the more charming. It was somewhere between a furrow and a pinch together at the centre and gave him an air of utter sincerity.

We drank too much. Talked too much. Or sometimes not at all, not for minutes on end, but it didn't disturb me or embarrass me or make me feel self-conscious. It only made me see what it could be like – silence between two people who were entirely comfortable in each other's company. It was like neither of us had ever been to London before. We were tourists on a city break determined to visit every museum and art gallery, buy tickets to every matinee and pop-up event. Andy even bought a postcard. It was of one of the artworks we'd seen at Tate Britain – a screen print from 1969 by Jim

Dine in grey tones with the image of a heart at its centre, which we'd stood for ages staring into, talking about what we thought it meant while everyone else seemed to pass it by.

We went for seafood in Borough Market. Afterwards, we took a walk along the river to settle our full stomachs, Tower Bridge twinkling in the background, his arm over my shoulders and mine tucked behind his back with the tip of my thumb slipping into the waistband of his jeans so I could feel his skin in secret. After that, I couldn't help but let the rest of my fingers follow, so we gave each other a look and went back to his place. I discovered the next morning, in an excruciatingly awkward silence in their shared kitchen, that Andy's housemate, who was supposed to be away, had come back early and had therefore been privy to a soundtrack that had been building up between two people who had barely been able to turn their faces away from each other. After we'd heard the door close behind him once he'd finally set off for work, we decided we should probably take a rest day and that the best place to do that would be in bed and that it really didn't make any sense for us to wear clothes or answer our phones or remember that the outside world existed in any way. So, for a whole day, we didn't.

But on the Friday, on very much the same whim we'd been on for the entire week, we took an impromptu train ride out of London. We went to Finsbury Park Tube intending to go to King's Cross to wander through Coal Drops Yard and eat at the street-food market. But when we noticed a train for Cambridge, we hopped on and our adventures continued. An hour later, we were admiring the college buildings and reminiscing about uni days. There happened to be rehearsals on at King's and we sat in the pews in silence and wonder at the heavenliness of the sounds we were hearing. We went to Jack's for cones and cups stacked high with gelato despite it being cold outside. And it was then, sitting on a bench on the riverside, that he broke off from whatever he was saying and turned to me. As if in slow motion, he extended his hand towards my face and nestled his fingers delicately into my hair just behind my neck, an area I suddenly remembered being called the occiput from Biology or a yoga workshop or somewhere I couldn't recall, and wondered how the unsexiest word on earth could be used for what was quickly becoming an erogenous zone I never knew I had. He brought my face towards his and kissed me. It was different to any of the kisses we'd been stealing throughout the week or even the very first one at the party. It was intense and lingering. I immediately felt myself turn to putty. I was suddenly completely malleable in this man's hands, at once in my body and out of it.

That was the one. The kiss that sealed it. After that I knew that we were *together* together.

If that was half-term, I couldn't wait for the Easter holidays.

You know it's fancy when the house has a name instead of a number.

Ivy Cottage sat at the edge of the village. It wasn't

particularly big or grand, but there was enough space in the back garden for a large tepee, a makeshift bar, a dance floor, tables and chairs and a vintage jukebox as well as the posh rented Portaloo stationed inconspicuously alongside the hedge separating us from next-door's paddock. Beyond the party, stepping stones led to a quiet little corner tucked away under a stone archway twinkling with fairy lights. The Beatles, the Beach Boys, the Bay City Rollers serenaded the crowd taking to the dance floor. I could see the woman of the hour, Aunt Jessie, bopping as energetically as her seventy years would allow while holding tightly on to the hand of a teenaged kid who I guessed must be her grandson, Ollie. It could only be a guess because Andy had fired off so many names on the drive there, and I had only so far been introduced to a few key figures, so my brain was spinning trying to remember who everyone was.

'Any exes on the guest list today?' I'd asked in the car, picking at the gel polish on my nails. I'd gone for a multi-coloured arrangement, one pastel shade for each finger. It was quirky and probably a little juvenile but, if nothing else, it would be a talking point behind my back if people at the party felt they needed one.

'You're safe on that front,' he said, smiling. 'Alex will be there so at least you'll know someone if I get sent out for more ice or something.'

I hadn't seen Alex since her birthday party and even then I had barely spoken to her because I had spent most of the night making out with her brother. The promise of her presence reassured me slightly, but it also reminded me that this would be the second birthday party I'd gone to for a member of this guy's family, and a month ago we didn't even know each other, so maybe things were going too fast. But I couldn't help that Andy's mother's older sister was reaching a big milestone so early on in our relationship or that Andy had asked me to go with him because he couldn't wait for everyone to meet me and it was going to happen sooner or later so why not just make it sooner. As nervous as I was about the whole thing, I was touched that he felt so excited, so ready to announce me as his girlfriend to his nearest and dearest.

Stepping out into the back garden, I suddenly worried that I'd chosen poorly when it came to my outfit. I had gone for a black dress and gold accessories. Fairly bold even by my standards. It involved tulle and layering and fell midway down my calf. It was a world away from the bright co-ords most of the younger guests wore, but my hair was tied back simply and I wore little make-up, so I told myself I could still easily fade into the background. Whether people would let me was another thing. And then I realised that it didn't really matter what I was wearing because, scanning the garden, there was no one else there who looked like me. And not because of my clothes.

Andy was right about the ice. The call for a replenishment came while I was in the Portaloo. He shouted he'd be back in twenty minutes and that I'd probably be able to find Alex sitting at one of the tables with his parents or with their older sister, Sasha, changing one (or both) of her twins' nappies somewhere in the house. I considered staying locked in the cubicle, but I decided that would not be a good look for the new girlfriend so I washed my hands and headed back out.

Alex wasn't in any of the places Andy had mentioned. She had disappeared off the face of the earth when I needed her most. Even though I barely knew her, she had been living in London for several years and hadn't been confined to the provinces like 98 per cent of the other guests, and that was enough for me to want to stay right by her side until Andy came back. I didn't want it to look like I was snooping around inside Aunt Jessie's house, so I put my big-girl pants on and went over to the bar to pour an elderflower and gin spritz from a Kilner jar with a tap, picked up a Gruyère twist and scanned for Andy's parents.

His mum, Andrea, had embraced me warmly when we arrived and his dad, David, had sounded sincere when he told me how glad he was I'd been able to make it. I held on to that as I sidled up to where they were talking to another couple. I arrived just as the other man was revealing the punchline to a joke. I didn't know whether it was better for me to laugh along with everyone else and swallow the awkwardness of everyone knowing I didn't know what I was laughing at, or not laugh and for him to feel obliged to retell the joke. So, I just smiled politely, stood quietly and turned to stare out to the dance floor until it was over, and I could get involved in the next part of the conversation.

'Layla, this is Richard. We went to school together,' David said, bringing me into the fold.

'Primary school. Can you believe it?' added Andrea.

'Nice to meet you,' said Richard, reaching out for a handshake before gesturing to the last person in the quartet. 'This is my wife –'

'Oh, he remembered this time.' They all chuckled. 'He usually forgets I'm here and I end up fannying around in the background until I manage to get a word in edge-ways to announce myself. I'm Sue.' Sue seemed like the kind of person who never struggled to get a word in edgeways. She had light brown, overly styled hair which fell just below her chin and flicked out at the bottom as though she had worn it in rollers for several hours before coming. Her nails were French-polished and her wedding finger was piled high with a gold band, a large solitaire and several eternity rings. I wondered if she could even bend it any more.

'Layla is –' David began before Richard, clearly the party's resident comedian, interrupted, nudging and winking at David: 'Your future daughter-in-law.'

I couldn't remember the last time I'd seen anybody wink who wasn't on a TV show. It made me deeply suspicious. It also set him and David off laughing and made some of my drink go down the wrong way, causing me to cough so much that Sue decided to take it upon herself to pat me on the back despite only having just met me. I could already tell that Sue and Richard were a particularly obnoxious breed of Home County-ers and I longed for Andy to come back or for the Portaloo to become free again so I could make a beeline. Thankfully, Andrea came to my rescue and gave Richard a mock telling-off, tutting at him and telling him to behave. She turned to me mouthing an apology then said something about the IPA being 7 per cent and David and Richard having had most of the keg between them.

'Only teasing. Pleased to meet you. Andrew speaks very highly of you,' came Richard's attempt at trying to fix things. I let out a nervous giggle and hoped someone else would say something so that I could become a bystander instead of the focal point. Andrea asked Sue how her eldest daughter was settling into London since she'd made the move. I breathed an almost audible sigh of relief. London was my comfort zone. It was only thirty miles from the Surrey village where Aunt Jessie, and just a few roads away, Andy's parents lived, but it had felt desperately far away since we'd come off the M25 and sped along single-track roads which it was supposedly okay to go down at sixty miles an hour.

'That's exciting. Which area has she moved to?' I asked, wanting to get stuck into my specialist subject.

'She's in Clapham. Oh, she absolutely loves it. She's at a magic circle law firm, got a nice set of housemates, and the drive between here and there isn't bad at all so she's back at least once a month. Best of both worlds.' I offered her tips she could pass on about the best museums, the best rooftop bars, the new productions, even the places they might be interested in going to when they went to visit her. I told her about all my favourite places, mentioned a few I'd introduced Andy to. And suddenly the conversation was flowing and I was glad I'd come. Andy could be getting ice from the South Pole for all I cared. I could handle myself and win everyone over at the same time. I would regale Andy with how much I'd impressed his family and friends over hog roast sandwiches when he got back. But then Richard thought of something he just had to ask.

'And whereabouts are you from, Layla?' he said.

'North London. Not too far from where Alex lives actually.'

'No, I mean originally? What's your background?'

Fucking hell. Really? I could feel my face getting hot and under my arms becoming slippery with sweat. Just as I was choosing between 'It's a great question, Richard, and, incredibly, one I have never been asked before' or something suitably vague like 'My background? Y'know – a little bit of this, little bit of that', a hand slid into mine. I felt it squeeze and hold on.

'Cold drinks are now available,' Andy declared. 'You're welcome.'

'Good lad,' Richard said, oblivious. He gave Andy a pat on the shoulder and ostentatiously tossed the contents of his plastic pint cup into the nearest hedge. 'You can crack open that bottle of Scotch you've been hiding now, Dave.' And with that the men went to the bar and the women pulled up seats next to Aunt Jessie who had hung up her dancing shoes and allowed the youngsters to override the jukebox with a wireless speaker and a playlist, leaving Andy and me on our own.

'All good?' he said.

'Yeah, great,' I said, biting the inside of my lip and making a conscious choice not to tell him what had been said while he was gone. It wasn't the time, and I wasn't even sure if he'd understand why it had made me want to be anywhere but there.

'Richard's a bit of a character, isn't he?' Andy said.

Before I could answer, we were swept up by Andy's sister, Sasha, and her twins. As we sat down to coo at the babies I checked my phone and saw a message from Sera: *How are things in the sticks?*

I smiled, felt my forehead soften and typed back: *Never leaving Zone 2 again. Don't care how hot he is.*

White. British.

I ticked the box and went to hand in the form. I shifted my eyes from side to side as I did so, gripping the clipboard for a second longer than I needed to. The receptionist smiled uncomfortably as if to say: *You can go and sit down now, you weirdo.*

I looked around. The room was full of other seventeen-year-olds. Hot young things. All tall. All clear-skinned. All silky-haired. All unlike me. Every one of them would have ticked the same box I did. The only difference was that they actually meant it. They weren't just passing.

That's probably not even the right word. Makes me sound like a character from *Show Boat*. That's not what I did. There obviously isn't the same need to *pass* in this day and age. No, it wasn't like that. Not exactly.

It was a stupid sales assistant job at Walterson & Sketch, mainly for the 40 per cent discount I'd get on their jeans if I actually got the job. I'd heard they did these group interviews that sounded more like auditions or go-sees for models and I was nervous even before I got there. But when I arrived and saw them all looking the same – being the same – I panicked. I assumed that's what they were looking for. White girls. I thought that was the customer demographic they were trying to appeal to and I convinced myself that if I woke up early and straightened my hair before every shift I would fit right in. I thought I knew what I was doing, ticking that box. But I didn't. I hadn't banked on the way it would make me feel. I walked out before my name was called and threw up in an alley by the side of the shop.

This long-ago episode was what I woke up thinking about the morning after Jessie's party. I wished I could burst back into that waiting room and just shout, at the top of my lungs, I'M NOT FUCKING WHITE! Probably a sure-fire way not to get a job, but pretty effective at silencing the shame I could still feel at the memory of that day.

Effective, but temporary, I noted to myself, as the party, the interview and Sera's words at brunch all began to coalesce and churn around in the pit of my stomach.

3

28.5 days until the wedding

'Why does it feel like I'm still wearing it?' I'd taken my wedding dress off ten minutes earlier but could still feel the weight of it on my body, pressing against my skin. I didn't know if that was a good or bad thing.

'Wait until you have to spend a whole day in it,' Mum said, looking up from her phone. She was flicking through the photos she'd just taken of me trying it on, even though it had only just happened in real life. As she looked down, I could see her glasses slowly slipping towards the tip of her glistening nose. I was roasting too. I prayed there would be more of a breeze the next time I had the dress on.

My mum hadn't missed accompanying me to any occasion I'd ever invited her to in my whole life, or at least that's how I remembered things. She made parenting on her own look effortless, like it was just one of many balls she was throwing up into the air and catching over and over again with little danger of them hitting the ground.

The tissue paper rustled under Erica's fingers as she wrapped it around the belt and hair slide I'd chosen to complete my look. Erica's wedding-dress boutique was tucked away off Essex Road. It was unpretentious, modern and almost impossibly tiny, with raw plaster walls, a cool stone floor and ylang-ylang candles infusing the air and relaxing the atmosphere. I'd fallen for her intensely bohemian vibe immediately after meeting her on the Piccadilly line when we were both a little the worse for wear. I'd overheard her leaving a voice message to her sister about the details of a dress she was designing for a minor celebrity and how it might finally help boost her followers on Instagram, which currently stood at 188, made up mainly of people who liked the photos she posted of her cat.

'I'll follow you,' I'd said when she'd finished recording. She looked alarmed.

'No, I mean online, on Insta. You were just saying . . . Sorry,' I said, feeling bad for eavesdropping. 'I'm one of those really annoying people who listens to other people's conversations about weddings. There's a name for us, I think. Brides?' She had chuckled warmly and seemed a little less fearful that I might actually follow her home. When she got out at Arsenal, she shouted back the name of her boutique as the doors were closing and waved as the train pulled away. I'd googled it as soon as I had Wi-Fi and scrolled through her feed of gowns and cats for most of my walk home from the station.

The next day, after confirming she could make me a dress in the five months I had left before the wedding, I signed her up. She was like a young Patricia Field with a touch of Joni Mitchell, but with a Tottenham accent. She'd let me co-design a modern, ivory, entirely sequinned gown with a sweetheart neckline. For my feet, she'd suggested a pair of electric-blue satin Manolo Blahnik Hangisis which caught the light as they peeped out with every step as I walked. I loved her for those unexpected touches – colour pops that added a sense of surprise and fun.

Erica placed the tissue paper into a box and the box into a bag.

'All set,' she said. 'Do you want to take these with you now or just grab them tomorrow at Sera's fitting?'

Brunch the next day was going to incorporate a dress fitting for Sera as chief bridesmaid. It was a surprise. I'd bought off-the-rack numbers for Poonam, Siobhan and Alex but I wanted to do something extra special for Sera. Every day, in the staffroom, she allowed herself five minutes to flick through the latest issue of *Vogue*. She'd heat up her ready meal and find a quiet spot then start to fold down the corner of pages with things that caught her eye. Homeware, heels, dresses. I'd never actually seen her in possession of any of the items she'd earmarked. I think the fantasy of possessing them was enough. Over the past few weeks I'd taken to going through the magazines afterwards, and taking photos of any dresses she'd folded down. I'd asked for her measurements, as I had the other bridesmaids, and had presented them to Erica one afternoon with photos of the clippings. 'I want to capture individual elements of the *Vogue* dresses but make something completely Sera. Do you know what I mean?' I'd waffled as she'd sipped and sketched. I knew she was going to do it, somehow find the time around making my dress, because she loved her job and because she said that Sera was the tallest client she'd ever been asked to dress and she wanted to do it for her portfolio.

Sera's dress worried me less than my own. I could still feel my lunch sitting heavy and undigested in my stomach, and I felt like a completely different size and shape to what I usually was.

'I'm not convinced I won't need more alterations,' I said, half genuinely, half seeking attention and reassurance from Mum and Erica.

'You're not going to change that much in the next four weeks, Lay,' was Mum's attempt, which seemed absurd. Surely, I was supposed to change in the weeks ahead considering the gravitas of the event. It was at once totally abstract and utterly terrifying. I'd been having a recurring nightmare lately where my legs buckled at the altar and I lifted my dress to find that they'd become tentacle-like, those of an underwater creature that wanted to get out of the church and head straight back to the sea.

'I might double in size. Or halve.'

'Babe, it's completely normal to think like that. You're perfect now and you'll be perfect in four weeks. Trust me. But we've got another fitting pencilled in, haven't we? So, don't worry.' I smiled at Erica to thank her for spinning me some of her tried and tested jitter-soothing spiel. It didn't help, it just made me feel un-special, another bride on the production line at the wedding factory, vain and fretful. I did enjoy her referring to me as 'babe' though, like she was signalling that we could stay in touch and be friends.

'Thank you for the pep talk. You might need to start adding those to the bill.'

'I keep telling her the same thing. Cha!' Mum kissed her teeth to punctuate her sentence which I knew would end with some kind of telling-off. 'You don't seem to hear it when it comes from me though,' she added, feigning upset to get some sympathy from Erica.

'That's all part of being the MOB – meant affectionately, of course.' I was a little annoyed that Erica was sharing our in-joke about the mother of the bride being on a par with a mobster. I couldn't remember who'd coined it first though, me or her, so I let her get away with it. Mum was still laughing as she made the final payment on my dress and accessories. She had insisted this would be her wedding gift to me the moment I told her Andy and I were engaged. It was just one of the many examples of how she had always tried to go above and beyond for me. Mum had enrolled me at ballet school at the age of three even though we couldn't afford it, and she hadn't let me see her disappointment that I'd chosen to give up and replace it with street dance before I graduated to pointe work. Instead she did something with that disappointment. She decided to focus on dance herself. After years spent in other jobs she'd been doing just to pay the bills, she had qualified as a dance movement psychotherapist and never looked back. All the questions about money – where it was coming from, how we could make it cover everything – were a little easier to answer after that. Anything but predictable, my mother.

I was glad I had another fitting and could leave the dress at the shop a bit longer. If it was at home, I knew I wouldn't be able to resist showing it to Andy. And then he'd show me his suit and we'd end up getting drunk and playing bride and groom dress-up and pretending to everyone that we'd eloped. On a deeper level, too, I didn't want it to just be another garment hanging in my wardrobe because it wasn't. It meant something. Hooking my arm into Mum's, I thought about these being the last days of things being the way they were, mother and daughter. Rita and Layla. Soon to be given away into someone else's care and protection. I'd felt in more and more of a rush to get to know my mother, that something was being lost. I wanted to try to express something about it to her but I felt self-conscious and didn't know if I fully understood what I was feeling.

'Let me look at you.' She took my face in her hands. Because she had something to say and I was going to listen, because it was probably going to be important. Because everything she said to me was.

'Oh, Layla. You're getting married. My girl, getting married.'

She brought me to her chest and held me there for a moment. The high street was busy and it felt like an incongruous thing to be doing as people passed by on either side of us, going about their business. I wriggled impatiently, my mind half on Sera and half on whether I should take the Tube or the bus, but I allowed my mother to have her moment, to breathe in her grown-up daughter and call to mind the first time my head had rested in the space between her chin and her clavicle like this, when the surgeon had placed minute-and-a-half-old me there, having pulled me from her still-open belly, and time had seemed to slow down, the pain and uncertainty of the hours before melting away. I squeezed her and then patted her back.

'No second thoughts?'

'Mum, can we not?' I said, rolling my eyes.

'This is grown-woman talk now, come on. Look at me.' I did and saw how earnest her expression was. 'Are you okay? Is this what you want?'

It felt like a strange question. Not because I thought she had anything against Andy but because it had never occurred to me before. I wondered if she might be picking up on all the crappy energy I'd brought to the boutique from the staffroom and was perhaps misinterpreting it as cold feet. Her mind had the ability to catastrophise in a heartbeat.

'Mum, I'm fine, okay? It's just Sera being a bit –'

'Oh, don't worry about her. That girl just loves drama,' she said. 'But seriously, are you ready? Are you happy?' I stopped squirming. I looked her in the eye and told her that Andy made me happy every day. Even on the ones he didn't particularly go out of his way to do so. It was just how he was. Like when he invented Pyjama Man.

Andy had started the tradition after I'd left for school one day and he'd realised he had to work late that evening. I'd arrived home at the exact moment my phone pinged with a text from him reminding me that he wouldn't be home in time for us to eat together and that I should sort myself out.

Sorry. I'll come and find you under the duvet later x

It was the second night in a row, the second week in a row too, that whatever project he was working on had encroached on the 'life' side of the work/life balancing act we'd been trying to achieve. So, I was pissed off. Not with Andy for having to work late, but with myself for being so readily available. I kept my response to a single word so that he'd know I wasn't happy.

Fine.

No kiss, which I regretted as soon as I hit send. I decided to have an early night without bothering to cook for myself, tutting as I went up the stairs. But then I saw what he'd left for me on the bed. I should've expected it, really, or if not that exact gesture, something at least. It was classic Andy. On his side of the bed, he had laid out his pyjamas. Pyjamas he hardly ever wore, preferring to sleep in boxers and a T-shirt because he hated overheating but knew he had to keep his shoulders warm so he wouldn't wake up chilly in the middle of the night. But a full set of pyjamas for this purpose worked perfectly. They gave the impression that he was lying there wearing them, with enough room on my side of the bed for me to curl up beside them. He had even placed a pair of his sunglasses where his eyes would have been and stretched out one of the sleeves to look like it was reaching for me. It was a ridiculous sight. Something a kid would do, not a 31-year-old. It wasn't something I'd ever tell my friends about. It wasn't a bunch of flowers or meal he'd cooked from scratch. It was better. It was an insight to the workings of his mind. The ability he had to make me smile when it was the last thing I wanted to do.

Mum traced her forefinger down the bridge of my nose, the way she did sometimes, and, laughing at the thought of what she was about to say before she had even spoken (one of her more annoying habits), she said, 'Okay then. Good. That's all I needed to hear. Go on now. Go and get drunk with the rest of London's teaching professionals. Lawd! To be a fly on the wall.'

We headed off in opposite directions, both of us glancing back a few times over our shoulders. Then Mum bellowed, 'And don't forget about Sunday,' like there was no one else around.

'It'll just be me. Andy's got to work.' I walked away backwards so I could still see her as she shouted back, 'See you. Love you, Layla.'

'Don't I know it!' I yelled back cheekily.

'Well, now London does too.'

'Didn't Grandad tell you never to shout in the street?'

'Cha! Cheek!' she said and I could hear her accompanying laughter trailing off in the distance as I turned and picked up my pace. I inhaled deeply, and the exhaust fumes of the three 43 buses passing by in convoy stung my nostrils. I narrowly avoided being hit by a scooter-mounted child whose weary father apologised to me in one breath and shouted at the kid in another, all while he tried to keep a buggy carrying his toddler on the pavement and out of the passing traffic. I smiled and told him not to worry. That smile came from how my city made me feel, the dirty chaos of it, the sparkling beauty of it.

I checked my phone. Still no messages. I thought about what Mum had said, about Sera having a penchant for the dramatic. While it was true, and we'd had minor spats, cross words, been in plenty of funks with each other over the years, something about how she'd been in the staffroom felt off. As I descended into the Tube station, feeling the light disappear and the moving heat of a departing train being pushed upward in my direction, I scrambled in my bag for my headphones so that I could block out the noise of my own thoughts for the journey.

I sat at the pub watching glasses being clinked by several teachers who had learnt of their promotions that day. None of them looked anything like Sera. The merriment going on around me suddenly interspersed with flashes of the grainy bodycam footage Sera had been watching on the news in the staffroom. Any sense of excitement I'd had about it finally being the summer holidays, the lead-up to my wedding or even just the fact that it was the weekend was in short supply.

I read the text which had buzzed through from Andy asking about how my fitting had gone, if there were any spare inches I needed to fill in my dress and whether we could do that later with burgers and beer on Stroud Green Road if work drinks didn't finish too late. We often ended up on the busy high street near our flat on a Friday night and I loved that it had become our stomping ground.

It's a date. Be there at 9 x I typed, wishing I could sack off the drinks before I'd even had one so that I could race to Andy and tell him what had happened with Sera, how strange the last day of term had been, all while washing down juicy, slightly pink patties the thickness of my thumb. I pressed send before clicking the side button and watching the screen turn black. But instead of putting it straight back into my pocket, I lingered for a moment. Seeing my uneasy expression reflected in the glass – colours dampened, shiny yet dull at the same time – made me want to crack the screen with the back of a spoon like a pot of crème brûlée. Looking into my own eyes, Mahad's voice suddenly replayed in my mind: *Are you albino?* It had caught me off guard a little. I wondered what he was trying to achieve by asking that, why it would even matter if I was. It also made me ponder something I rarely did because of the futility of it. *What did my dad look like? And why had I never tried to find out?* But before I had the chance to analyse those silent questions in the secrecy of my mind where I never had to let anyone know I cared about the answers, a real voice from outside it began asking me something.

'What's happening with the hen, Lay?' it said. It came from Siobhan who was pulling up a stool at the table where no one else had noticed me slipping quietly into my daydream, barely partaking in the debate about when the new PE substitute had started sleeping with the groundsman.

'Wish I knew, Shiv. Wish I knew.'

4

28 days until the wedding

After finally extracting myself from bed, I wandered into the bathroom where Andy was already halfway through getting ready. I laid my hand on the bare skin where the top of his buttocks met the small of his back. I felt his warmth and briefly rested my head against him while I looked at his reflection in the mirror as he shaved, the razor running across his cheek and down his neck in a swift, smooth motion. He rarely allowed himself to be seen with stubble and Saturday-morning hockey was no exception.

'Ah, she's up, is she?' he said. He smiled and tried to kiss me but I ducked away just in time before he could transfer any bristly, white foam onto my face, which had really been his intention.

'Hope you move faster than that on the pitch,' I teased and headed back into our bedroom giving him a cheeky glance over my shoulder.

It was a sanctuary that room. When the time came to move, I'd try to find some way of transplanting it, in its exact form. It had a high ceiling, en suite bathroom and a large window complete with window seat which looked out over nothing but the greenery of other people's back gardens. It was also big enough for a super-king bed – one we generally didn't make the most of because of the way we curled around each other in one corner of it most nights. On nights when we'd had a tiff over something – like the way he always left empty packaging in the fridge and cupboards or the way he would use the living room for work calls instead of the spare room for which we were specifically paying extra rent to use as a home office – on those nights, the size of the bed really came into its own. Then I would firmly stick to my side leaving Andy to his, and keep a gulf between us so that our bodies didn't accidentally touch in the night and falsely indicate that all was forgiven and he could get away with the same behaviour again. Anyone who said *never go to sleep on a fight* obviously wasn't aware of the passive-aggressive, self-gratifying buzz of doing so.

I sat down on the ottoman at the foot of our bed and began to tackle the pile of unfolded laundry which had been sitting there for most of the week. It dawned on me, as I separated my clothes from Andy's, pairing socks and rolling them into little balls, that there were only going to be three more Saturdays like this one, before the Super Saturday that would be our wedding day. The evening before, when I'd told him about the Sera argument – no, not argument, clash, thing, whatever it was – and how confused it had left me, I realised how upset I was about it. I'd told him I knew she was project-ing all the disappointment about the promotion onto me but she hadn't even texted me to apologise after-wards when she realised, even though I'd gone out of my way to send one to her saying, *It's fucked up about the job. Should've been yours. This place doesn't deserve you. Lay x.* He'd listened to all of it, nodded, ordered dessert for us, and let me offload. I couldn't remember him saying much in response, but maybe that's because I'd barely stopped talking. I did remember his hand on top of mine, though, there in the middle of the table at the restaurant, and him squeezing it occasionally, and I remembered feeling better without necessarily feeling like anything had been fixed. But now that it was the start of a new day and with the whole summer ahead, everything seemed to feel lighter. This was due, in part, to the way I'd been woken up. Andy had snuck out of bed early, leaving me there to lie in. I'd opened my eyes and rolled over to find a tray bearing loose-leaf green tea swirling inside my favourite teapot – the small glass one with its matching cup – and a miniature jar of honey like the kind you get in fancy hotels, and finally a croissant. It was from a bakery we'd stumbled on by accident on one of our meandering walks, and I'd told him their buttery, flaky pastry was the best I'd tasted this side of the Channel. He always made a point of remembering it when I said that something was my favourite. I loved how he collected those snippets, insights into me, and filed them away, pulling them out of his hat whenever he wanted to make me feel good.

I heard the tap turn on briefly before several quick splashes and a satisfied groan coming from a refreshed, smooth-skinned Andy. I smiled to myself and continued to Marie Kondo our T-shirts, knowing that any moment

54

now he would come back into our room, see me there, still in my lace-trim satin shorts and camisole, and decide whether he had enough time to do all the things I'd seen flash through his mind and across his eyes as he'd turned to watch me leave the bathroom a few minutes earlier. I didn't look up from my folding pile, but hummed along to the music playing in the background, pretending to be oblivious, giving him time to weigh things up. I could honestly say that there had never been a Saturday morning, or any other time in our relationship, when I had been too tired, too busy or in any way uninterested in having sex with him. The sex felt different depending on the mood or time of day or how much time we had available, but it always felt good. If he opted in now and allowed himself to be a few minutes late for practice, I could tell it would be over in moments, that both of us would be left breathless, and all the neatly piled clothes would once again become a heap on the floor at the foot of the bed.

I put my running shoes on and left the flat with Andy, trying to keep up with him as he rode his bike out of our cul-de-sac and joined the main road. But he was too quick and I started to lag behind. I saw him turn to give me a cheeky smile over his shoulder as if to say he'd won our unspoken race, before disappearing round the corner and off to the hockey pitch in Hampstead.

Sera and I had had our Saturday brunch ritual going strong for the past few years. We'd usually exchange texts when we woke up to goad one another into doing a pre-brunch workout to justify everything we planned to eat later on. Sera opted for T25 in her living room, while I liked to run along the disused railway to Highgate along Parkland Walk. The sweat helped me clear my head, like it was being drained. No matter what, brunch was uncancellable. It could not be deviated from, postponed or bumped. In lockdown, we even had Zoom brunches. It always trumped everything else. We would be buzzing from Buck's Fizz by twelve and lost in conversation about the old days, the ones to come or what had gone down at school that week, until three. But that morning, with no pre-brunch messaging, I was seriously lacking motivation. A run would at least give me something to blame the tightness in my chest on, not wanting to acknowledge the real reason for the trepidation I was feeling. I was pinning quite a lot on how Sera would react to the dress I would soon be surprising her with. I hoped it would make her feel special where the interview had made her feel cast aside. Everyone likes surprises, I told myself, as I reached the entrance to the trail. I put my earphones in and pressed play on the 'Don't Wanna Run' Guided Run in my Nike app, and even though I didn't want to, I did.

She looked at it. Just stared at it. But didn't say anything for a long time. She hadn't taken her jacket off or put her bag down despite having been at Erica's studio for twenty minutes already.

We'd met at the station and I immediately started rambling, asking her how her evening was, trying to make everything okay. She didn't mention my text, just said she'd switched off her phone and spent the evening with Caleb. He'd turned up, cooked for her and they'd vegged out on the sofa watching TV. She was quiet, didn't ask how I was or how my night had been. I bought her a coffee from a hole in the wall in case she needed the caffeine and we made our way down a high street once voted fourth in the Top Ten of Britain's Most Depressing Roads.

The studio was in the basement below the boutique and was a cross between a haberdashery and a teenage girl's bedroom. Reams of coloured fabrics marked with chalk lay draped over benches. Incense tinged the atmosphere, evoking yoga studios and stalls at Shepherd's Bush Market. Erica's cat prowled around her ankles and occasionally rubbed himself along a piece of fabric, one of which left traces of glitter across his grey fur. I couldn't help but think about the musical and wanted to sing a few lines of 'Magical Mister Mistoffelees' but it wasn't the right moment.

'Make yourself at home,' Erica said, smiling at Sera, while she tinkered with the hem after the big unveiling. I decided to step in to help Sera do just that, scooping the strap of her bag off her shoulder. She finally peeled off her jacket, and then looped back round to the dress which hung magnificently in the centre of the room.

'What do you think?'

'It's nice. Yeah, beautiful.' Sera circled the dress, stopping to check the corners of her mouth for stray Vaseline in one of the mirrors on her way past.

'You know it's for you, right?' I said with a nervous chuckle.

'What did the others say about theirs?' said Sera.

'They, theirs are . . . Basically, don't tell them you got a fancy one, okay, because theirs are from Debenhams.'

She looked the dress up and down, stepping closer to it but not too close, it seemed. The garment was the hottest of pinks – vibrant, neon almost – a single block of colour except for within the folds of the silk where it caught the light. There, it looked silver, molten, as though precious metals were being poured from a height before us. It had been cut for a loose fit and fell to a floor-grazing hem made up of three layers. It would make her look as if she were floating. And from behind, the scooped fabric and rows of three delicate spaghetti straps for each shoulder would frame her back as if it were fine art. She could really show it off on the day by sweeping her hair into an updo. There were no other adornments. It didn't need any. The dress was just like her. Bold. It was about colour, simplicity and grace. Somehow, it even managed to flatter the hanger.

'Is it too pink?' I probed.

'Nah. I could pull it off.'

'That's what I'm talking about!' I said overzealously, trying not to give too much weight to the way the word 'could' had landed with all the vague, distant possibility of a choice that had yet to be made. I brought my left thumbnail to my mouth and clicked it between my teeth repetitively. Erica was now hovering the way a salesperson at Ikea might when stuck serving a couple who were having a domestic about exactly how they'd configure the Billy bookcase they'd spent several hours deliberating over.

I could feel her looking from Sera to me, from me to the dress. Me. The dress again. Sera. She wanted me to take the lead. Coax from Sera her feelings, concerns, gut reaction to the dress. She wanted me to broach the obvious: was she going to try the thing on or not?

Just then the glitter cat sidled over and tried to caress Sera's leg but quickly realised that he would quite possibly be kicked or lose his tail if he persisted. The studio buzzer sounded; Erica silently thanked fuck, responding almost before it happened, scurrying off saying something about a delivery, which I imagined she'd try to draw out for as long as possible. Sera's attention floated away from the dress to the room around her. She fingered containers of buttons, strings of sequins, the red plastic baubles at the ends of pins protruding from little cushions along a workbench. She admired half a turquoise blazer being worn by a headless dressmaker's mannequin in the corner. In a bid to get *her* head back in the game, I said:

'Are you going to try it on?'

'I didn't realise that was what we were doing today. Wedding stuff. I'm not really in the mood to take all my clothes off. Get dressed again, that kind of thing.'

'It was a surprise, so I didn't want to, couldn't, that's why I didn't . . . Never mind.' I didn't want her to pick up on my disappointment that she hadn't screamed with delight at first sight of the dress, like she had when she FaceTimed me after Caleb had bought her a pair of Louboutins. All I'd been able to see on the call were bright red soles and all I could hear was high-pitched squealing. I half considered telling Erica to fish my dress out so that I could put it on to show Sera how easy taking her clothes off and putting new ones on was. But I didn't want to seem facetious, even though I would only have been trying to be playful, fun, like I usually was on a Saturday with Sera. Like we both were. Usually. Maybe she's tired, I thought. Or hangry. Should we have done brunch first and the fitting last? Or maybe she had the wrong knickers on and didn't want anyone getting a glimpse of them, even though I'd seen her parade around in her granny pants and little else on plenty of occasions. However she was feeling on the inside, on the outside she looked fine. Chic yet casual, wearing a polka-dot jumpsuit, strapless and stretchy, no bra. Her hair was scraped back into a messy bun and her skin looked dewy and fresh. She turned back to her dress, or the one I hoped would be hers, felt the silk with her fingertips, lifted the fabric of its skirt curiously, letting each individual layer float back down again. Somehow she was making the dress look better simply by standing near it. I knew she liked it. She had practically salivated over photos of elegant, one-of-a-kind dresses like this, made lovingly by passionate designers, every day in print. This one was real, and yet she was acting like I was asking her to put on her school uniform again.

I suddenly remembered the bottle of prosecco I'd asked Erica to chill. That's what we needed, both of us. We needed to loosen up. We needed bubbles. I retrieved the bottle from the little fridge, grabbed two flutes from the shelf above it and rushed over to Sera with them. 'One for you,' I said, mindful of popping the cork in the opposite direction to the dress. 'And one for me. We can't play dress-up without bubbles.' I held out my glass and waited for her to do the same. 'To da chief!' I declared and, although I think the nickname made her wince slightly, she chinked me back and we sipped. I felt my shoulders slide down a little and told myself she simply needed time to settle in and also, probably, some assurance that I wasn't about to shaft her with the bill for an expensive-looking gown she hadn't asked for, like some brides might.

'So, ready to try on your present?'

'Fine. Might as well,' she said.

Erica rushed back in brandishing a parcel to make it seem like she had left the room for a legitimate reason and hadn't been listening just outside. She ushered Sera into a large, semicircular fitting area and pulled the curtain across to give her some privacy. I exhaled and clapped my hands together in an over-the-top movement I was glad no one had seen, and began to pace around the room.

'How does it feel, on?' I called over. 'We wanted it to feel weighty, but, like, weightless at the same time, didn't we, Erica?' I was trying to fill the silence on my side of the curtain with words that would make me feel better instead of thoughts that were running away with themselves to places I was scared of. But neither Erica nor Sera took any notice of me. I could hear a few mumbles, pleasantries, a polite laugh here, an 'excuse my cold hands' there. Erica popped out to get some pins and bulldog clips but gave me no indication of her initial thoughts, or Sera's. I tried not to read into anything but folded my arms and tapped my fingers against my biceps impatiently, anxiously, in expectation. It was the expression on her face rather than the dress on her body I would be looking at when she finally emerged. As Billie Holiday began playing over the speaker, my mind flashed with something I'd once read about her. How she was, according to jazz critic and long-time friend Leonard Feather, 'sweet, sour, kind, mean, generous, profane, lovable and impossible'. The Sera I knew was all of those things. For as much as I loved her, and for all the ways in which she could build me up, there was no denying that she also had the ability to do the opposite when I least expected her to. I hoped this wasn't going to be one of those moments. The curtains parted, but insignificantly and briefly. Erica dashed out and retrieved some heels from the display in the shop and nipped back through to the fitting room again. This time, on her way past, she mouthed the word 'amazing' which made me do an involuntary mini fist pump. I began to let my head bob along to the UKG which had discordantly replaced the torch singing all of a sudden, took a sip of my prosecco and waited. I was starting to enjoy myself. I felt another piece of the wedding puzzle falling into place, another tick on the to-do list my life had become. My dress, done. Flowers, check. Shoes, tick. Bridesmaids, sorted. Well, almost. I exhaled with a huge sigh imagining Andy and me in San Sebastián in four weeks' time, brandishing shiny new rings on our left hands.

When the curtain hooks rattled again, they were thrown open all the way. Sera emerged with her head held high, her fingers delicately gripping the skirt so that she could safely cross to the mirror which covered a whole wall. I could tell nothing from her face. But her body language, her body within the dress, put me on edge and seemed to hint at something I couldn't put my finger on. Something that made me feel sorry for all of us – myself, Erica and Sera. She looked statuesque. Powerful, like the dress had amplified her innate ability to crush me with little more than a word.

She asked Erica how long it had taken to make, how she'd come up with such an amazing design. It was all Erica, Erica, Erica. So, when our host graciously gestured to me and told Sera it was a joint effort, I was hurt but not surprised when Sera tossed me an empty smile. Things were not going to plan.

'You look unbelievable, Sez,' I said. I thought about following it up with 'Seeing you in that, Caleb might turn my wedding into an engagement party, you get me?!' but it sounded clunky and disingenuous, and it would not be okay for Caleb to pull a stunt like that, so I left it.

It was when I took my phone out and tried to take a photo of Sera wearing the dress, or, rather, a reflection of Sera wearing the dress in the mirror, that things really turned sour. Sera inexplicably adopted the same expression I'd seen her use when she'd had the misfortune of being forced to use a public toilet.

'Can you delete that please?' she said.

I thought she was joking, being bashful, worried that I'd post it. Even when I told her it was just for me, to show my mum, maybe, she insisted it was erased and peered over my shoulder to check that it had been. Tectonic plates were shifting. She took one more look in the mirror, did an about-turn, let the skirt pick up speed and air like a flamenco dancer on an empty stage in an empty bar, dancing for herself. She lingered for a moment with her head looking back over her left shoulder, taking in the way the neckline scooped.

'Nice,' she said. 'Shame.'

I wasn't sure what she meant, but before I had a chance to ask, she began to walk back to the fitting room, more nonchalantly than she had exited it, I thought. The sound of splitting fabric was almost violent. She had decided not to pick up the hem as she walked this time, not even a little. One of the stiletto heels had pierced the silk millefeuille, tearing it several inches. Erica, ever the professional and firmly in 'the customer is always right' mode, quickly moved to free the heel from the fabric so that no further damage could be done. Sera kicked off both shoes and apologised profusely. To Erica rather than me, which felt in keeping with the morning so far.

Once again, I began to say words on the other side of the curtain in an attempt to quell the awkwardness as well as my shock and embarrassment. Erica assured us the wound in the dress was no more than a snag – 'It'll take me five minutes to fix that, I can do it with my eyes closed' – and that we shouldn't worry because that kind of thing happened all the time. 'All the time, honestly,' she said. Her lies were a kindness I was grateful for.

Sera put her jacket back on, put the strap of her handbag firmly over her shoulder and waited for me to get my shit together so we could leave. On our way out, we crossed paths with the next client. She smiled at me before practically running over to Erica's creation for her, a simple strapless number, all in black, with cut-out details just above the hem. It was stunning. I saw in her reaction all that I'd wanted to see in Sera's. Then the door closed behind us and I imagined Erica launching into a foul-mouthed tirade about her previous clients.

The eating part of the brunch took place a few hundred metres up the road at a Turkish restaurant. Ridiculously underpriced, heavily laden platters were placed in front of us bearing eggs, freshly baked bread, honey and yogurt, spicy sausage, olives, halloumi and hot, feta-filled tubes of filo pastry.

'Finally. Let's eat,' Sera said, digging in. I wasn't hungry. I tried to pick at bits but mostly sat still, quiet, amazed that she still hadn't apologised for what had happened in the studio. The brattiness, the ingratitude. The fucking weirdness, frankly.

'Why wouldn't you let me take a photo?' I said, stabbing at an olive with a cocktail stick.

'I dunno. I'm having a fat day.'

I scoffed. 'I've literally never heard you say that before.'

'It's true. That's why I wasn't really feeling the whole fancy dress-up thing.'

'Okay, well, I'll find out when Erica can have it fixed by and we can book in again,' I offered. 'If you like it, that is?'

She loaded her fork with spicy sausage and dipped it into golden egg yolk before lifting it to her mouth. She hadn't fully swallowed when she finally said, 'Look, Lay, can't I just wear the same as everyone else? And aren't they paying for their own? What's wrong with me doing that?' And then, quietly, almost inaudibly, she muttered, 'Don't need your man buying me dresses.'

'My . . . Andy? Andy's not paying for it. I am. I've been saving up.'

'Oh,' was all she said in reply. I was so annoyed at her referring to Andy as my 'man' instead of his actual name that I had to muster the courage to ask her why she was acting the way she was. Andy was a big fan of Sera. He saw the way she made me light up. He appreciated that we had the kind of bond that most people longed for but rarely found. Occasionally, he would text her to ask if Caleb might be interested in playing hockey when his team was a player short or to ask her advice on gifts she thought I'd like. I thought Sera was coming round to him too. Sure, there were times when she would nitpick his clothes or his laugh, or the fact that he seemed to be on a 'crusade', as she put it, to diversify his workplace. She seemed ever so slightly wary of him but no more than she had been of every other male I'd hooked up with since my first kiss at the age of thirteen. Or so I'd told myself.

'You will wear it, won't you?' I asked.

There was no answer. She gestured to her full mouth to indicate that she was chewing and not prepared to engage in conversation with me at that moment. The only sound coming from her was the squeaking of halloumi.

'Sera? Seraphina?' I demanded, this time full-naming her so she knew I wasn't fucking around.

I was dumbfounded. I had burnt my tongue on hot feta and, nearby, there was a couture dress with a gaping hole in it. But mostly, I was completely, utterly lost.

5

Before

Sera was the person I was most excited to tell. We'd chilled a bottle of fizz for the occasion. Andy poured some out into each of the three flutes on the table as Sera hugged me lightly.

'Nice rock,' she said to Andy, smiling half-heartedly in his direction but without making any other kind of congratulatory gesture towards him. 'Didn't need my help for that one then?'

'No, luckily I couldn't mess this one up. It's come down through my family, so –'

'Really? How did I not know that?' I said, tucking into the *croquetas* in the tapas spread I'd assembled for the occasion.

'I did mention it but you were pretty busy screaming your head off,' Andy said, nodding to Sera and trying to get her on side with a 'what's she like, eh?' kind of expression. Sera knew exactly what I was like, and gave him the same look back in return. 'Screaming,' he continued, 'and jumping up and down in the middle of the –'

'He did it in the middle of the bridge, by the Japanese maple –'

'Formerly, the most zen spot in London –'

'In Waterlow Park –'

'Until you turned up, that is –'

I hit him playfully as we spoke in relay, each cutting in to grab the baton, tripping over ourselves in excitement to share snippets of the story. Sera tried to keep up, her eyes moving from Andy to me each time one of us spoke before she gave up entirely. I could hear how annoying we sounded, how sickly sweet the whole scene was. Us, holding hands across the table, faces beaming, finishing off each other's sentences. Something I couldn't remember doing before, or maybe we had and I'd been so wrapped up in myself I hadn't realised how embarrassing it was. It felt like, overnight, I'd become one of those smug, overly happy people who can't understand why everyone else isn't walking on air and permanently smiling. A fiancée.

'It rained though,' I added, to try to tone things down a bit.

'I'm not sure we'll be allowed to go back. You probably gave all the peacocks a heart attack,' Andy said.

'He's exaggerating,' I said.

Sera looked up. 'Cute. You guys are . . . cute.'

Then she folded her arms across her chest for a moment before taking in both our faces, releasing one arm and raising her glass.

'Cheers,' she said.

'Cheers,' Andy echoed.

'Cheers,' I added, all the while staring at the glass of cava Sera had passed over in favour of the water glass she had decided to toast with instead. I tried not to think about what bad juju it was and instead placed the last *croqueta* into my mouth. Whole.

The engagement party was so delayed it almost made more sense just to skip ahead to the wedding. But, after all the lockdowns and false starts and all the abnormalities about the new normal we had been forced to exist in for so many months, it was important to me to mark it, our promise to marry each other. I wanted to celebrate it and I didn't want our families and friends to have to meet for the first time on our wedding day. I wanted people to have a drink together, to get to know each other, to like each other.

It was an alfresco gathering, held a couple of hours before dusk so that the sky over the Italian Gardens in Hyde Park would look its most beautiful. When it came to park locations, Andy had made a bid for it be in Waterlow or Finsbury or even Highbury Fields to keep it local and also, I think, to show off how much green space we had to choose from. He hadn't seemed to miss being south of the river too much over the previous nine months which was yet another reason I felt so sure that the choices we were making together were right and the wedding would soon be another triumph. I'd based the idea for the engagement do on something I'd seen on Instagram. I'd even asked a bartender friend if he'd be resident cocktail maker for the event. I'd planned the whole thing perfectly in my head and I was hoping it would pan out the same way. When it was finished we'd go home, just the two of us, and I'd feed him cake and then any part of my body he wanted and we'd congratulate ourselves on having successfully pulled off what was basically a mini wedding reception.

In Andy's corner were his parents, his sisters, his brother-in-law, Aunt Jessie and her family, Best Man Dan, a handful of groomsmen from uni and a couple of people from work. In mine, I had Mum, the bridesmaids – Sera, Poonam and Siobhan – Caleb (gracing us with his presence), a few old faces from uni and some more of the Heartview High faculty. I'd practically begged Sera to help me set everything up but she said she couldn't and would probably miss the start of the party. She'd been intent on dragging Caleb to any flat viewings she could get for two beds in new, concierged developments offering Help to Buy in the Greater London area, and they had a full day of viewings before the party. She knew in her gut that he'd dig his heels in with excuses about everything that was wrong with whatever they saw. How they were too expensive, or flimsy, or hadn't learnt anything from Grenfell when it came to cladding, but she was prepared to go through the motions if only to have something to throw in his face about how she'd been putting in the effort compared to him when it came to thinking about their future.

Luckily, Poonam had been our loyal foot solider for the afternoon. She'd helped me decorate little tiered plinths which we used to rest each of the Ottolenghi-inspired salad dishes on, so that it looked like the front of one of one of his restaurants. We'd even strung fairy lights to the low branches of the tree I'd earmarked as the perfect spot. I'd prayed no one else would be sitting there when we arrived to set up but had no qualms about politely asking any squatters to move along, was even prepared to pay them in money or burritos if I had to. I'd made a playlist and a pavlova and I was ready to party.

I was happy to see that Sera and Caleb had arrived while I'd been off collecting my mum from the wide-open green space she'd managed to lose herself in.

'Finally. I thought I'd never find you,' Mum had said as I approached her.

'Technically, I've found you. I dropped a pin. Didn't you get it?'

'You know I can never follow those little blue dots anywhere, Layla,' she said and we made our way back to the party.

Once we'd rejoined the others, Mum made a beeline for Sera, embracing her and saying a quick hello before I introduced her to Andy's parents for the first time. They bumped elbows instead of shaking hands, which I thought was nice and seemed to break the ice. After a few minutes, Andy's dad had managed to make my mum laugh and I began to feel myself relax as Andy and I watched on. We caught each other's eye so that we could acknowledge that what was happening was a big deal but also going smoothly and we didn't have to worry.

I started to notice that Sera and Caleb weren't really spending any time in each other's company. In fact, they were almost repelling each other, like magnets turned the wrong way round. Sera chatted to Poonam while Caleb was several metres away in deep conversation with someone else's plus one. If we'd been in a room, Caleb would have been trying to take it over, as usual. I could hear his voice, intentionally louder than the music and everyone else, but I let it slide. The vibes were, generally, good, positive, and even though hosting usually gave me mild anxiety, I was able to breeze around in my black maxi dress and my sparkly flats checking whether people needed their drinks topped up, and telling them to enjoy themselves, eat food, save room for cake.

'How did the viewings go? You got here quick,' I said to Sera when I was finally free of Andy's old uni house-mates, and out of Caleb's earshot.

'Is it obvious that we're not talking?' she asked. She was her usual well-put-together self, hair loose and parted at the centre. She kept tucking it behind her ears as if it was irritating her, tutting whenever a few ten-drils escaped. She had thought about her choice of heels. Wide, not stilettoed, so she didn't sink into the grass.

'You two? Why, what was the problem this time? Location? Service charge? Not enough room for his man cave?' I nudged her as I teased. She let me do both.

'He could choose any of those flats and I wouldn't argue. I'd pack. I'd pack up and go, like, now. I hate that.'

'Hate what?'

'That he has that power over me.'

In a moment, the mood of the conversation went from light and playful to deep and dark. Sera wasn't the kind of person to submit to anyone else's will easily. But she was right, there was an energy about the two of them, together. It seemed intense. But the fact that it had always been that way, that she seemed fine to comply, had always meant that I just let her get on with the whole thing.

I heard the music notch up in volume. I cast a glance around to make sure that it wasn't disturbing any of the other picnickers nearby and relaxed a little more seeing that the party was taking care of itself. Andy was smiling with a beer in one hand and a burrito in the other. The oldies seemed happy getting to know each other and most people were on their way to being deliciously drunk. I could allow myself the time to watch the last few particles of daylight going up in embers in the pink-orange sky knowing that it was really happening. I was really engaged. To the most wonderful man.

Towards the end of the night, I could see that a huddle had formed which consisted of Aunt Jessie, her daughter, Andy, Best Man Dan and Sera. From where I stood, a few metres away, only half listening to what my mum was saying to Andrea about dance therapy and self-expression, it looked like Aunt Jessie was holding court, smiling as she spoke and linking arms with her favourite nephew. Sera looked distinctly not into whatever was being said and didn't seem to be pitching in to the conversation. I'd suffered the same fate at Jessie's birthday party when I got left alone with her. I'd had to listen to her describe in detail the perfect conditions for growing runner beans in the back garden and would have done just about anything to make it stop, so I guessed Sera needed rescuing. But part of me also half wondered if it was all a bit much for her – the party, the happy families – when she was clearly in the middle of a rough patch with Caleb. I didn't like to think it, but at that moment I wondered if she might be slightly jealous of me. Of all the deadly sins available, envy had never featured in our relationship before. There was plenty of gluttony and occasional wrath but I'd never wanted anything she had nor she I, on the face of it. We were equals, two halves of a whole. What if she was now looking at my life with green eyes, growing bitter about the parts she wanted but didn't have? But it was only a thought. A passing thought that would go away again, like a fly being batted towards an open window and finally finding its way out. Apart from an engagement ring and someone to split the rent with, I didn't actually have anything she didn't have. Not really.

But as I sidled over to the group, threading my arm through Andy's and placing it around his waist when I reached him, the two of us the picture of premarital bliss, I understood why Sera had her screw face on.

'Well, all I mean is, she's very fair, isn't she?' Aunt Jessie was saying. 'Oh, your ears must have been burning,' she said quickly, noticing me, but without altering her course. 'I was just saying, your mother – who I must go and introduce myself to – she's so much darker than you. And I think it's all fascinating. You just don't know what colour the babies might be.' Then finally, when I thought it couldn't get any worse, she topped it all off with 'Very fair, I should think' and took a gulp of wine.

I looked around at the assembled faces. Jessie: tickled

pink by her own observation. Jessie's daughter: an apple who hadn't fallen far from the tree. Best Man Dan: thinking about getting another beer. Andy: worryingly unreadable. Sera: horrified.

And as for me, if someone had taken a photo of the moment and shown it to me later, I would see myself looking small. Incredibly small. So small it was as if I hadn't been there at all and I could pretend it had never really happened.

6

27 days until the wedding

Once a month, on a Sunday, Mum and I had a little tradition. Come hell, high water or even passive-aggressive arguments with your best friend, these Sundays were sacrosanct. We would catch the 8.50 train from London Euston and arrive at Birmingham New Street roughly two hours later. We would then jump into a cab and go the five miles or so to Erdington, north-east of the centre, passing signs for Villa Park and going over Spaghetti Junction where we would be dropped off at a parade of shops. The shopkeeper, recognising us as Roy McKinnon's family, would greet us by name, ask us how we were and say something about 'all that madness going on in London' before shaking his head and chuckling to himself, while we chuckled to ourselves and got on with picking up our usual shopping list: bun, cheese, whisky and ginger beer. The final stretch of the journey would be completed on foot up the steep hill that was Grandad's road. At Grandad's, reggae rose from the house like steam rising from coffee morning to night. It was always on so loud it ushered us towards it from the bottom of the street. It made you feel like everything was going to be alright, within that house, with the world.

After a morning of cooking, and some light jamming or watching the news, awaiting our arrival, Grandad would spend the rest of the day with us smashing dominoes down on the table so hard it could break in two. We always arrived hungry. The kind of hunger that could only be satisfied with *that* oxtail, in *that* seasoning with *those* dumplings. And the coleslaw that went on the side – the no-frills kind from Iceland that cost £1.50 for a family-sized container – and muted the burn of the perfectly balanced flavours in Grandad's gravy. Every so often, Mum or I ferried plates of food to and from the kitchen at the back of the house to the sitting room at the front, with its bay window looking out onto the impossibly steep street and the other terraced houses lining it. Occasionally Grandad would take a sip of whisky from a glass that looked like it hadn't been washed since the seventies and sometimes an eruption of 'Touch 'im!' would come from his direction in an accent so thick with Jamaican lilt that I couldn't believe he'd been in England for sixty-seven years. 'Touch 'im' told us he was winning the game. I didn't know what it meant in a literal sense, but the vigour it was relayed with clearly conveyed the opposite, that no one could touch him, he was so far ahead that he could never be caught and the other players should sit back and take note, go through the motions, lay their dominoes but not actually expect or hope to win. Winning was never in my sights anyway. I didn't have the heart to admit to him that I didn't really know how to play. I mean, I knew how to play – matching one set of dots to another – it was easy to make it look like I was a legitimate player, crouched around that rickety coffee table, scratched, burnt and stained with the bases of a thousand whisky tumblers and spliffs that had rolled from ashtrays.

But I knew there was more to it. There was strategy and skill. In cards, you get card counters. Well, Grandad was a spot counter. He knew exactly how many 6s, 2s, doubles and blanks were left in each player's hand. I'd been playing since I was tiny, and I still hadn't worked out how he did it. But it was fun, and we got through the best part of a bottle without really noticing. It was time, together time, time to reminisce. Talk about who was still left on the island and whether he'd ever go back, what it had been like to work down the pit and under cars. How pain felt. The pain when a child dies, or a wife leaves, the pain of loneliness. All those things disguised as a game. Of matching spots to dots and blanks to nothingness.

'Y'alright, Bab?' Grandad used the word as a term of endearment for me – his only grandchild – his nephew in Jamaica when they spoke on the phone and some-times for my mum. Within that word was every ounce of love he had for his pickney-dem, and it never failed to make me feel safe.

I did my best not to feel blue on that particular Sun-day. Sera hadn't called or texted since our brunch the day before. Usually, on weekends when Sera was staying with her mum, there would be a selfie of the two of them together, Sera and Dorea, both smiling and waving at me with accompanying captions saying they wished I was there or that they'd just watched some old, grainy camcorder footage of the two of us as eleven-year-olds practising a dance routine. We'd learn them from music videos or shows like *Sister, Sister* and *Moesha*, rewinding specific sequences over and over again, until the ribbon in the video tape became hot and tangled and eventually beyond repair. It felt novel to us that girls who were black and brown could carry an entire show, make us laugh, make us think and, on top of that, teach us how to sing and dance. We never once saw anyone do all that with a British accent.

It was rare for Andy to work on a Sunday but things had kicked off on a project and he said it was unavoidable. I tried not to sulk too much – he'd be stuck at home in the spare room at the expense of visiting Grandad. And especially when he'd spent most of the previous evening trying to soothe my anxiety over the dress fitting. I'd found it sweet, if annoying, that he'd been in Sera's corner the whole way through, subtly hinting that I should try to think about things from her point of view, that she might be feeling under pressure trying to organise a suitable send-off for her best friend when she clearly had other things preoccupying her and possibly more going on with Caleb than she was letting on.

'So, why can't she just say that then? And I did offer to take the hen do off her plate, just for the record,' I'd said, shooting the messenger without meaning to. He took it in his stride, like he so often did, and continued to let me prop my feet up on his thighs on the sofa while he flicked through the bewildering number of options available for our viewing pleasure.

'Don't worry about it. It's not like she's not going to organise your hen,' he'd added, without looking away from the screen. 'It will all be fine, I promise.' Everything he was saying made sense and I wanted to believe him, really tried to. So why did it feel like he was wrong? Like everything was.

Thinking about Sera made me stare off into the middle distance in Grandad's front room. Not even the bass from the stereo seemed to be able to jolt me back and Grandad asked again if I was 'alright, Bab?' I was glad he was so willing to accept it when I said I was this time. He switched to asking after Andy. Grandad loved Andy, which surprised me at first because he hadn't enjoyed meeting Mum's last serious partner and the way he had kept his outdoor shoes on in his lounge and even taken it upon himself to turn down the volume on the record player. He was never invited back again. But Andy had done something miraculous to Grandad. At their third or fourth Sunday meeting he had come to the house bearing a bottle of whisky. Andy had asked my mum and me what he could bring and we told him that Grandad always liked to have a bottle of High Commissioner to open. There was always one not too far away, ready to seize, unscrew, pour until he had finished it, sometimes entirely unaided. But Andy had arrived at my grandad's house with small beads of sweat gathering at the very top of his forehead, looking nervous, clutching a beautifully wrapped box of something that was not the recommended High Commissioner. As I watched Grandad de-ribbon, unwrap and unbox the expensive bottle from a small whisky producer in the Highlands, my eyes moved from Mum's face to Grandad's and then to the bottle and back and forth in several small, undetectable flicks so that I could take everything in and try to think of a way to apologise on Andy's behalf before running to the local shop to correct the error. I could sense my mum biting her tongue, the kiss of her teeth confirming that she thought Andy foolish for going off-piste. But before I had the chance to intervene, Grandad stood up, the bottle in his left hand and a smile growing steadily across his face, and erupted into laughter. He then proceeded to slap Andy on the back in half a dozen of the most affectionate and sincere blows I'd ever seen him deliver to anyone, confirming his delight that someone had finally bothered to spend a bit of money on his favourite thing in the whole world when he could never afford to with his modest pension. My mum and I didn't get a drop. That was Grandad's and Andy's. A loving cup shared by them and nobody else.

While I updated Grandad on what Andy was up to, Mum picked up a record from the stack propped up against a houseplant that seemed to grow several inches up the wall in between our visits. I'd never once seen Grandad water it but I could imagine him doing so, a private act of care-giving, each and every day. It was the only living thing he shared his house with and he wasn't about to let anything else in his life die. He had lost his only other child, Mum's half-brother, a decade earlier in a motorbike accident.

Mum slid the record out of a dog-eared sleeve which looked no thicker than tissue paper and bore no title or artist. She held it by its edges as she blew lint from its surface. This ritual made the music sound even better. There were so many records in that room that you could listen to a different one every day for a full year. Dub, reggae, soca, 'chenga-chenga' – not an official genre but so-called by Mum because of the way the guitar strings were plucked and pinged, the way they made you bounce your shoulders up and down and bop and spring at the knee as you moved around the room.

With our soundtrack thronging, we finally got stuck into putting the world to rights, conversation so deep, you wondered if you'd stay lost within it forever. It moved from the ordinary – the neighbours, their indiscretions, hearsay at the corner shop – to the extraordinary – how Grandad had once single-handedly pulled a man from fallen rubble on a building site; from politics – whether we'd ever see a black prime minister (not in his lifetime he assured us) – to the past – back to Jamaica, his beginnings, the origins of him and therefore each of us sitting in that room. He paused for a moment to take a sip. He barely touched his food when we were together and always said he'd eat properly in the evening after we left. It was enough for him to see us enjoy what he'd cooked, watch us lean into the cushions of his sofa, bellies full, heads lightly buzzing from whisky and ginger beer or cans of Red Stripe from the fridge, dozing off blissfully. His family. Provided for. He coughed a little and rubbed the left side of his abdomen with his hand.

He looked like he was feeling around for something, a tender spot, which he found and prodded a few times to check how sensitive it was.

'Y'okay, Dad? You got some pain?' Mum asked, trying her best to play down the concern in her voice.

'Mi alright, Bab. Mi alright. Mi tek after mi daddy. Him neva sick.'

The room fell into silence. It would soon be time to leave so, for just a moment, I let my eyes close and my head fall back onto the top of the sofa to soak up the serenity of that place, enough to get me through the week ahead, the sorting, the doing, the thinking, the talking.

'Him a, a, a, a – him a policeman. Daddy. Policeman, ya'know,' Grandad said after a little while. 'Him neva cough, nah splutter, nah sniff like him did wan' fi sneeze. Neva.' He sat back in his armchair as though considering the notion for the first time, his father's immunity to illness, his invincibility. I let his words float into my ears and reach a level of understanding deep in my body, like there was a special place for his wisdom within me where everything made sense.

'Every morning, him run up and down pon di sand. Barefoot. Bare back. Baring him chest an him soul fi all tuh see. Him always sey him just as him meant to be. Everyt'ing alright wid di world. He did tek a likkle drink from time to time but everyt'ing in moderation. Everyt'ing alright if unu 'av self-control. Him always had money wen he did put his hand inna 'im pocket. Sand 'tween him toes. Peace an quiet wen he want it. Fruit tree, free fi him to pick, growing just there inna 'im

84

yard. Chicken a-run round him foot and him own bricks, him four walls round him. Roof ova him head. Him always sey, if you 'av your own home, a likkle patch dat is yours, den what unu 'av is peace. And dat is what mek unu feel rich! Not more money and more dis and dat. Your own home is like a likkle piece of heaven you find on earth.'

Then silence took hold of the space once again. The music had stopped. I wasn't sure when. It had simply faded away as Grandad spoke, it had stepped back and let him take the floor with his words.

'No, my father neva got sick,' he came again. 'Not once inna him whole life. Di first time him sick, him dead.'

I opened my eyes suddenly, taken aback by how easily and unexpectedly Grandad's musings had strayed into talk of death. Mum hadn't been jolted by it in the same way. In fact, her eyes seemed to sparkle in the afterglow of any talk of Jamaica, like she was right there on the beach, running alongside her own grandfather. I knew she thought of Jamaica as a kind of Mecca or at least an amalgam of all the good things about the Notting Hill Carnival – which she never missed – without the rain or the constant threat of cancellation by the council. It was as close to Jamaica as she had ever come, and Grandad had only been back twice for funerals – his father's and his older sister Cynthia's. We often talked about going together one day, who we'd stay with and where we'd drink, but I could never tell if either of them ever really had any intention of making the trip, no matter how much

I went on about it. It had become one of those things they joked about, that they'd always come back to, but it wasn't a real notion. No tickets would ever be booked, no distant relatives informed that they'd soon have visitors.

Grandad got up from his armchair. His hand remained in the same spot on his side as he shuffled across the room in his slippers. He cleared his throat and appeared to wince in discomfort. Mum and I locked eyes, both of us noticing that he wasn't his usual spritely self. Before he was fully out the door, Mum gathered up the used mugs from the coffee table, to make it seem less obvious that she was following Grandad to talk to him in private about why he seemed out of sorts.

'I'll come with you, Dad. Make another round.'

'Alright, Bab,' and Grandad pinched her arm lovingly and waited for her to pass through the door first like the gentleman he was.

'We've got bun and cheese, remember,' I called after her. 'On the side.'

I didn't follow, just stayed in the front room to give them a few minutes to themselves. They'd talk as she boiled the old tin kettle over the gas hob, while he peeled back the sticky plastic wrapping clinging tightly to the dark, fruity bun. I'd bought pre-sliced mature Cheddar to go with it to save any messing around. For some reason, I always forgot about the bun until just before home time. Always. I could feel my taste buds beginning to spring into action at the thought of it. I made a mental note to wrap a couple of slices up and take them home for Andy. He probably wouldn't want a big evening meal.

Bun and a cup of tea would cut it. He'd want to get to bed early so he could be fresh for the start of a new week. Those evening lie-ins, as I called them, were just one of many little habits we'd formed together – one which probably made us sound like we were old before our time and officially the world's most boring couple. But where I might've cared about that before, with other guys, I didn't any more, not with Andy. With Noah, a boyfriend I'd dabbled with when I was twenty-six, I'd had a panic attack one Friday night, after finding that we were in bed by nine thirty, both reading books in silence in his king-size bed. I broke up with him the next day and swiftly went on a forty-hour bender with Sera which ended in a warning from a community support officer for smoking weed outside Ministry of Sound at 4 a.m.

When Mum and Grandad came back into the room in mid-flow, my mother was using the tone of voice she used when she knew she was right and the other person was irrefutably incorrect and would be proven so shortly. But Grandad was simply laughing. Grandad had a thousand different laughs. This one wasn't rude or dismissive in any way. It was the kind that meant Mum was worrying over nothing.

'You need to get someone to look at it. If you won't go to the GP, let's at least call 111. They can tell you what might be causing the pain.'

'Wha mi seh? Mi alright! Mi nah si no doctor-man who go tell me fi go away. Or mi-a cry wolf.'

'Where are you getting that from?'

'Plenty. Plenty o' people, dem. Anyway, di las' t'ing di

doctor dem-a need right now is more patients. Dem a-busy wid all o' di Covid. Cha.' Cha was Grandad's version of a full stop, and he clearly wanted to leave the matter there. But Mum scrunched up her brow as she sipped her peppermint tea, the bag still floating in the dark green water. She was concerned. I could see her mind whirring to assess the level of persuasion she would need to get him to agree. She sipped, and sipped and sipped, and then replied:

'They have a duty of care –' which is as far as she could get before Grandad kissed his teeth with such force that I thought they might all be sucked back into his mouth, which would at least justify an ambulance I thought silently but didn't offer up to try to break the tension. Then he slapped his leg pointedly and sat back down in his chair.

The room was shady, the sun sitting low in the sky. It was several moments before he moved again, this time stretching over to the coffee table for some bun. It was clear from his pained expression that he was trying not to groan in front of us. Still, Mum knew then that she had to let it go. But she would try again the next day over the phone, and the day after that, and the one after that for as long as he told her that the pain persisted or, more likely, until he lied that the pain was suddenly gone. Or until our next Sunday visit came round and she could see for herself, with her own two eyes, that he was once again like his father, never sick, and doing nothing to warn us of danger afoot.

7

Before

On one of these fabled Sundays, when I was eleven years old and had just started at secondary school, before he'd shooed me out of the front room so he could secretly roll one of his funny-looking cigarettes, I asked my grandad if we were Scottish. It was like the time I asked my mum why I wasn't 'blue' like her when I was around five and colour-blind or colour-confused, or simply unable to articulate how I saw my mother's dark brown skin compared to mine, pastel beige and unremarkable. I'd been prompted to ask the Scottish question because a teacher had said that my surname signified that we were clans folk, or near enough.

Mr Gregor wore his family tartan around his neck without fail every day he taught me in Year 7. It was impossible not to realise he was Scottish. He explained to me at great length during a Geography lesson, as the rest of the class worked quietly on something to do with a map of the British Isles, that the McKinnon clan was a branch of the Gregor clan and that I should ask my father all about it, as 'all good Scots know their clans'. I told him I would, because I was too embarrassed to correct him in the middle of the hushed classroom. So I held the question in my mind until the following Sunday, back in Birmingham. Grandad's reply had shocked me.

'No, man. Dat de slave-man name.'

Two waves of shame passed over me in that moment. The first, because it had never before entered my pretty, blonde, eleven-year-old head that anything to do with that had anything to do with me. That time in history you read about in books. The second, because I was embarrassed that it did.

But mostly, all I could think about was how much I wished I could forget the answer. How much I wished I had never asked the question.

8

21 days until the wedding

It was 31 July.

The thought of the following day being August, the month of my wedding, made me want to stop the world so I could get off for a minute. Or five. Or a few days. A week tops, just to give myself a breather. It had been a busy and laborious week. A week in which I vowed never to go to Hobbycraft or any of its competitors ever again. On Tuesday, Poonam and I had gone in for two items only: a pack of 3D papier-mâché numbers to place on each of the tables at the reception and a can of gold spray paint. Ninety minutes and £157 later, we emerged, wondering what the hell we'd filled our bags with. I was also feeling weary because Poonam had badgered me about the hen around the entire shop.

'She's on the case. It'll probably just be drinks. Really pared back. Low-key. But fun. Really fun. And, hey, at least it'll be cheap,' I'd said, in an attempt to soothe her well-meaning questions about Sera finally letting her know the when, what and where. Why it was taking so long and who I was kidding were different matters.

'It's your last taste of freedom, Layla. It's supposed to be the most amazing party of your life.'

'I think you're confusing that with the actual wedding, Moony.' I'd started calling her by her family nickname – Poonam meaning 'full moon' in Hindi – when I heard her niece use it soon after we became friends in the middle of our MEds at Imperial.

'You do know we're going to Ibiza for mine, yeah? Summer 2025. Put it in your diary.'

The fact that Poonam didn't even have a boyfriend was meaningless. I knew we would one day, maybe in 2025, maybe the year after, find ourselves lost in lasers at Amnesia, with her in a plastic tiara and a Bride-To-Be sash. It made me feel like a failure that Poonam's hen was more of a sure thing than my own.

If it hadn't been for last night, I might have given Sera the benefit of the doubt, tried to believe that she'd been beavering away behind the scenes all week long. A week after the end of term was a fair grace period to set the date, book a place, distribute the information to the bridesmaids, I thought. But instead of a progress report letting me know whether we'd be going to a cocktail-making masterclass or getting sweated on by Magic Mike (I didn't even care which any more, I just wanted to have something to tell the others), Sera had replied to my link to our Saturday brunch spot – King's Cross, just opened, 4.8 on Google, buttermilk pancakes – with one of her own. A link to a programme on BBC iPlayer and a text saying: *Speaking of food, here's some for thought*. I didn't click on it straight away. I slung my phone onto the sofa non-chalantly and answered the door to the delivery guy. With Andy at a leaving do and a Friday night to myself,

I'd ordered in. A double portion of crispy deep-fried squid and garlic-oil-drenched morning glory. Green noodles, I called them, so I could feel virtuous and like I'd made a marginally health-conscious choice. It looked so appetising when it arrived, I photographed it before eating the entire thing in a matter of minutes sitting cross-legged on the living-room floor. After that I took a long bath. I liked to linger in the tub after pulling the plug out. As the waterline moved down my body, it took with it a little of the sense of foreboding I had about Sera's cryptic message with each slurp of the drain until finally all the water had disappeared. Then I rubbed peppermint lotion into my feet and wrapped myself in my dressing gown before sitting down on the sofa to half watch the programme and half jot down ideas for my speech for the wedding, the one I wanted to seem impromptu but which would in fact be planned with military precision, would make people laugh and possibly include an a cappella love song.

Britain's Forgotten Slave Owners. I realised as soon as the title appeared on the screen that brunch was no longer going to be brunch. I watched both episodes back to back and cried throughout. And afterwards. In fact, I felt like part of me might be crying forever. It was a bit like *Who Do You Think You Are?* but with a distinct lack of C-list celebrity. It was like a *Who Do You Think We Are?* All of us Brits. A *Who the Hell Do We Think We Are and What the Hell Is Our Country Built On?* That's what they should've called it, this documentary looking into the compensation paid to British slave owners after

Abolition, when they found themselves out of pocket, when it became illegal to trade in human lives. To keep Africans prisoner to do their bidding. To harvest their sugar cane. To make their rum. But it didn't end there. The documentary talked about another endeavour undertaken by the show's historians and researchers. And I knew instantly that was the real reason Sera had sent me the link. They had set up a database for people – ordinary people, the very same who might buy a family member a genealogy kit because they'd run short of ideas for their next birthday; unimaginative people who don't understand the gravitas of things – to look up the names of everyone who'd received one of these compensation payouts. I started to wonder if Sera's aim in sending it to me was to make me feel like a bad person, to position herself as the good one out of the two of us. I felt stupid, a very precise kind of stupidity. Like I'd been caught in a lifelong act of pretending that the past had nothing to do with me, couldn't touch me and certainly had no part to play in my relationship. The irony of being a teacher and feeling particularly uneducated immediately made me feel sick and unsafe in my own company.

The documentary had set the scene by showing the presenter handling instruments used to torture, the horror of the middle passage, the natural beauty of the Caribbean islands compared to the hellish realities of what had taken place there. But at the crux of it was the new research which had been conducted by a London university into the legacies of slave ownership and the way the money paid to slave owners as compensation after Abolition sank like seeds into the soil of the British Isles. There, it germinated and stretched its roots into our foundations and infrastructure to the point where what we saw around us today could no longer be considered clean. And then there was the database. The names of the individuals, the families, who'd received compensation for the loss of their assets – the enslaved themselves. The fact that my surname was probably in there. Or rather, Andy's. It became all too apparent, as the credits rolled, as I stared on aghast, the containers from the Vietnamese takeaway discarded at the foot of the sofa beginning to smell sour, that I had failed to do my due diligence.

I quickly decided that the database was a can of worms I shouldn't open. But it simultaneously seemed to take all my willpower, and very little at all, not to load the site and type in our surname. It wasn't that I thought I'd find anything incriminating – life wasn't that cruel, surely. But I was scared. Scared that if, for some reason, the database did present me with worms, worms whose concealment within their can had kept me safe all these years, including the eighteen months Andy and I had been together and especially the last six while we'd been engaged, I would be nothing short of fucked.

I always liked that we already had the same surname, Andy and me. It was our thing. There'd always been something beautiful about it. Something that linked us before we ever even met. Before that programme, things were good. We were good. Everything was normal. I was a girl about to marry a guy because I loved him and he loved me. Now suddenly it was different. I wished I could un-watch it, forget about what I'd learnt from those two hours of television, delete the dangerous new knowledge about the database from my mind and simply go about my normal everyday everything.

So, I turned off the TV. I put a wash on, flossed my teeth, watered the plants. Pushed the thought of it away. I constructed a few choice sarky comments in my mind to send to Sera like 'historical research into my future husband's surname is above and beyond your chief bridesmaid duties WTF!' But then, before I knew it, I was logging on with intent. I used my work laptop in the spare room with the door closed and the doorstop in front of it so Andy wouldn't suddenly appear over my shoulder. I was being calculated about things, I could feel myself thinking up excuses if he ever found any clue that I'd researched him like this. I held my breath and typed in the letters, M-C – quietly berating myself as I did so about being stupid, doing a stupid thing, K-I-N, something I should be embarrassed about. Did I not have enough going on without this? N-O. How had I found the time to stalk the ancestors of my future husband for evidence of their ownership of mine? We weren't – N – even married yet and I was already sneaking around. Already kind of lying to him. ENTER. And there it was. McKinnon. White, Scottish McKinnons. Reams of them. I slammed my laptop shut.

It all felt tainted then, like it was all falling apart. All because I couldn't leave well alone. Suddenly there was this film of murkiness covering everything. You couldn't touch anything without getting some on your fingers. You couldn't just wipe it off on your jeans. Part of me was embarrassed to be making an issue out of something that was nothing. But if it *was* nothing, why was it making me feel this way? Maybe I should have felt more embarrassed that I could possibly think that this thing, this unspoken, ugly, dark 'nothing' that I'd unravelled in the fabric of our relationship, was inconsequential. Maybe, in reality, it was everything. I wondered what Andy knew. Had this information been an open secret in his household? Could it really be true that the financial comfort enjoyed by him, Alex, Sasha, his parents, the twins, and – even more mind-fucking than that – by any children Andy and I might one day have, was in part due to this compensation? Not to mention the profits his ancestors had made off the backs of the enslaved people they owned in the first place. I climbed into bed, pulled the duvet up to my chin, and, even though I felt like I'd been lying awake for hours, my eyes wide with worry, somehow I was out for the count before Andy walked through the door.

There was demolition work going on next to the station as I made my way to brunch. The building that had stood there before was now only half a building. The vision of that destruction – fully furnished rooms ripped apart, the foundations of concrete walls dangling precariously over piles of rubble below – felt like a bad omen for my meeting with Sera. I wanted to pick up a hard hat to protect me from whatever might come flying in my direction once we were face-to-face. I was glad Andy hadn't really thought to ask what I'd done with my Friday night in before he'd left for hockey. If he had, I would have lied. Would've just pretended everything was fine and I'd watched a forgettable film, eaten my takeaway, done some tidying up and gone to bed. It was nice to be able to save myself an untruth; it made me feel more trustworthy somehow.

I arrived at the restaurant shortly after eleven. The hostess gave me the option of a table outside in Granary Square or tucked away indoors. I scanned around trying to see if Sera had already staked her claim somewhere but I couldn't find her. Something about sitting outside on the plaza in the sunshine felt too relaxed given how awkward this was going to be, so I manoeuvred inside and pointed to a table in the window which gave me a view of the door and the square as a safety measure. It was apparently good etiquette for job interviews to allow the candidate to have an escape route in their sightline which they could choose to use at any point. The restaurant was fairly empty, although every other table had a small metal tent in its centre with the word RESERVED across it so I imagined it would soon fill up. I hoped she wasn't running too late, hoped she was actually going to show up.

When she finally arrived, she was in the middle of composing a text or an email on her phone which must have been urgent as she wasn't prepared to take her attention off it to make eye contact with me as she sat down in the seat opposite.

'Hey,' she said in greeting, after clicking send, even though the moment had passed.

'Hey. Did you get a chance to check out the menu? Think we should do the bottomless or just –'

'I'm not eating,' she said, as if it had been obvious.

I looked at her wordlessly, all the unsaid things rushing to the space between my eyebrows, the place my yoga teacher always referred to as the 'third eye', which only ever made me feel like a character from *Star Wars* instead of an enlightened yogi. For a moment it felt like all the things I could say, would say, were held just there, perfectly articulated, eloquently stated, bravely backed up. After my search on the database had brought up what seemed like a never-ending list of McKinnons last night, there had been no let-up in my mind catastrophising everything. Trying to pre-empt what Sera was thinking, what she was going to say to me. Whatever was about to happen, it probably wouldn't change the feeling that I'd done something wrong. Or Andy had. It was this icky, heavy feeling that I couldn't get rid of. But I didn't know what it was – the crime, the misdemeanour – I couldn't seem to express it, not even to myself.

Just then, the waitress appeared at our table, saving Sera the effort of having to engage with me just yet. 'A Bloody Mary. Please. That's all,' she said in a clipped manner. The waitress shifted her eyes to me, so without thinking I pointed to the fried chicken and waffles on the menu and immediately regretted my choice. I smiled at her so it didn't feel too odd that I wasn't speaking, and, with that, she left saying, 'I'll bring some water for the table.'

Within minutes, I was sure I could smell my order, my portion of fried chicken and the fluffy doughiness of the waffles filling the restaurant. I felt nauseous but hungry at the same time. I wondered if I should raise the documentary straight away before the food arrived. It just wasn't practical to expect to be able to eat and argue at the same time if that was where we were headed. But confrontation was something I went out of my way to avoid. It usually fell to Sera to do any confronting, which was (usually) one of the perks of being her friend. She was fidgeting in her seat. I could tell she was thinking about picking up her phone but was trying to resist the urge. It wasn't our normal comfortable silence. It felt loaded and ugly. The waitress came back and placed Sera's drink down in front of her and a jug of water in the middle. I watched the condensation fall down over its curves and pool at its base.

'So, did you watch it?' I asked, surprising myself. I was certain she'd wanted to be the one to ask this of me, and I felt oddly powerful getting in there first. I was constantly sending her articles based only on their headline without having read them myself, which was totally pointless when Sera wanted to discuss them with me later and couldn't because I didn't know any of the details about the new potential cure for cancer or whatever it was about. I was hoping this was another one of those situations. Just another one of those things we did.

'Of course,' she said. 'Caleb and I watched it together.' She tapped her nails against her glass and traced her fingertips around the rim. They'd probably checked out the database as well, probably had a laugh together about how stupid I was. How late I was to the party that was my own life.

'I did too,' I said quickly. 'It was shocking. I didn't know that . . . about the money. That it was how they . . . It was good. Really good. Good to know.'

'Good to know? Right.' I saw her eyebrows flick up briefly, almost imperceptibly. It felt like everything I was saying was the opposite of what she wanted to hear. I wished I'd prepared something in advance, something I could recite, like a review. Why had she landed it on me like that? I wanted to tell her that I'd been home alone last night and if she'd bothered to call round instead of text we could have watched it together and evaluated it like adults. Or teachers. Or, crazier still, like friends.

'I mean, obviously I knew most of that stuff,' I lied. 'Kind of. Bits of it anyway. It was really interesting.' The meaninglessness of the word 'interesting' lingered between us as I poured myself a glass of water and finished it in one go. I poured another one. It wasn't until I had almost finished the second glass that Sera finally spoke again.

'Don't you think it's a bit of a wake-up call? Because, lately, Layla, I don't know . . .'

The waitress appeared over my shoulder to place my plate just beneath my nose. I greeted the arrival of my food with a semi-audible 'fuck'. The girl was so unimpressed with me that she didn't hang around to offer me any condiments and I knew she wouldn't be popping back to check how everything was going with my meal. I stabbed at the beige stack of food in front of me with my fork, severing a piece of fried chicken and a cube of waffle in one go. It was dry and chewy in my mouth and I longed for something to lubricate it with, but I had no idea what the right sauce was for such a ridiculous meal. Still, I was glad I had something to do as I thought of what to say. I chewed and thought. Chewed and rephrased. Chewed some more. Finally my mouthful was so well masticated I began to worry that I was grinding my teeth to a fine powder. So I swallowed and cleared my throat. And then I stepped up to bat.

'Lately, what? What's wrong?' I said.

'Marrying your oppressor is what's wrong.'

Involuntarily, I began to laugh. Nothing was funny. Nothing. But my disbelief at what she was saying seemed to manifest itself as laughter and there was nothing I could do about it. I put my knife and fork down on the plate, sat back in my seat and looked at her.

'Okay, that was a bit over the top,' she conceded. 'But having the same surname. You being who you are, knowing where your name comes from, all that stuff your grandad told you, him being who he is. I could have told you something like this was going to come out.'

'Really?' I said, incredulous.

'Yes. And maybe you would have found out on your own eventually. But all of a sudden you're moving in together and getting married. I'm just, I'm worried about you. Like, the way you're shrinking yourself to fit in with his family.'

'I'm not shrinking myself,' I said, while scanning my mind for all the instances when I might have appeared to make myself smaller, less visible around them. There were several to choose from.

'Okay then, just to give you an example, you're planning to straighten your hair for the wedding, aren't you?'

'I don't know yet,' I said. I was.

'Don't you?' she said, not letting up.

'Maybe. But only because that's the look I'm going for. Not for the reason you think I am.' But it was. I sipped my water meekly, eyes lowered.

'You're my friend, yeah. I want you to be okay. I want you to feel like you can be yourself. You've got to think about whether you're making the right decision, that's all I'm saying.'

Then, for what felt like the hundredth time that week alone, I decided to give her the benefit of the doubt, asking, and only half meaning to sound like a teacher speaking to a twelve-year-old when I did, 'Is everything alright at home, Sera?'

'Don't you have any respect for yourself?' she shot back at me. 'For your heritage? For your friends, like me? Or your mum? Do you even watch the news or do you just pretend to know what's going on in the world? Marrying someone linked to your family's oppression like that – being owned again – that ain't right.'

The look on her face made me feel pathetic and lost, trapped in a moment I couldn't get out of. But she seemed so in control, her words so perfectly formed. I suddenly felt completely alone. In a busy restaurant. In London. With my best friend. I had no one.

'The answer to all of those questions, if you'll let me

speak, is yes. But who's being "owned again"? Where are you getting that shit from?' The fact that I had managed to string a sentence together felt miraculous to me.

'I thought you were a black gyal, deep down, Layla. Rita's daughter. Roy's granddaughter. My friend. That's where you come from. But . . .'

'But what?'

'Why are you acting so white?'

I felt hot, like my blood was reaching a dangerous temperature inside my body. My hands were shaking. I couldn't remember ever experiencing a physical reaction like that to the mere sound of someone's words.

'Are you seriously telling me you are pissed off with me because of a TV show?' I asked.

'I'm not pissed off.'

'Then what?'

'Y'know, you can be so naive sometimes, Lay. It's the way you're acting, like the past has nothing to do with you. You can't feel good about marrying someone whose ancestors might've owned yours. And even if they didn't, they sure as fuck owned someone's and that's pretty messed up too.'

'I thought you'd come round to Andy. I would never even have met him if you hadn't forced me to go to a party I didn't want to go to. Andy's a good guy,' I said. 'He's decent and he's kind and he cares about things.'

'Oh, don't get me started on that. Mr Diversity and Inclusion. Since when is it his place to get more black people into his company? Has anyone there asked any actual black people what they think? Or is it just for show? To atone for the sins of his ancestors?' The last part seemed to be more of a throwaway remark. Like something she was testing out but didn't necessarily want me to hear. But I had and my eyes widened at the sound of it. She really seemed to be gunning for Andy. I shifted in my seat, pushing my plate to one side so the space between us was clear.

'Is this why you aren't organising my hen? Because you hate my fiancé so much?'

'Seriously?' she said, staring me out, making me wish I hadn't gone there. 'Are you seriously still considering marrying him?' It was an extreme I couldn't have imagined her going to. But she went there anyway.

'Are you joking, Sera? Andy has done nothing wrong.' I couldn't actually believe we were having this conversation.

'But he's part of it, isn't he?' she said. 'Look at his family. His aunt basically thanked fuck you're light-skinned at your own engagement party, Layla.'

'She's seventy,' I said, not quite shouting, but aware that other people could hear me. 'And I can't believe you're using that against him. *He's* not like that.'

'Well, I can't believe you're going out of your way to make excuses for her. For any of them,' Sera said.

The look Sera gave me then told me everything I needed to know. Her mind was made up. I was going to have to choose between my wedding and my best friend. Between losing my soulmate and losing my soulmate. The thought that I might actually be deprived of Sera made my brain feel like it was having some kind of spasm and I began spouting anything and everything that entered my head without filtering it first, to try to claw back the things I felt slipping away from me.

'I don't have to take his name, at the end of the day. I mean, obviously I already have it, I have the same one, but I don't have to retake it. The act of retaking it is what I feel like you're mad at me about. That's right, isn't it? Because we could actually be one of those couples that chooses their own married name. Have you heard of that? Or I could take Andy's middle name – Mason, it's Mason, which sounds like a surname, doesn't it? And, same initials, so that's a plus, a bonus. Whatever. Or – no – I mean, this is going to sound a bit – but I could speak to my mum about looking into our family tree a bit and see if we could trace things, back, back, back, back, back to our African names. I'd be up for that. Because that way we'd be bringing it full circle, like, honouring them, I mean, Andy might be up for adopting that name or something. Bit modern. But he's very progressive.'

Sera gave me a look I'd never seen before. Under the table, I pinched the loose skin around my left wrist between my thumb and forefinger in an act of self-consciousness, as though I needed to check I was really there.

She sipped and said, 'You're not taking his name. You're keeping it. Like some fucked-up kind of Stockholm syndrome.'

There was no official end to the brunch. We both wanted it to be over and we were both complicit in letting it fizzle out, in letting the other person get quieter and quieter, sinking further into their phone or picking the dry skin around their nails until it was over. In a slow and uncomfortable series of snide remarks, scoffs, tuts and passive-aggressive stares into the middle distance, we managed to ask for the bill, mutter some fakery about seeing each other soon, saying hi to my mum or her mum or some other unpleasant pleasantry, paid said bill and, somehow, make it out of there alive.

I imagined Sera choosing not to take the Tube and walking the length of Caledonian Road so that she could call Caleb or one of the new names I'd been hearing lately – Reena, Emma – who I'd never met because Sera had never introduced me to them – and giving them a blow-by-blow account of how things had played out. The new names were people she'd met at the Black Teachers Assembly. She had made it clear that it was her thing and not mine. She kept telling me I wouldn't have time to contribute in the way they wanted people to, so I'd never really tried to get involved. And I hadn't really noticed what had been bubbling away between the two of us because I'd had other things to attend to. Namely my wedding, which now seemed like it might derail eighteen years of friendship.

After I left the restaurant I went to sit by the fountains in Granary Square. The rain I'd expected never came and cirrus clouds hung like nets of lace across the crisp blue sky, so I sat on a bench and watched the water shoot into the air and fall back to the ground in waves as toddlers, some in swimsuits, others in nappies, pitter-pattered around each spout in fits of pure joy. I thought about calling my mum but she worked Saturdays and, besides, I wasn't sure I wanted to tell her what had happened. She'd probably say something thought-provoking yet neutral in a bid to make me see Sera's side, but that wasn't what I wanted. I wanted to be angry at her. Actually, I wanted to be unrelentingly furious with her. In what universe does your best friend try to ruin your marriage before it's even begun? I wanted to rage at her for finding some historical quirk to disguise the fact that, in reality, she didn't like Andy. I didn't know if she ever had. And if Mum had even hinted at seeing where she was coming from with all that, I'd only end up going off at her too.

I called Andy and he answered immediately. His voice was welcoming and loving at the end of the line. He asked how brunch was and if I'd sorted everything out with Sera.

'All good,' I said and felt the sweat building at the sound of the first big lie I had ever told him. I couldn't be honest about what had happened with Sera because I knew he would never forgive her for upsetting me. And not just that. I wanted to protect him from it.

Sometimes, after brunch, Sera and I would play movie roulette at the nearest cinema, asking the cashier to sell us two tickets to a film of their choice that was starting within the hour. We'd then go to the nearest newsagent and buy bags of Butterkist toffee popcorn and pre-mixed cans of G&T to sneak in. The best were films we'd never heard of before or ones with subtitles. We'd usually come out slightly tipsy, berating the film and the person who'd sold us the ticket, saying how we'd never do that again but both knowing we probably would, the very next week, because it gave us a little thrill and was something we only did with each other. I told Andy that Sera was just buying the tickets. That she said 'hi' and I'd see him at home after the film.

Now that I'd lied to Andy about where I'd be for the next few hours, I wondered how I should spend them. I could feel a wave of sadness building up in me and I knew I needed to get a grip so that I could think things through properly and decide on a course of action. That was how my brain worked. Where there was a problem, there needed to be a solution and a plan. I wanted a swift resolution so that I could get back to finalising the wedding and spend the next three weeks in a state of reverie, not getting stressed out like other brides-to-be. I was determined to enjoy the run-up to my wedding no matter how selfish that seemed.

I hoped that what had happened in the restaurant was just one of those things we were going to talk about a long, long time from now. Talk about and laugh about, somehow. A knotty, interesting thing which would make people say 'really?' and 'that's crazy' when I told them at parties. I hoped it wasn't the insurmountable friendship destroyer it felt like at that moment. I stared into the spray coming off the fountains. Sera and I were not broken. Not yet. But we were bowing under a strange new pressure. She hadn't slept with my boyfriend or betrayed my trust. She hadn't upset me by telling me my wedding dress was ugly or stood me up. We hadn't pissed each other off or had a serious bust-up in the normal sense of bust-ups typical of successful, professional women of our age.

But maybe what had happened was worse than all that. She'd told me I wasn't black enough to be her friend any more, or I didn't act black enough. Or I didn't respect the parts of me which were black. Maybe these things were all the same, but on that bench, I pored over it all, second-guessed everything, in an attempt to get to the heart of the matter. She wanted me to choose being black over being white, and not marry a white guy, or at least not one whose family might've owned mine. The notion was either completely understandable, rational, a kindness one friend was doing another. Or dangerously toxic. An abuse of trust. An unthinkable ask. I wondered what Dolly Alderton would make of it if she'd received it as an anonymous letter to her agony aunt column. I'd like to think she'd at least say, 'Ooo – that's a good one,' before diving back into her pile and responding to one about someone's anxiety about their boyfriend of two years developing a sudden secret porn habit, the writer being a virgin and unsure what to do about the whole thing.

I began to remove my Stan Smiths and then my socks. I stretched my legs out and wriggled my toes to let the passing breeze weave through them. I rolled up my baggy boyfriend-cut jeans to the middle of each calf, feeling the dryness of my skin and making a mental note to apply copious amounts of coconut oil after my shower that evening. I made sure the straps on my yellow cross-body clutch were pulled tight so my phone wouldn't get wet inside before gingerly stepping out into the nearest fountain. I was the only unaccompanied adult doing so. I wanted to be a child again for a moment. To be unburdened from all the shit adulting meant. I pretended I was that girl on her first day of secondary school, lucky enough to already have made a friend. Someone who would tell the others not to laugh at her because anyone who laughed at her 'sister' would have her, Sera, to deal with. And while the laughter grew because we didn't look like real sisters, we felt sisterly inside and didn't care what the outside world said about the outsides of us. Back in the days of my colour-blindness.

9

Before

There was a flurry of texts from Mum asking me if I'd heard and whether I'd seen the video. I told her I had but it was a lie. After hearing the news on the radio, I had made the decision to actively stay off the internet so I didn't stumble onto the video anywhere. I didn't need to be a spectator witnessing a man's final moments on earth. But even without seeing it, I didn't seem to have much trouble conjuring up imaginings of the scene that had unfolded across the Atlantic as London slept. The fear on his face. The scared animal-man-child-being he'd been reduced to in front of the world's gaze. In front of his killer whom he'd begged to stop killing him. It gave me a feeling I couldn't shake. A feeling I couldn't quantify. And to add to it all, I didn't know where Sera was.

We had arranged to meet at Highbury Fields to do a few laps and try to enjoy the bank holiday – the beginning of half-term – as far as lockdown rules would allow, but she didn't turn up. There'd been no text to say she was running late, no missed calls and she wasn't answering any of mine. I wondered if her phone had run out of battery on the way there, or if she was ill and needed looking after but hadn't been able to let me know for some reason. But whatever the reason, it was completely out of the ordinary for her not to show up and I was worried. I tried texting Caleb as casually as I could, without seeming overanxious or alarmist in any way, but when he didn't reply within a few minutes, I decided that no Covid rules were more important than finding out if my best friend was okay and I jumped on a bus and rushed to Sera's flat.

Eventually, the door was opened. Her head was wrapped in a brightly patterned silk scarf. Tufts of unbrushed hair escaped through some of the gaps and the scarf had become loose and dishevelled at the sides. Her eyelids were heavy. Puffy and swollen and red along the lines of her eyelashes. She wore a dressing gown I didn't recognise over a baggy, faded Prince T-shirt and shorts which looked too big for her, like ones Caleb might play basketball in. I headed straight into the kitchen, watching her slope off down the corridor to the living room. I ran the tap for a glass of water and looked in the fridge to see what I could put together. The kitchen was immaculately clean. There were no takeaway boxes on the surfaces, littering the floor or in the recycling bin as one might expect, so I decided I should make every effort to feed her immediately. I heated a pan, added olive oil, some chopped garlic and onions. I rinsed the contents of a can of chickpeas and added it to the softening alliums before pouring in enough vegetable stock to cover the contents.

I left the soup to simmer and went into the living

room. I didn't say anything. Neither of us did. I just stood and observed her from the doorway for a few moments, all curled up, foetal, as she watched the news on the TV by the fireplace which no longer housed a fire but a wilting cheese plant. She looked at the screen, or through it really, like a child mesmerised by the scenery rushing past the window when they first take a train. She looked weak as she lay there on the sofa. 'Mauger' as my mum would say. A patois word which always evoked images of stray dogs with prominent ribs and threadbare coats. I went back to the kitchen, seasoned the soup and then tasted it. It was simple but flavourful, a thin broth I hoped would revive or at least comfort the shell of my friend in the other room. Seeing her eat a spoonful would make me feel better. I found half a lemon which was dry and faded in colour but still held a little juice and squeezed it over the bubbling mixture in the pan.

I didn't need to ask her what was wrong, as we sat there sipping soup on the sofa. I searched the pale broth for sunken chickpeas and saw Sera doing the same. I felt like a mother watching her ailing young child as she tasted, chewed, slurped and swallowed what I'd put in front of her. She wasn't the kind of person to let the weight of the world sink her, but this had. His death had clearly plunged her into a deep despondency. I could feel her sadness and a part of me felt bad for going about the day normally, even getting out of bed, instead of staying at home to watch the news loop and repeat, incrementally adding new details with every passing hour as more was learnt about the dead man and the cop. The counterfeit $20 bill which had started it all; the cries of 'Tell my mom I love her. I'm dead. I'm dead' which had marked the end but also the new beginning that followed. I wanted to tell her I got it, that it had punched me in the gut too. But instead we just sat together and watched. I reached for her hand and squeezed it tightly. I was grateful to feel hers spring to life to reciprocate.

'I can't stop watching it, Lay. I can't stop – can't stop trying to work out why. Why do they treat us this way?'

I tried. I really tried but I couldn't find the answer either. Again we fell silent. Again we squeezed. Still we watched. Until finally, Sera said:

'Something big is coming next, Layla. Watch. It has to. Because – because . . . it just has to.'

'So, let's meet at eleven tomorrow,' Sera said at our new normal Zoom brunch.

'Tomorrow?'

'The protest? It's starting at the US Embassy and heading to Trafalgar Square. You are coming, aren't you?'

'Yeah. Of course I am.'

I had never joined a public gathering in protest of anything before. I had a vague memory of Mum taking me with her to lay flowers outside Kensington Palace for Princess Diana when I was five years old. And we'd gone together to lay flowers at Grenfell. Those had been sombre, mournful events. They were a kind of protest, one could argue. No less full of rage and upset. The idea of marching seemed important but also scary and big, like something I had only seen on news footage and at the cinema, with crowds of people walking through the streets behind community figureheads, linking arms, unafraid to take the first blows from the opposition or the police. But I knew I had to be part of this. No matter how far I disappeared into the crowd, how insignificant I seemed to the cause, I wanted to be one of the people using their presence to show that things had to change.

Little did I know, my body had other plans for me. A migraine attack. I hadn't had one for years, but as soon as it began, I was in no doubt. It came with the same warning signals it had back then: zigzagging shards of light across my eyes, obscuring my vision. A persistent tingling sensation down my left arm. A crushing sense of anxiety and an almighty stabbing pain in the side of my head which confined me to bed for the rest of the day. I called Sera first thing in the morning when the aura started, in tears partly because of the loathsome feeling the migraine was bringing on but mainly because of the disappointment that I would be missing it, and that I was letting her down.

I was still apologising the next day. I called her full of questions to find out what it had been like. Who had she gone with? Had she seen any arrests? Had she stayed until the end?

'Just wish I could've been there,' I said, unable shake the FOMO I was still experiencing.

'Forget it. If you're sick, you're sick,' she said.

'Although I seem to remember you didn't have any trouble dragging yourself out of bed when you were supposed to be recovering from that laparoscopy in second year when you desperately wanted to go to a gig. But, hey. What can you do?' I didn't know what to say. I was shocked by what she was insinuating.

'Anyway. Glad you're feeling better,' she said, less accusingly. 'And don't stress about it. There'll be plenty more marches. Plenty.'

10

20 days until the wedding

'Communication. Communication. Communication. It's what it's all about,' James bellowed and clapped his hands together. It was a punchy opener for the final session of the marriage preparation course Andy and I, along with three other couples, had attended every Sunday evening for the last four weeks. Punchy and directed specifically at me, or so it felt. Like he knew somehow that I had spent the last twenty-four hours doing whatever was the absolute antithesis of communicating with Andy. But at that moment in time, I couldn't have communicated with him even if I'd wanted to (which I didn't) because he wasn't there. He was late.

Attendance on the course was a prerequisite of where we'd be getting married. I'd been going to the Roman Catholic Church of St John the Evangelist in Islington with my mum on and off since I was a child. She'd switched us to it despite it being a bit further away from where we lived after our local church told her they would only baptise me if she changed the spelling of my name to match how it appeared in the Bible. Her love of Eric Clapton won out, and we became semi regulars at St John's. For Mum, church seemed to be about quietening down the constant chatter of the world around her. I knew she prayed, but she didn't preach, didn't shout it from the rooftop or deliver readings during Mass. She simply drew strength from her faith when she needed to and tried to put that out into the world in her own way. Grandad's relationship with God seemed to extend only to the framed psalm hanging on the wall in his front room.

Nostalgia had a lot to do with why I still occasionally found myself in the pews at Mass sitting next to Mum. It was a special place. I had been christened in its font and had received my First Holy Communion at its altar, so it felt only right for my next rite of passage to be there too. And although Andy didn't subscribe to a religion or regard himself as particularly spiritual, he did at least seem to have an appreciation for ecclesiastical architecture.

'Actually, I always like to credit a fourth C for ours surviving the last twelve years, darling. Chocolate!' Lydia tittered to round off a joke she'd probably made a hundred times or more over the years. But chocolate was actually one of the reasons I enjoyed coming to the sessions and her joke segued nicely into the arrival of the box of M&S biscuits they always laid on. The ones you needed to use a chisel on to break through the thick, brown casing on the outside of each one. I took two as the tray was passed around, telling myself it would help to soak up some of the alcohol. I was approximately one espresso martini away from being drunk. I'd put a hard stop on drinking with the three out of four bridesmaids who were still speaking to me around 16.00, telling myself that I could sober up from my lightly bubbling state during the journey from Soho to Islington. But that hadn't happened. In reality, I'd stopped drinking at around 17.14 before jumping into a black cab at 17.15 somewhere near Brewer Street, praying I'd get to Lydia and James's house for 18.00 without being sick on the back seat.

Alcohol was the tactic I'd gone for to deflect attention away from Poonam, Siobhan and Alex all receiving the notification SERA LEFT on the group called 'Lay's Hen' on WhatsApp earlier that day. I'd glossed over it with a very dubious lie that Sera had been the victim of one of those phishing cons and she'd had to get a new phone. I'd pretended not to see the way Poonam was looking at me as if to say 'Why are you bullshitting?' or how Siobhan and Alex had sought out each other's eyes while I was speaking. I was just grateful they were keeping their suspicions to themselves so I didn't have to deal with them. Alex, I knew, wouldn't be asking questions about Sera because she had launched straight into a monologue about her neighbours forcing a change to the on-street parking regulations through the council, putting her at some kind of inconvenience or disadvantage I couldn't really understand. I was, therefore, very much within the realms of inebriation as I sat on the sofa for our final class at marriage school, crumbs spilling out of the corners of my mouth, desperately hoping that no one would notice, while the other couples sat holding hands, or finding some other way to show how prepared they already were for wedded bliss.

James and Lydia were regular parishioners. I'd seen them at church with their two children, Arlo and Rosalie, who were eight and ten. They'd been running the course from their sitting room for the past three years. It was something they wanted to do, they said, for their parish, and it had the added benefit of helping them to regularly reflect on their own marriage. They were on the one hand very conservative, devout people, and on the other, hippyish and completely cringey in most things they said and did. Like the way James would sit on the floor by Lydia's feet sometimes, even though there was ample seating available. He'd prop an elbow up on her knee while absent-mindedly rubbing one of her feet as he spoke. It sometimes felt a bit much on a Sunday. I tried to tell myself it was sweet and I didn't want to gouge my eyes out at all.

But they seemed to take their roles as custodians of our future nuptials seriously and I appreciated that. It was like they had our backs, they really wanted us to be good at it, being wives and husbands, and although I wasn't quite sure how that kind of thing could be taught and learnt, I was learning. Something was going in, making me think about the daily grind of it, beyond the wedding – when Andy has forgotten to take the bins out again or I've spent too much money on scented candles. And it amused me to see the way everyone would squirm in their seats and come over shy whenever the word sex was mentioned.

A certain level of participation was expected of the group, individual couples and individuals within those couples, so it would have been better to have had a clear head. As I waited for Andy to burst in apologising and blaming the Sunday service on the Overground when really I knew he'd probably spent too long gaming, or had fallen asleep on the sofa bingeing on sport, I wondered if I'd ever see any of the people around me again after that day. There was Elise and Felix. Together five years. Engaged for two. Marrying in September. Who may or may not have realised that they had a body part touching the other person at all times. Next to them, Victoria and Zak were taking the whole thing very seriously. They never forgot their notebooks and matching fountain pens. They'd been together for two years after meeting at one of their church's monthly quiz nights which they planned to commemorate during their reception with a round of questions about their relationship to see how well their friends and family knew them. With prizes. I pretended to hate the idea when bitching to Andy after the first session but secretly wished I'd come up with something as cute for ours. Then there was Katya and Paul, who were nice. Really nice. A bit too nice in my opinion. They'd told us we were all welcome to come to their big day after a particularly touchy-feely session earlier in the course, but it turned out to be an empty invitation as they hadn't mentioned it again since. Not that we could have made it. Andy and I referred to them as our wedding-day twins because they would be exchanging vows within an hour of us at another local church on Saturday 21 August.

'As per previous weeks, let's spend the first few

minutes reflecting on what you took away from the last session and then we'll talk about what we'll be covering this evening. The final hurrah!' James said, before turning to Lydia to ask her something I couldn't make out.

Challenges. That was what we'd covered in the previous session. Essentially, all the shit things. For worse, for poorer, in sickness, those bits, as opposed to their jollier counterparts. James hadn't actually used the D-word at any point when he was asking us to consider what we might do in the face of infidelity, financial problems, disagreements over where to live, but all the talk of shit getting real suddenly landed it right there anyway, right in front of us with a thud. We'd all looked at each other fearfully. Felix, with his Cheshire cat grin and wispy hair, had tried to lighten the mood by saying that divorce was now most prevalent among the over-fifties and we were all barely in our thirties so it wasn't something we had to worry about for a couple of decades. But apart from that, it had been the quietest the group had been. The downs (from the 'ups and downs' that people always claimed they'd be able to get through in their wedding speeches) weren't what most engaged couples wanted to spend their time talking about. In the last three years I'd attended six weddings. Two destination, three registry and one church. There had already been one divorce and one affair among them. Still, I told myself that those kinds of things happened to other people, they would never happen to us. Breaking up before we got married though. Oh, that was still a distinct possibility, I thought to myself, sitting there, checking my phone for arrival updates from Andy and, secretly, a grovelling text from Sera, as I continued to process the database. The documentary. The disapproving friend.

Finally, at 18.11, Andy scooched into the seat next to me, making his apologies and kissing me on the cheek. A kiss definitely trumped all the hand-holding and knee-rubbing I'd been sitting amid, but it also made it completely evident to him, being within an inch of my mouth, that I was tanked up, prompting him to whisper in my ear, 'Big day with the girls, was it?' I put my finger to my lips and shushed him with a naughty glint in my eye. Lydia shook the pile of handouts impatiently, anxious to get on with the session. This one was called 'The Influence of Family and Childhood on Your Marriage'.

'Bit late for that, isn't it?' I asked jokily but completely rhetorically. Wrong crowd. Thankfully the question was mostly lost in the hubbub as people took their handouts, sipped their tea, dunked their biscuits. The only person who'd heard the mild scoff was Andy. I hoped he wouldn't laugh. If he did, he'd set me off and then we'd really be in trouble and the other couples would wonder how the hell we'd ever manage to matriculate at marriage university with them.

For the most part, I thought that the influence of my family and my childhood on our union would be positive, already had been. I was just glad it wasn't called 'The Influence of Ancestry and Friendship on Your Marriage'. From Andy's perspective, he'd lucked out, not having a father-in-law around to have to impress, please or prise me away from. Just Mum. Like

Grandad, Mum had fallen under Andy's spell very early on in our relationship. I'd called her the day after we first met, and without mentioning anything of him or the party, she'd heard the smile in my voice and said I sounded different. Then when I next saw her, she said I looked different too, not physically different exactly, but there was something in the way I was carrying myself that she hadn't seen before. She'd later told me that she knew from that day that Andy was the one. The three of us had since established a cute kind of three musketeers vibe. We would sometimes meet for dinner on a Friday night. On one occasion, when I was the last to arrive, I lingered for a moment on the other side of the restaurant before making my way to the table, watching from afar the two of them sparring, laughing, talking about work, politics, the state of the world. I loved the way they got into debates, how neither was afraid to challenge the other, or stand down to avoid putting me in the middle of something. And as for my childhood, though it had been untraditional, it had been happy. And so had Andy's. As a family, they had travelled widely, camped, cycled. They were an outdoorsy bunch whose motto seemed to be to see it, try it and learn from it, and to make the most of life. All things I wanted to feature in our marriage, in how we'd raise children. And together, on the surface at least, our two families seemed to get along which is really all you can hope for.

I opened the handout and scanned the first page for the group exercise. I huddled up towards Victoria and

Zak as I read it out. 'Discuss any marriages among your families or close friendship groups which inspire you and list their qualities,' it said. 'Who wants to kick off?'

'My parents. Without a shadow of a doubt,' Zak said, more to Andy than to me or Victoria. 'The last few years have been . . . yeah, don't really know how they made it through but they did. I want to be able to do that. Get through anything, y'know.'

'It's my mum and dad's thirty-fifth anniversary next year,' Andy reciprocated.

'Coral,' Victoria chirped up, like it would earn her a point. I tried not to laugh.

'How do you know all these?' said Zak, sounding a little exasperated but also titillated by his fiancée's general knowledge.

'They're having a massive do, hiring out the estate they got married at. I guess I'm kind of hoping we can follow in their footsteps a bit,' Andy said, smiling at me as he spoke. The reminder that they were planning a big blow-out party in the Highlands at the old McKinnon seat was unwelcome. Andy's family hadn't owned it for generations and it had long since been a hotel but suddenly the thought of going made me feel sick.

'Okay, wrapping up with your final thoughts for that one,' Lydia announced before picking people at random and asking if they wanted to share any of their examples.

'Layla, would you like to go next?'

'Sure, we've written down Andy's parents. And, er, Andy's sister and her husband. Those two. They're both really good ones. Weddings. Marriages, I mean. Married people.'

'And anyone not related to Andy? Your relatives, perhaps? Or any friends?' James looked at me. Actually, it felt like everyone was looking at me. Andy included.

'Nope, ran out of time,' I said and looked to Victoria in anticipation of it being her turn next.

'That's okay, Layla. Anyone you can think of now? Not to put you on the spot, but if you don't mind sharing, is there a married couple you find to be role models, people you might look to for advice or support?'

I suddenly felt very sober and very flushed. I crossed my arms over my chest. I couldn't think of a single example. Dorea was technically still married but only because Sera's dad had walked out on them in the middle of the night and never come back. They guessed he was still alive but didn't know where and didn't care either. Dorea had at least mentally divorced him if not killed him off completely in her mind. She had no plans to remarry so the legality of the thing didn't matter to her. She was unencumbered by it. So, I thought about giving the names of the 92-year-olds who lived next door to Mum. John and Patricia had been married since 1946 and hadn't spent a night away from each other since, they said. But apart from the pleasantries we'd exchange when we passed each other on the balcony, I didn't really *know them* know them. I wondered if I could make everyone laugh by citing our hosts as the model man and wife, a couple Andy and I could hold up for the way they seemed to understand the many levels of what it meant to be married.

I looked at Andy and felt a little embarrassed that I was so mute on the matter. I was the reason we were there. Me, wanting to get married in that church, and yet it was also me who had arrived steaming and with fuck-all married friends to show me how this thing was done. I took a deep breath, shrugged my shoulders and looked James straight in the eye.

'Beyoncé and Jay-Z.'

'You're quiet,' Andy said expectantly. But I stayed that way for a little longer.

It was ten past eight and getting cold. We jumped on the bus. Andy followed me up to the top deck. He knew I had a thing about sitting upstairs, right at the front. I liked to imagine I was driving the bus from above. I enjoyed being in prime position, seeing what was coming before anyone else did and feeling like I was on a theme park ride. My tendency towards childishness as a fully-fledged adult was so strong that I worried about myself sometimes. Would I ever feel my age or would I always be holding on to the past? Could I ever be a mother when I couldn't possibly see myself growing up in all the ways I was supposed to? Maybe marriage would have that effect. Shuttered shopfronts began to whoosh by as the bus took us along Upper Street and back towards Finsbury Park.

'How were the girls?'

'Good.'

'Alex alright?'

'Yeah.'

Quiet again. It had to be that way because every time I spoke, I thought, I should be speaking about one thing and one thing only. What would I call it? The ultimatum. That felt too dramatic. But at the same time, it wasn't far off what Sera was giving me. But I couldn't. Didn't know which words to choose, didn't know where I would even start. At the very first wedding preparation class, just a few Sundays ago, we'd discussed the importance of talking and listening, generally, in life, but particularly in marriage. It seemed like such an obvious thing, saying what was on your mind. Listening to the views, wants, grievances of the other person. Thoughtfully considering them and using this new-found knowledge to move forward in some way. To save arguments, make decisions or just get to the end of another day, not divorced. And I was doing precisely the opposite.

I could easily have got out of my own way and made Andy's attempts at a normal conversation easier. 'What about our first dance song? . . . Any ideas yet? . . . What are you planning to do next weekend while I'm on my stag?' were some of the things he tried to coax me with. But for the first time in a long time, I didn't want to talk about anything related to the wedding. All I wanted was to be alone with my thoughts to work out what was going on and the part I was playing in it. I wanted to teleport myself home and into the shower. Rinse the day off, the whole week. I carried on looking out the window. Andy had taken his phone out and was scrolling through Twitter. It felt like a missed opportunity that Twitter hadn't been something they'd bonded over, Sera and Andy. They could have compared notes on who they followed and were followed by, had full-blown conversations about it that I wasn't involved in because I wasn't on it. I would have liked that, I think, wouldn't have minded feeling left out if it meant they'd found some common ground, a shared interest. I knew Sera followed him because she'd let me Twitter-stalk him using her profile just after the house party. I suddenly got worried that Sera might have taken to the platform to talk about what was going on with us, canvassing opinions from her followers on the hypotheticals of your bestie mixed-race friend maybe marrying a guy descended from the very plantation owners who used to own her family. I dreaded to think what the hashtags would look like. I peered over his shoulder trying to see what he was looking at. But before I could, he closed down the app in a flurry, reached over to push the bell twice so the driver didn't pull away, and grabbed my hand, saying, 'Come on, we're getting off.' Even though we had barely gone two stops. I didn't protest.

'I know a place,' he said. 'This'll cheer you up.'

Within a few minutes we were stood outside what was no more than a hole in the wall big enough only to accommodate one person, a small fridge, and an array of bottles containing spices and sauces. The hole was emitting a divine smell. Salty, fatty and acidic all at once. A hot grill sizzled behind the lone chef. The brown skin of his face was punctuated with crystalline blue eyes which he used to smile at us as we approached. He wore a white turban around his head and an apron covered in the remnants of previous orders and a hard day's work. A small group of people milled around nearby before falling away, as one by one they were summoned to collect their orders. Andy ordered two lamb kofta wraps; one with extra pickled cabbage for himself and the other without onions for me.

'A kebab?' I said with a tinge of unnecessary bitchiness he politely overlooked.

'You'll see. Back in a minute.'

I watched as he headed over a zebra crossing and into a twenty-four-hour Nisa. My fingers twitched for my phone but I thought better of it and left it in my pocket. Andy returned seemingly empty-handed just in time to confirm that he wanted chilli sauce on the wrap with the extra cabbage and garlic sauce on the other. When they were ready, he took my hand once again and gently pulled me along the cobbles in Camden Passage. We walked through a small park but bypassed its benches and carried on. A homeless man in a sleeping bag read a tattered copy of *Brighton Rock*. A few paces beyond him, I turned on my heels and went back to put a £2 coin in the disintegrating coffee cup in front of him. He turned a page and changed position without acknowledging me. I thought about giving him my lamb wrap, but by the time I caught up with Andy, the moment had passed and I knew it would be a kick in the teeth to Andy's impromptu mystery tour, which was clearly a bid to make me feel better.

We emerged onto another Dickensian-looking residential street whose houses each had doors of a different pastel colour. I practically peered through the front window of the one with the pink door, forgetting that a real person would probably be inside. How would I feel about someone doing the same while I was trying to enjoy a relaxing Sunday evening in front of the TV? Then someone slammed a window above my head and it felt like they were emphasising the fact I should continue walking and mind my own business. And then we were there. Canalside. A perfectly positioned bench awaited us under an old-fashioned street lamp.

'Not bad, right?'

I shrugged like it was nothing, even though it was the nicest stretch of canal I'd ever seen in London. No graffiti, no dodgy characters around. It was a shrug too far and I could tell I was killing Andy's vibe with how I was acting. He looked at me with raised eyebrows, before shaking his head and muttering under his breath, 'Fuck sake. Be like that then.' And, fed up with me, he turned his attention to his kebab instead. My bad mood had finally put him in one and I thought about telling him what was consuming me. I would tell him, I thought. As soon as I'd finished eating. I would get it off my chest. I watched as the breeze made ripples in the canal. It looked like red wine, heavy and dark. I extended my hand, placing it on his knee, and leaned my head against his arm.

'Sorry I've been off,' I mumbled.

'S'okay. Look, we've graduated from wedding school. That calls for a toast.' He pulled two ice-cold bottles of sparkling water out of his jacket pockets. We did our usual air-toast choreography, which we now did over even the smallest of things as a kind of in-joke, echo, harking back to when we first met – like getting through a Monday, or agreeing on what to watch on TV – and sipped. He leaned in to plant a kiss on my temple and then settled back against the bench before acknowledging a passing dog walker. No. I couldn't do it. There was no way I was going to ruin the moment by bringing up any of the Sera shit.

I don't know how much longer we sat there. He seemed a bit more accepting of my quietness, which I was grateful for. We walked a little way down the canal and then got off so that we could loop round and get back onto Upper Street. Eventually we reached the busyness and bright lights of Angel, a cross section of Londoners on their way home from their own Sunday evenings spent out and about.

I felt my phone buzzing in my pocket and let go of Andy's hand. He carried on a little way ahead, turning round to mouth that he was going to pop into Sainsbury's to get some bits. I knew as soon as I heard Mum's voice that something was wrong. She wasn't crying but she sounded close to it, her breathing ragged and strained between sentences. Mum had taken herself up to Birmingham after what she described as an infuriating phone call with Grandad that morning. She'd decided that going there immediately was the only way she was going to get to the bottom of his symptoms, which he still hadn't contacted the GP about. She had taken him to the walk-in centre, despite his tutting and grumbling, despite everything in his body language suggesting that it was the last place on earth he wanted to be. In the consultation room, after the invasion of the Covid test alone had made it seem like he might bolt at any moment, he had initially refused to remove his jacket or lie on the clinic bed to be examined. But eventually, after the kind of persuasion and reassurance a mother might use on a toddler who's lying on the floor in the middle of the supermarket and refusing to move, he had acquiesced.

'Distended,' the doctor had said, padding around Grandad's 78-year-old flesh, one surgical-glove-covered hand on top of the other. 'Ultrasound,' he surmised. But there was a waiting list. It could be a week or two, possibly longer. At this, Grandad had kissed his teeth, slapped his knee and looked at my mum as if to say 'Si. Wha mi tell yuh?' The receptionist had given Mum a number to call first thing in the morning to see if she could get a cancellation. She was going to stay the night, make the call in the morning, be there just in case she could get him seen that day.

'That's all you can do, Mum,' I said, trying to make her feel better, trying to keep my own fears under wraps about what a scan would show or how much worse it could get before he finally got seen. 'Sounds like you did well just to get him through the doors of the walk-in centre . . . Mum? Are you still there?' I knew she was, because I could hear her breathing, but she wasn't speaking. I could imagine the concerned expression on her face, as it pressed against her iPhone. She was probably standing in the bay window, gazing into the middle distance down the street, where she'd played as a child, before she'd known anything of illness and waiting lists or suffering, being cared for rather than having to be the one who cared. Sometimes I wondered if she ever regretted leaving Birmingham. She'd moved down with an old boyfriend who wanted to make his fortune in London, where all the money was, where all the jobs were, he'd said. But really, she was only interested in where he'd be, so she had left home and everything that was familiar. She followed him with no plan for what she would do if and when (when being the case just six months later) they broke up. But the start of a new decade had seemed as good a time as any to change her life. Deep down, she had been looking for an excuse to break out of her old one, to rid herself of the expect-ation to become a nurse or a secretary while everyone else was still suffering the effects of the riots a few years earlier on any hopes or aspirations Birming-ham's youth had for their futures. And she knew people in London before she got there, even if she could only count them on two fingers. An old school friend and a distant cousin whom they'd travelled to visit by coach when she was growing up, the memory of which I distinctly remember seeing flash across her eyes on our way past Victoria Coach Station one day. Anything else she knew about London had been learnt from episodes of *Desmond's*. But after a brief stint in Peckham after the break-up, she had moved north of the river to be near her friend. She had been there ever since.

Finally, her voice filled my earpiece. 'Dad was scared, Layla.'

'Nah. Grandad ain't scared of nothing,' I said light-heartedly, laughing a little, hoping that the next time she spoke I would hear a trace of a smile in her voice too. But instead she went quiet again and I knew it was time to be serious. 'What do you mean scared? Because he might need an operation or something?'

'No, no, not like that. It was – I don't know – I've never seen him like that before. He was twitchy. Suspicious. Of the doctor, of the person at the front desk even.'

She had probably had a long day. A train journey, taxi rides, coaxing Grandad, translating medical jargon. She needed to rest and everything would feel better in the morning. I thought those things and wanted to say them too, as much to myself as to her. But she was expressing something real. Something she had seen her father feeling.

'If they were really worried they would have sent you to A&E. Everything will be alright in the end,' was all I could come up with. But I meant it. Or hoped it at least.

'And if it isn't?' she said.

I could see Andy walking back with a bag for life stretching against its contents in one hand and a large bag of crisps, which he was shaking enthusiastically, in the other.

'Then it isn't the end yet,' I said into the receiver.

16 days until the wedding

Usually, I'm a huge fan of eating and romance. The fact that Andy had booked us a table for lunch at the restaurant where we would be having our wedding reception involved both, but I had slowly been losing my appetite over the previous four days. Four long, Sera-less days which I had mainly spent repeating the letters W . . . T . . . F . . . over and over again in my head, kissing Andy goodbye for work and breathing sighs of relief when I had the place to myself so I could get on with stalking his ancestors online.

I had completely forgotten Instagram existed and now pored over the database any chance I got, using different combinations of facts that I knew about Andy's family to see the results it listed. Like the entry which showed £1682 being paid out to one Duncan McKinnon on 26 July 1837 for twenty-eight enslaved persons on a plantation in Jamaica, and his address at the time being the old estate we'd all soon be partying at for Andrea and David's thirty-fifth wedding anniversary. Yes, like that one. That was a particularly low moment. A moment which had entered my mind again just as Andy had begun to peel off my clothes on the sofa after coming in from work one evening, making me recoil and tell him I wasn't in the mood, had a headache, wanted an early night.

'Are you okay?' Andy said now. I had felt his gaze on me in a concerned way since we'd sat down at the table so I knew this question was coming.

'Huh?' I said.

'You're barely eating.'

I quickly scooped up a forkful of cured meats and artichoke purée, chomping demonstratively to make the point that I was actually eating, if he'd give me a chance. He furrowed his brow a little, suspicious of my behaviour, tore off a piece of focaccia and dunked it into some olive oil, waiting for me to respond.

'I just have a lot to do today,' I said, with more of an edge than I'd intended. His shoulders appeared to cave in slightly and he looked a little crestfallen. I felt like I'd just kicked a small, defenceless little bunny while wearing a pair of steel-capped boots. I wasn't busy at all and I sounded whiny and ungrateful.

'Well, I'm the only one actually in the middle of a working day,' he mumbled. He was getting pissed off with me now, which I couldn't really blame him for. 'What exactly do you have to do? It's all pretty much there, isn't it?'

I struggled to think of anything either taxing or particularly meaningful from my dwindling list that couldn't be ticked off in an afternoon, so I was glad when he followed up with 'I think you're just worried about your grandad.'

'Probably,' I said, feeling even more wretched for using Grandad as an excuse.

'It's good that you're off school so you can spend a bit of time with him. He'll be fine. He'll be walking you down the aisle in a couple of weeks, trust me.'

I was booked onto the 9.48 from Euston to Birmingham New Street the following morning. I would be picking Grandad up from home in a taxi and escorting him to the hospital for his 13.45 scan. My mum had been calling for a cancellation all week and had finally managed to get one but she couldn't miss work and I'd jumped in to offer to take him. I felt bad for having been more preoccupied with Sera than my grandfather, his pain, how he'd tried to keep it from us.

'How could he be so stupid not to talk to me when this started happening?' Mum had said on the phone the night before. She'd never called him stupid before, had never raised her voice to him in my company, had never been annoyed or burdened by him. There was a tenderness between them I envied. Friends whose fathers would pick them up from school, films depicting superhero dads who saved their daughters from sex traffickers, those sorts of fathers had never really sold me the idea that I was missing out on something. It was only seeing Mum and Grandad's bond which had ever made me think that having a father of my own might be nice. But I knew she hadn't meant it. She was worried about him. She just wanted him to get checked out so she could make a plan of action.

I looked at Andy, trying to make me feel better, eating

our wedding food. He had this ability to somehow always appear hopeful, always find just the right words. I desperately wanted to un-know what I had learnt about the plantation and just be normal with him again. I told myself that by the time he got back home from the stag in three sleeps' time, I would no longer be this sulky, silent, consumed version of myself. I'd be the one he'd signed up to marry. The fun one who had things to say. Cracked a fucking smile every now and again, maybe. But how could things be normal again? I was becoming more and more obsessed with the database, and not just the McKinnons it held dirt on but everything to do with the compensation payments. How the people compensated had used the money, what had happened to the enslaved people and the sheer implausibility of the fact that government debts from the compensation were not fully paid off until six years ago, in 2015. I felt an imbalance in my relationship with Andy. I felt soiled not only by the idea of the money and the possibility of its connection to him, but by the ownership of human lives, the maltreatment of enslaved people. The children. The women. I felt like a traitor. If anyone in the black community ever found out, not to mention my mum and grandad, I would be looked at shamefully and told I was not my ancestors' wildest dreams but, in fact, their worst nightmare.

'We should fill our boots now. The bride and groom never get to eat at their own wedding apparently.' He laughed a little at his own observation before the waiter came over to ask how it was going and if we had any questions about the food. I let him take the lead, zoning out, hoping the conversation would move on to sports or something else they didn't expect me to be part of. I looked down at the tablecloth and picked at the scattered crumbs like a desperate bird.

After we'd eaten everything, the chef who would be cooking on the day of our wedding came bursting out of the kitchen to see us. 'You like?' she asked. She was rotund and smiling, stretching out her arms like she was greeting two old *amici*.

'You like. Of course you like,' she repeated, this time dropping the inflection at the end and insisting on what she knew to be the case. She reached our table and placed a firm hand on each of our shoulders. We nodded enthusiastically as she effused about the sweetness of the Vesuvian tomatoes, the crispness of the *gamberoni fritti*, the frizzante, the clams, the way each dish she had selected celebrated the season and complemented each other. She was like a proud mama, listing the accomplishments of her children.

'Simple food. *Ma molto buono*, no? I can't promise the marriage will always be so simple, but the food, yes. Why not?' She laughed, a hearty, genuine laugh. I could manage no more than a fleeting smile and a short blast of air through my nasal passages to approximate a kind of laugh-like noise at her little quip. Yes, Maria, it was far from simple, I wanted to say. I would've given my right arm for simple. Simple would have been glorious. Like a plate of tomatoes dressed in nothing but oil and salt. She glossed over any awkwardness with a triumphant yell of '*Giorgio, caffè. Due caffè.*'

Giorgio was there brandishing two espressos on tiny saucers and a pot of brown sugar before we knew it. Maria took her leave then, walking backwards to the kitchen most of the way, so she could blow kisses in our direction as she went, leaving Andy and me looking at each other as if to say, 'Is she for real?'

I'd given up caffeine in a bid to detox before the wedding, so the next time I saw Giorgio the waiter, I asked for fresh mint tea. It came, and I stared at the leaves like I was trying to read my fortune.

'I promise not to end up in any strip clubs while I'm away, so you don't need to worry,' he said.

'I'm not,' I said, shrugging a little, realising that my steel toecaps were firmly on again in spite of myself. I looked around the restaurant and tried to visualise everyone in that space in a couple of weeks, but it was like waking up in the middle of a really good dream and trying to restart it again in exactly the same place only to find the remainder turning into a nightmare.

'I know Dan's got that stupid "no contact" rule for the weekend but I've told him if you need me – for anything, Grandad, something to do with the wedding, just, because – you can call me about anything,' Andy said.

In truth I was conflicted about him going away. I both did and did not want to be alone. It felt awful to be carrying it without being able to let him know what I knew, why I was struggling with it, or to find out what he thought. But every time I almost did, all I could hear was how ridiculous I would sound. How accusatory. What kind of response would I actually be looking for? There was the possibility that he would take it completely seriously, suggest we examine things, our relationship, delay the wedding until we'd had a chance to process everything. Or he could take it not seriously enough. What if he batted it away? What if he ridiculed it and raised his eyebrows and told his parents that Sera and, by association, me were trying to drag their family name through the mud. I wanted my life to go back to the tiny, indiscernible speck among all the other lives being lived in the world that it had been only a week ago.

Soon, he would ask me what I had planned for the rest of the day and I would need to have something ready. I usually loved the summer holidays and the freedom they brought. The summer before Andy and I got together, Sera had said she wanted to fly to Bilbao for lunch, like Kano had described on his last album. I thought she was joking but she actually booked us flights, not for lunch but for a weekend, and we'd bowled around the Basque country getting drunk and eating steak. Her middle name could have been 'on a whim' the number of times she had simply decided something in a moment and done it. I would miss being taken along for the ride if we didn't manage to work things out. The thought of which scared me.

'You can call me, okay, Lay?' he repeated. Then he reached around the table and took my hand, pulling on it slightly so that eventually, reluctantly, I stood up, so that he could guide me towards him. I perched on his right knee and he wrapped his arms around my waist and kissed my forehead. The staff were all in the kitchen.

I could hear only the occasional clink of plates and water running. Lucio Dalla was quietly lamenting Caruso's unrequited love. The same song had been playing the last time we'd eaten there. Before. Before, before. Back when I hadn't looked at a screen telling me that the McKinnons who once lived at Ballyoche House had also overseen a plantation in the same parish in Jamaica that my grandad was born in.

'I'm gonna miss you,' he said, looking at me so earnestly I felt like crying and spilling my guts. I felt like asking him if I could come to Bucharest so I could have a change of scenery, be away from everything and stop thinking about things for just five minutes.

'I miss you already,' I said and rested my head on his shoulder so he couldn't see my face.

15 days until the wedding

They had come for him in the night. He'd been in his pyjamas in a deep sleep. It had just gone 1.38. An odd time to choose. Unnecessary in its exactness. They'd used a battering ram to open his front door causing curtains elsewhere to twitch but no one to rush to his aid. They gave him enough time to dress in his only pair of jeans and a brown jumper which had a hole in the left armpit. Enough time to put his dentures into his mouth and his feet into his shoes, but not enough time to find his glasses. Probably a good thing, really. The blurry vision might have allowed him to imagine he was still sleeping and merely caught in a bad dream. He asked questions like *Who are you? What's this all about? Why is this happening? What are you doing all up in my house? Where are you taking me?* The replies which came informing him that they were the police sent on behalf of immigration officials can't have done much to reassure him. It had never been clear to him whose side the police were actually on, so Kenneth had always just chosen to keep out of their way so he would never have to find out for himself.

Grandad had already heard all this from a lady called

Celine and now I was hearing it from her too. Celine was at Grandad's when I arrived to pick him up for his scan and before I could even introduce myself she was congratulating me on convincing him to go to the doctor and admonishing him for not taking her advice to go sooner. She would sometimes pay him a visit to do a bit of cleaning around the house, make sure he had enough food in, wash his clothes, cook for him or just keep him company, take a drink, play some cards. She often did the same for Kenneth and others in his group who had come over from the islands. They sometimes met at the local pub or each other's houses to play dominoes and talk.

Celine had been the first person to read aloud the words saying that Kenneth was 'an illegal immigrant' who must report every month to immigration officials. He had done so. Celine could attest to that. She had dropped him off and picked him up on several occasions. They wanted documents which proved he was a UK citizen. Celine had helped him trawl through his paperwork, managing to piece together a few payslips, his tenancy agreement and documents about his pension. Celine had contacted his doctor's surgery to request a letter stating how long he'd been a patient. She had even found a handful of photos of him as a young boy on a day trip to Weston-super-Mare with other children from his primary school. But it had not been enough. He had not satisfied their requirements to be granted leave to remain and was sent 'back' to Jamaica, nearly fifty years after he'd arrived in England. He had been fighting to return ever since.

Grandad excused himself, quietly kissing his teeth as he went. A gesture directed at Celine I assumed, but not loud enough for her to hear over by the bay window where she was lifting and replacing trinkets and photo frames after giving them a cursory wipe with a duster.

'That was a couple of years ago now,' she added.

'That's terrible,' I said, while thinking that the amount of time that had elapsed seemed completely at odds with the amount of detail and sense of urgency she'd recounted the incident with. I wondered if she missed him. Kenneth. I struggled to keep up with her other stories, all reeled off at pace as Grandad flitted in and out trying to get ready, tutting every so often at what was being said. The things she'd heard, things friends had heard. Things they feared might happen to them. Someone's pension payments suddenly stopping, another being denied cancer treatment, told it would not be something the NHS would be able to offer her, despite having always paid her taxes. She would have to go private, something she could not afford to do, or back to Grenada, something she did not want to do. Another had been told not to return to work until they had the correct work permit, despite having worked for the company for ten years as a contractor.

'That'll be why he's been acting up like this – Roy,' Celine said, lowering her voice while Grandad was nowhere to be seen for a moment and she could get away with it.

'Acting up?'

'Y'know, digging his heels in. Not getting checked out

by the doctor. He probably thought, if they've done it before – the Tories – well, y'know. Probably thought he should be keeping his head down just in case.'

In some ways it made complete sense what she was saying. I was sure the only reason Mum had managed to get him vaccinated in the end was because it hadn't involved the hospital or a doctor's surgery but just a trip down to the Afro Caribbean Millennium Centre. The person administering the jabs was even a regular there, so for Grandad it probably felt nothing like the scary government machine pumping Pfizer into people's arms. The fact that a report had been published into the Windrush scandal, apologies (of sorts) made to those who'd suffered, promises of compensation (yet to be paid) made to the people affected hadn't repaired the damage. It had been a hot topic of conversation at many of our Sunday get-togethers. But the elderly have a way of holding on to things, beliefs, fears, engrained routines, and who can blame them.

'Mi ready. Come, Bab,' Grandad announced practically halfway through the door, complete with flat cap and coat. He looked like he'd had enough of Celine and her opinions and gossip for one morning. The look of relief on his face when he saw the taxi waiting outside was plain to see. She came to wave us off from the doorstep. 'See you both. Mind how you go,' she called, her lightly Brummie accent warm and sincere. 'And don't worry, Roy. They can't do anything to you. Nothing at all.' With that she closed door of the house, we closed the door of the cab and the taxi drove away.

Grandad was quiet for the entire journey and while we waited for his name to be called in the hospital waiting area. Finally, he shrugged and kissed his teeth again, huffing, 'Celine cyan't hold her tongue.' It was true, Celine liked to talk. All that hearsay. All those tales of friends as well as distant acquaintances and strangers, people from Birmingham and around the country, other black British Caribbean émigrés. I put my hand on his and squeezed it tight. 'That's all over now, Grandad. Besides, Mum would have made sure you were safe. You wouldn't have been in any danger. I promise.'

'You nuh know dat. Cha! Anyway. It nuh matter. Don't go worry yuhself bout me.'

But I was worried. It seemed like he had been consumed by all of this for a long time. And worse than that – I hadn't picked up on any of it because I'd been in my own world. Why had I never asked him about it? Not just general chit-chat – the kind of politics going on somewhere else, to someone else – but about how it actually affected him as an individual. I'd wanted to use the time in the waiting room to make sure that he was still happy to give me away at the wedding, but in the wake of everything Celine had said, it seemed unimportant. Selfish. Irrelevant even. And would he even want to give me away? What if he disowned me for going ahead with the wedding knowing what I knew now? Everything he was scared of today was basically the aftermath of what I'd been researching. The government that had made compensation payouts to former slave-owning families was essentially the same government that had been shipping his mates off to the Caribbean after they'd answered the call to help rebuild the country following the war. The hypocrisy of it turned my stomach.

The air smelt sterile and surgical. The walls were white, dirty white in parts, with scuff marks every so often, where wheelchairs or gurneys had been parked up against them. We had arrived fifteen minutes early for the scan but something told me that we would be called in late and we should be prepared to be there for a while. I looked at the large wall-mounted clock above the front desk. Andy's plane would be landing soon. Just at that moment, a text came through from him. It was a long line of *x*s followed by the words *Can't wait to have you back in my arms, Beautiful.* I could, I thought cruelly, while inexplicably missing him at the same time. Grandad adjusted his position in the chair, winced and rubbed his abdomen, letting out a low groan.

'The painkillers are probably wearing off, Grandad. Do you need more?'

'No. No. Mi fine. Mi nuh want fi mess up anyt'ing dem might see inna deh.' I didn't know much about biology but I didn't think it worked like that. Still, I didn't want to push him. I was just glad he was there and he was on his way to being seen.

'Shall I get you some tea from the vending machine?'

'A likkle water,' he said, so I got him some from the cooler nearby. He chuckled as I handed it to him.

'What?' I said, chuckling too but not knowing why. His laughter was infectious. His whole face lit up and his eyes sparkled.

'What unu call dis?' he said, eyeing the paper cone holding the water. It looked ridiculous in his hand. Flimsy and not fit for purpose. He knocked the contents back in a single gulp and crushed the cone before throwing it across the aisle where it landed firmly in the bin. Even in his discomfort, he was still the coolest grandad ever. I watched his finger tapping against his knee. Not impatiently – he seemed to be tapping along to a tune in his head. Something he'd play on one of our Sundays, I guessed. I wished I could hear it. Wished I could be inside his head with the music and all the knowledge that came with age and hindsight.

'You were born in St Catherine, weren't you, Grandad?' I asked.

'Yeah, man. We always bin deh, in-a St Cat'rin', man. Mi even got a plot of land deh.'

'Really? I didn't think you ever wanted to go back.'

'Dat not why mi own dat land, man,' he said. I let it hang in the air for a moment in case there was more, in case I was missing something obvious. But nothing came.

'Then why? Why buy it?' I said.

'Because – because mi c'yan.' He stopped the finger-tapping, smiled to himself. The plot of land, the green and lush landscape of the Jamaican countryside, he could see them. I wanted to see them too.

'Grandad. Do you ever wish you hadn't left?'

'If mi neva leave, mi neva would-a have unu. Your modda. I born as British. Mi did come here British. I did put plenty into di mum country, but mi did get plenty outta she too. This is my home. Even when dem try tell wi – Kenneth, all-a dem, man – even when dem try tell wi sumt'ing different. Y'un'a'stand, Layla?'

Did I understand? Did I really?

'Roy McKinnon. Roy McKinnon?' I couldn't see where his name was being called from. It snapped me sharply back into the room. I began to flap a little, trying to gather up our belongings, help Grandad out of his chair and signal to whoever was calling that Roy McKinnon was indeed there, shouldn't be listed on her clipboard as a no-show, that I had a mother who would make heads roll if Roy McKinnon didn't get the attention he needed.

'Cum, Bab. Dem callin' mi.'

Finally, the blue-clad young radiologist came into view and registered that we were making our way over.

'I can come in with you,' I said to Grandad, keeping my voice low. 'I can just sit behind the screen, if you like. If you want me there, I mean. Or do you want to do this on your own?'

He didn't say anything. Just hooked his arm through mine, nodded his head in recognition of the woman waiting for us, and walked right past her with his granddaughter firmly in tow.

Someone would call him to discuss the scan results as soon as they were available, we were told. In the meantime, he could continue with the ibuprofen and the warm compresses when the discomfort was too great. He should eat only what he could manage. Soup was ideal, nutritious but easy to digest, until his appetite improved.

Grandad didn't want to get another taxi. He wanted to catch the bus to Corporation Street, like he used to whenever he went to town. He wanted me to take him somewhere. Or rather he wanted to take me somewhere. The Bull Ring, he said. There was a market there. Better than the one he'd started going to in recent years because it was closer to his house. He no longer felt as confident as he used to making the journey to town on his own. He occasionally got Celine to go to this market for him, the good one with the good stuff, the fresh meat at good prices, fresh fish, gutted, scaled and cleaned on request. Fresh, crisp bunches of baby spinach which stood tall, never drooped. Scotch bonnets with shiny, taut skins, no wrinkles. Ones that would pack a punch in the cow foot soup he planned to teach me how to cook when we got home to last him until Mum came again over the weekend.

When we got to the market and I saw the look of homecoming on his face, I felt better. Mum had told me how much the city centre had changed from when she was a girl, let alone compared to Grandad's younger days. We'd had to weave our way through the sprawling shopping centre, all bright lights, glass and people rushing around too quickly and teenagers shouting into their phones, and I was worried the covered market stalls Grandad had described to me, which were around here somewhere – but exactly where, he couldn't remember – had been bulldozed and replaced by a John Lewis. When we found them, he looked more at ease. The mishmash of stalls were mostly run by older traders, not quite

Grandad's age, but certainly of an age where they'd seen a fair bit of life. They had held steadfast in the face of developers trying to move them along and build flats where they sold fruit, five knickers for £3 and DVDs when no one had a DVD player any more. They never called in sick, knew their elderly customers by name, never knowingly undersold anyone.

'Roy. Roy. That you? Good man. 'Ow ya doin'? I thought I spotted a familiar face,' called one of them. He ran the veg stall, wore a tatty beanie hat and a smile which revealed a missing tooth and stretched the hundreds of tiny grey bristles covering his chin out into a long thin line. The money belt he wore around his waist jingled as he waved at Grandad. He reached over his produce with a bent arm so that they could bump elbows. A compromise for their usual handshake. Still, it was brotherly and familiar and there was something touching about the whole scene. I stood a couple of metres back, didn't want to interrupt them. I wanted to watch Grandad do his thing. We rarely left his house during our Sunday visits, except maybe to go the short distance to the local park to do a lap of the lake. I didn't know how long he'd known this man, when he'd last seen him, whether their acquaintance went beyond commenting on the weather, the changing face of the city or the pandemic. But in a way, I didn't need to. I could see that Grandad belonged in that moment, in that place, just as much as the other man.

Poor Kenneth, I thought. Who were they to tell him he didn't belong there as well?

*

It was ten o'clock on a Friday night and my mum was working again, sitting in the kitchen on a bar stool typing on her computer. She had stopped to eat and listened intently as I told her about my day with Grandad. Celine. The scan. The market. The soup. I hadn't stayed to eat in the end. I'd done the prep, the chopping of the vegetables, the seasoning of the meat, all with Grandad coaching me from a chair nearby. I'd left it simmering and Grandad comfortable, assuring me he could finish it off and that he wasn't feeling too bad, that he would eat some and probably go up to bed shortly afterwards. I'd hugged him goodbye, taking care not to grip him too tightly and aggravate his tender tummy. I'd pulled back into Euston a little after eight, and headed straight to Mum's for the night. I was glad I'd stayed with Grandad and cooked for him, just being around each other, mostly quiet but together. And even though I felt like I was carrying something in the back of my mind that was affecting everything about me, colouring my days and making me anxious and unsure of things, Grandad's house was still able to work some of its magic, cocooning me, calming me down, slowing my breathing, giving my brain a chance to rest. Mum seemed lighter too, for the knowledge that Grandad had had his scan and was now firmly in the system.

'But why didn't he tell us how afraid he was?' I said, still feeling bad. 'He could have talked to us instead of living like that, in fear all the time.'

'Do you know anyone who likes to admit when they're frightened of something? It's just how he is. I tried to talk to him about it and he always ended up walking out of the room so he didn't have to listen. I had to leave it alone after a while.'

'It's my fault. I didn't even ask him. I saw it all on the news and I didn't give it a second thought. I mean, he's got his passport. But I didn't even bother to – And he's my grandad. I should've been –' My voice broke. I immediately tried to disguise it, running the tap and rinsing off the last of the cutlery in the washing-up bowl.

She stopped typing, and out of the corner of my eye I could see that she had folded her arms across her chest and was staring at me with her head slightly tilted to one side.

'You're young. It is not for you to worry about.'

'I'm not that young. Too wrapped up in myself is what you really mean.'

'Layla, you're a good granddaughter. You love him and you look after him. You can't take everything on.'

I fell silent. Still feeling wretched despite her best efforts.

'Speaking of which,' she said, 'do you need me to help with any of the last bits for the wedding?'

I knew she was trying to cheer me up. It was a kind offer, but an empty one. I could see the stress lines on her face and the way she was clenching her fist involuntarily. She looked like someone who didn't have the capacity to take on anything else.

'Everything's fine,' I said, turning my back on her, wiping down the sink area the way I knew she liked it.

'The dress! I completely forgot – what did she say? Did she like it? I thought you were going to send me a photo.'

There were some biscuits on a plate neither of us had yet touched, so I lurched over to them and put a whole one in my mouth so that it was suddenly full and bulging at the cheeks. I chewed slowly, hoping she'd see that I didn't want to speak with my mouth full, which was still a pet hate of hers from when I was a kid, and maybe she'd start typing again and forget she'd asked me anything. It didn't work. She was waiting.

'Sorry,' I muffled through a mouthful of crumbs. 'Hold on.'

I forced the mass down my throat where it felt bulbous and uncomfortable. I was either going to lie or I was going to tell her that Sera had raised some concerns that I was potentially marrying the descendant of our ancestors' owners, which I had recently discovered might be valid. I had a good relationship with my mum, I told her most things. It wasn't clear what exactly was stopping me from telling her this, although it had a lot to do with the fear that she would agree with Sera not me. But the excuse of not burdening her with another drama was solid enough for me. I told her Sera had tried it on but she needed another fitting and wouldn't let me take any photos until then. But that she liked it – loved it – the colour, yeah, everything.

'That's good. That's good, something to make her feel good about herself, especially when things are on the rocks again with what's-his-name,' she said. Just like that.

Like she fully expected me to know the latest, that it would be something I was on top of, as her friend. Her best friend.

'I hope it's ready in time. Only fifteen sleeps to go,' she said, with one of those excitable grins all mothers of brides are prone to, and promptly went back to her screen. At that, I excused myself from the kitchen and went to the bathroom and locked myself away.

I took a shower in lukewarm water. I dried my body slowly and absent-mindedly with a towel the texture of Ryvita, cursing my mum for never using fabric conditioner, before opening my old chest of drawers to find a set of pyjamas I first wore when I was sixteen. They still fitted and I wore them every time I stayed in my old room. I wrapped the Ryvita towel around my damp hair and knelt down on the floor, peering under the bed. My wooden trinket box was still there, peeling stickers and nail varnish splodges still adorning the outside. I'd been round to Mum's plenty of times recently, but it had probably been three or four months since I'd stayed over and several years since I'd had any desire to go through this box of keepsakes. I put on the TV but muted it – the movement of the lights and colours made me feel less lonely. Then I flung myself onto the bed and removed the lid from the box. Inside it, there was an invitation to my christening and a CD with no indication of what I would find on it. There were a few old postcards, some of which were addressed to my mum from trips with Sera which I'd reclaimed as reminders of what we'd got up to, the atmosphere, the exuberance present in the subtext of the words I'd chosen. There was nothing of Andy in the box. I had a separate one for that under my real bed, my current bed at home. But this was *home* home. I reached for my handbag and pulled from it the folded piece of paper I had scrawled on during the train ride. It had tumbled out of my head and onto the paper at speed. It was the recipe for cow foot soup, Grandad's personal recipe. With his exacting quantities, his particular method, his timings. I tucked it into the box and replaced the lid.

A combination of the darkness I found myself in, the distance I felt between me and Sera, how deeply I missed Andy and how out of sorts my grandad had been that day made this an ideal time to cry again. But the tears refused to come, so instead I opened the browser on my phone, visited the database and clicked on the ad I had noticed the day before for a walking tour of the City of London. A walking tour with a twist. The next one was taking place tomorrow. There were still tickets. I could just fit it in before my hair appointment in the afternoon. In three clicks, I had purchased a ticket. Spending time with Grandad had shown me something I had failed to see before: how I'd been missing the mark, looking in all the wrong places for all the wrong things. I had forgotten that there were two sets of McKinnons. Andy's and mine. I'd been pursuing Andy's because it seemed easier somehow.

I had to change tack. I needed to get my head around the Jamaican McKinnons too.

13

14 days until the wedding

My great-grandmother's great-grandmother was a slave. She slept in quarters, cheek to toe with others like her, without anything to call her own. Not even breathing space. At twenty-nine, my great-grandmother's great-grandmother probably wasn't dreaming about her wedding day. No. She might have been thinking about the one she was due to attend. Not as the bride. Not even as a guest, but as a gift. No, 'gift' makes it sound nice. Kind. Thoughtful. Tied with a ribbon. She was property being given away, handed over to another master on his wedding day. I had read that people like her weren't even allowed the basics. Soap to wash themselves with, for example. They weren't allowed mirrors. Did she even know what she looked like? Perhaps the overseers feared the enslaved would spot how similar they looked to their oppressors if they ever caught a glimpse of their own reflections? One nose. One mouth. Two eyes, albeit set in darker skin, but nevertheless human, like them. Or maybe it would have given them an opportunity to gaze into their own eyes just long enough to find the resolve to rise up. That's what I was thinking about as I looked at myself that day, in the glass pane of the bus shelter on my way to the City. After I'd booked the walking tour the evening before, I'd stayed up for most of the night. I'd set myself up with accounts on Ancestry, My Heritage and FindMyPast, starting a tree for my family following my grandad's line as far back as I could. I'd looked around the International Slavery Museum in Liverpool, if virtually, feeling bad I hadn't known it existed let alone visited in real life during the three years I'd studied there. I had watched online lectures on how it is possible to find links to slavery in everyday objects, everyday surroundings and everyday interactions. In fact, it's almost impossible not to. I'd carried on scrolling and googling and reading into the early hours while my mum slept. I'd been tempted to knock on her door, wake her up, start asking her questions about our ancestors, anything she knew that might lead me to where they'd lived and who, exactly, they'd 'worked for'. But instead I stayed firmly stuck down the rabbit hole I'd found my way into.

I would have preferred to sit down at the bus stop instead of staring at myself in the glass but the bench was occupied at one end and dirty at the other. So, I stood there, leaning, brooding. I had to keep reminding myself that I wasn't on my way to brunch with Sera. I still hadn't heard from her and I had no idea what to say so hadn't reached out to her either. The ongoing silence between us was palpable. It almost thrummed. No doubt she could hear it too. Was she out brunching with someone else instead? I let myself imagine she was so that I could feel angry at her for a moment, working myself up into a sulk that she'd probably been looking for a reason to replace me for months and the McKinnon name debacle was as good a reason as any. But I knew I was being childish so I tried to switch my thoughts to something more productive. It would take me forty-five minutes to get to St Paul's on the bus, during which time I would try again to populate my family tree. There were also resources on the database I could look into. I could even email the researchers to see if they could share details about the enslaved people the McKinnons of Ballyoche House were compensated for in 1837. It was worth a shot. Then I'd arrive for the tour, maybe hang around to see what else I could get out of the guide, one to one, before hot-footing it to my appointment with Bianca for a trim and a treatment. Tomorrow, there were place settings that needed to be made and the table numbers still needed their coating of gold paint. Why had I been so peppy and overeager about hand-making everything?

I picked myself up out of my slumped position and rolled my shoulders back, inadvertently cracking my neck as I did so. Then I went for another crack on the other side, this time deliberately. There was a satisfying crunch as a little bit of tension was released. Perhaps it was the last of the negative self-talk I'd had ringing in my ears since the night before saying that everything I was doing was pointless. Suddenly I felt fired up. Before I had a chance to second-guess myself, the number 17 arrived and whisked me away.

It was 10.58 when I arrived at the meeting spot. The Pret in front of the cathedral where around ten people stood waiting, smiling knowingly at newcomers to tell them they were in the right place. I wondered if two minutes was enough time for me to dash inside quickly and get a hot drink and a pastry. I had visions of the group leaving without me and having to lead myself around the narrow passageways of the City, piecing together a few facts using Google and Wikipedia. I couldn't miss it. Also, today was the final one before the theme changed from 'Slavers in the Square Mile' to 'Walks with Wren'. It was cold. Fine rain, the kind that somehow manages to soak you right through, was beginning to fall despite the forecast saying it would be dry. I put my hood up and used the cover it provided to get the measure of the people I'd be spending the next two hours with.

The tour had attracted an interesting – mostly white – demographic. Among them, a pair of middle-aged women and a lone twenty-something guy in corduroy trousers rolled up at the ankle, sporting a beard. He was someone I would've described as a hipster, but he would probably have been offended at the thought of being one, which I found to be the case with all hipsters. And then a trio of black girls in their twenties. They had arrived separately, two of them thanking the other one 'so much for organising this' and laughing and joking as though they went way back. I overheard the tour guide discreetly mention something to one member of the group, a mother carrying her baby on her chest in one of those harnesses that always made me nervous about the new significance a trip or fall could take on when you have another human attached to the front of your body. She said that with older children, she would usually ask the parents to take their child to one side, out of earshot, at two or three points, as the nature of the information becomes graphic and inappropriate for young ears. But she was satisfied that the baby wouldn't understand what was being said so there was no need. My knowledge of early years learning begged to differ but I didn't say anything. Instead I tried to blend into the group.

Claudia, the guide, had a pained expression on her face as she gave her introduction, explaining some of the stops we'd be making along the way, how important the tour was to her, how far-reaching and long-lasting the effects of the slave trade had been. I thought it was sweet how she contorted her face in that way, to demonstrate her sadness, her regret at the whole unfortunate business. Then she attempted something I wasn't prepared for and immediately made my heart rate pick up. An ice-breaker.

'Before we set off – and this is entirely optional of course, there's no pressure – but I do like to find out a bit about you, if you will.' She chuckled and so did most of the group. There, ice broken, I thought, but she continued. 'What brings you here today? Why this tour?' She paused for dramatic effect. 'What's got you curious?' Another pause. 'Anyone? Don't be shy.'

Reluctantly, Hipster Kid explained that he'd taken his friend's place last minute because they had Covid and he had nothing else to do today. Then one of the middle-aged women told everyone she was there as research for a project she couldn't talk about unless we were all going to sign an NDA which she may as well have kept to herself. And *I'm here so I can help my best friend avoid marrying a descendant of her ancestors' owners*, I thought about saying. But even adding the lie, removing myself, didn't help the whole thing sound any less batshit in my head so I kept my hood firmly up and looked down at my feet until the threat had passed.

Starting off at St Paul's – 'The crown of the Church of England' – Claudia said, gave her the opportunity to talk about the Church's role in the slave trade. Because it, the institution, had been, essentially, a slave owner. 'Just like the Bank of England. And Lloyd's of London. And Greene King Breweries. Among countless others.'

I made a mental note to never find myself in the Camden Head again.

'One argument the slavers and pro-slavers used time and again was that slavery was justified because enslaved people were not Christians. And the Church stood by. Participated even.'

She went on to tell us about a Church-owned outfit called the Society for the Propagation of the Gospel in Foreign Parts operating on Barbados, which would even brand the word 'Society' across the chests of any slave who attempted to be anything less than passive. Running away, inciting rebellion, that kind of thing. I looked up at the huge dome, my mouth gaping slightly as my neck craned. There was still a faint hum in the air from when the bells had rung out at eleven o'clock. It defied belief to think of bishops and priests complicit, active, in the slave trade. And just the mention of black bodies being branded conjured such graphic images that it made me wince.

'Branding, by any definition, I'm sure you agree, would now be classified as torture,' she surmised, her voice low and sombre.

'Dap,' came a resounding gurgle from the baby. And with that, we moved on to the next site.

As we walked, I got caught behind the trio of friends. It was sweet how excited they were to be together. They would have mini catch-ups on all their gossip and the goings-on in their lives as we travelled between sites. Their dissertations and interdisciplinary projects, the new self-care routines they were honing, how their families were. It was joyful what they were offering up and getting back from each other. Seeing this exchange, how enlivened they were, made me smile sadly to myself thinking of Sera. I wanted to loop my arm through theirs and assimilate myself into their squad, no questions asked.

Claudia said she wanted to show us some interesting sites in the abolitionist story as well as the slave trade's and we duly arrived in a small courtyard.

'This is where it all began,' she announced with a flourish, arm extended proudly. We looked on, not seeing what she was seeing, waiting for her to let us in on the significance of an eighties-looking office block and the goods entrance she was gesturing to. It turned out to be the site of a former Quaker bookshop and printer's which had hosted the first meeting of the Society for

Effecting the Abolition of the Slave Trade. The very same bookshop which had published the famous drawing of the *Brookes* slave ship. I knew all about the *Brookes* but had forgotten why until that moment. I'd passed by an antiques shop once. Mum and I had decided to go on one of our excursions to Notting Hill for the day to check out all the charity shops, because they always had the best donations including designer labels complete with tags. This particular antiques shop had already closed for the day, making it even more enticing to stop and peer into. At the time, I had a bit of an obsession with anything old (except for people and fruit). Keepsakes, toys, snuffboxes. Old cameras gave me a certain thrill. Even now, one of my guilty pleasures was bingeing on episodes of *The Repair Shop* and letting myself cry without wiping any of the tears away when a family member had to collect the repaired item on behalf of the elderly owner who had dropped it off because they'd since died. They would never get the chance to see their heirloom restored to its former glory.

Through the window, I remember running my eyes over a mahogany sideboard (because Mum had tried to guess the price), a collection of coins in a pristine presentation box, a porcelain doll – creepy, bespectacled – and a model ship. I learnt from the small engraved plaque underneath that it was a miniature representation of 'THE BROOKES – 1781'. I also remember the urgent feeling I had to look it up afterwards and the top hit being the famous diagram the abolitionists had used as their campaigning tool, urging society to open their eyes to the true horrors of the slave trade and eventually compelling the government to bring it to an end.

The model had had tiny sails positioned alongside so that air would funnel towards the inhabitants below, and the bow, though tarnished, was in perfect proportion. It had looked like it could recreate the final voyage of the real *Brookes* from Cabinda to Montevideo, very capably, without incident, even though that was the voyage which finally led to it being condemned as unseaworthy. It was a shame it had not first been condemned as un-human-worthy. For a moment, I wondered, if I had lifted up the upper deck, whether I'd have found 454 perfectly carved human cargo shackled together inside. I was glad the shop had been closed so I couldn't have found out.

'Enjoying it so far?' came a clipped voice trying to get my attention, snapping me out of my daydream. It was another of the group's lone wolves. I hadn't noticed him until he'd asked Claudia if we could wait for him while he ran into a pub along the way to use the toilet. He looked to be the oldest person there and wore a smart suit jacket complete with pocket square. We started walking again, making our way to a crossing to keep up with the rest of the group.

'I don't know if enjoying is the right word, but, yeah. Glad I came,' I said, pleased, deep down, that someone had decided to talk to me. 'What brings you on the tour?'

'Frankly – and I'm not ashamed to admit it – I'm here because of the movement.' I had to look at him for a moment longer to see if he'd clarify which movement he was talking about for the avoidance of doubt. 'Black Lives Matter,' he confirmed. 'Which, let's face it – it's the main reason they're putting this whole thing on, I suspect. Not to sound too cynical about it all.' He was suddenly in flow; my question had opened the floodgates it seemed. I listened without interjecting, not entirely sure where he was going to go with it but keen to find out.

'I really want to, to, to . . . get it. I want to be –' and then he said it and I was a little taken aback to hear it – 'woke.'

I could see he meant well. And who knows what else he had lined up to help him to wake up. Books? Marches? Immersing himself in black culture? *Good for you*, I thought to myself, ready to wrap up the conversation, get back into my bubble and absorb all the other sites we had to see and what Claudia wanted to tell us about them.

'Well,' I said, fairly sure he wouldn't be able to spot a Hozier lyric but it still being the most appropriate thing to say to someone who'd just unabashedly revealed their desire to be this particular type of new version of themself, 'it's not the waking that counts. It's the rising.' And when I heard myself say it, I realised I was saying it as much to myself as I was to him.

About halfway through, Claudia described one particular account of a crossing from West Africa to the Caribbean. The conditions were base and basic and the disposition of the cargo, or 'people' as they were also known, was 'distressing to say the least'. It was recounted that a crew member became so infuriated, driven to distraction, maddened almost, by the sound of one of the stolen children's incessant wailing that he duly tore the child from its mother's arms and threw it overboard. 'The mother of the child, a one-year-old whose cries were interspersed with sucks of milk at her breast, replaced his cries with her own, only they were worse, much worse, and could not be quelled. But her fate was not to be tossed into the sea to be reunited with her babe, as she begged for, but to complete the voyage and be sold upon disembarking, for she was simply too valuable.' The language skills of the youngest member of our group may have been rudimentary, but his mother's were not. I watched the colour drain from her face as she listened. I saw her hands wrap so tightly around her own one-year-old cargo that I was scared she would crush him. It didn't matter that it was hundreds of years earlier or thousands of miles away from where she stood, I could see her living it. It was her child being taken from her and her child being thrown away like a bundle of rags. She welled up, silently. Everyone saw but no one asked if she was okay. Maybe it was because there really was no way she could be. Claudia avoided catching her eye. We set off for the next landmark and the mother slipped to the back of the group. By the time we stopped again, I looked around and she was gone. I imagined she'd simply slowed down, widening the gap between her and the group, before disappearing down the steps of Mansion House Tube, trying not to replay what she'd heard over in her mind. When we finally arrived at our last stop, Claudia pretended not to notice that we were a smaller group than when we'd set off. Maybe she lost a few along the way on every tour she did. She didn't let it distract from her finale. The culmination of the experience we'd all been on together. The City's only real recognition of its involvement in the slave trade. A sculpture etched with a poem entitled the 'Gilt of Cain'. Claudia drew our attention to the way the financial terminology the poet had used – stock, bond, acquisition – also encapsulated the slave trade, the experience of the enslaved, the commodity of them. I photographed it, every section, every word.

'The past is never dead. It's not even past,' she said, wrapping up with a quote by William Faulkner. If that was all the tour had taught me, I would still have got my money's worth. It echoed faintly with what Sera was trying to tell me, I was surprised to admit to myself. She had used different words, delivered to me in her own, very Sera way. But it chimed. It still didn't help me decide what to do about it though. The past may not be dead, but it was haunting me.

I stayed for a little while after the group had dispersed. The absence of them was filled with something. An atmosphere. A quiet. Something I needed to feel. A picnicker was finishing up his sandwich on a bench near the sculpture. When he left, I took his place and looked at the grey columns of the artwork. They were like sugar cane, tall and proud. I tried to imagine them swaying in the warm Jamaican breeze on a real plantation. Perhaps the one my ancestors had toiled on. The one they'd sweated on. Cried on. Died on. My eyes settled on the plaque, the metallic bas-relief of the poem glinting in the sun.

When I was eight years old, I wrote a poem about a snail. It began with the line, 'Slowly, slowly slides the snail.' I couldn't remember the rest, but could see in my mind's eye with perfect clarity the sugar paper I'd written it on and which I'd then cut into the shape of a snail, complete with a shell I'd created from another piece of paper and stuck on top. The reader had to lift the shell to reveal the poem. I remember the sense of pride I felt at what I'd made. Smugness, too, maybe, that I had gone above and beyond anything my classmates had managed to make. That, not only was I a writer, I was also an engineer. An artist. A child prodigy. In my late teens I'd written rhyming, sickly sweet love poetry to a boyfriend who, in hindsight, hadn't deserved it. I remember him being impressed by it at the time, telling his friends that his girlfriend was 'the most incredible writer', wearing me like a medal he'd done nothing to win. I read the poems again after we broke up and was embarrassed that I'd committed such sentiments to paper. In a moment of deep depression and embarrassment, I'd rid myself of them by burning them in the too-small flame of a scented candle. Those were the poems I could remember writing. And as for the ones I'd read, none had ever made me shiver before. Not like the one in front of me. My eyes fixed on one line. I couldn't tell whether I was reading it or it was reading me: *Break the bond the bind unbound lay bare — the truth.*

I stayed on the bench until I understood what it meant and then I got up and traced along the shape of the lettering with my fingers. It was cold to the touch and smaller than it should've been, in my opinion. Each letter should've been as large as a single windowpane on the Rothschild Building. The entire poem should have been plastered across it in red paint.

'What have you been using lately, Layla?' Bianca asked, holding up one of my tresses and rubbing the ends with a disapproving look on her face.

'Nothing really. Some leave-in conditioner some days. Other days, nothing.'

'It's dry as a bone. I told you to stick to coconut oil. How many times I gotta tell you? You might have a white girl's face, but you got a black girl's hair. Y'get me?'

She was right. She had told me that. At my last appointment eight weeks earlier, and at the one before that, but I'd ignored her. I'd allowed myself to be swayed by some clever advertising for Frizz Ease and their new campaign featuring someone who looked a bit like me if I squinted and looked through one eye. My hair and I regularly fell out with one another. It started when I was nine after a boy in my class had pointed to my face in the sea of other faces in the annual whole school portrait. 'Look, there she is. There's Layla. The one with the sticky-up hair.' I tried gels and jams, mousses and hair glues, anything I could borrow from other girls in my class or steal from my mum's room to get my hair to be less visibly unappealing. In the end, aged thirteen, I was finally able to wear my mum down enough to agree to relaxing it. It wasn't her fault that the sodium hydroxide, when mixed with the ammonium thioglycolate plus the sodium thioglycolate, overshot my hairline slightly, burning my skin. I gave up on chemical straightening before I really got started. It felt like it was for the best. I moved on to GHDs and blow-drying to get the kinks out instead. There was also the time I stopped using conditioner because the girl with the shiniest hair in Year 9 had told everyone that that was her secret. Sera was horrified that it had escaped my attention that Little Miss Shiny Locks had white hair (in characteristics as opposed to colour) and I did not. 'So why are you listening to her?' she'd asked me with a bewildered look on her face. 'Layla, why don't you ever just do you? Huh?' she'd said, before taking me to her friend to get my hair cane-rowed at the front and plaited down in extensions at the back. I remembered the weight of them. I remembered the feeling of swinging them over my shoulder as I turned my head. And I remembered the look on the face of my manager at my first Saturday job in a cafe which served drinks while people painted bowls and mugs. Her mouth said, 'Wow, who did your hair? It looks . . . interesting.' Her face said, I'll be giving you non-customer-facing duties until it's gone.

Sometimes, I got the impression that Sera thought my life was easier than hers because my skin was lighter. In lots of ways, it was, but if she really knew the extent of my insecurities growing up, maybe we wouldn't be where we were now. Whether I should call myself half-caste because that's what I'd heard other people describe me as, or whether I was, essentially, a black girl because I had only known my black family. Biracial. Mixed heritage. Dual heritage. Or no more than the token character in a Pepsi advert because it added something a bit exotic. Maybe I was beautiful, but not in a conventional way, perhaps even a bit strange to look at. I was always asked where I was from . . . No . . . no, where I'm *really* from. Because it was obvious there *would* be something – an interesting mix of this or that – that everyone was entitled to know about. I was the one who didn't know which box to tick on the form.

I wish I had told her that one of the worst things about it was the look strangers gave me when they saw me with my mum. Something about the two of us acting like mother and daughter not computing because of the contrast in our skin. I wish she'd known about the woman who had peered over the side of the pram Mum was pushing after leaving hospital with me to inspect its cargo. Me. Six-day-old me, fast asleep. Tiny hat on my tiny head, arms either side of my little face like an incredibly small weightlifter raising dumbbells in the air.

'She's not yours, is she?' the woman had said, looking from me to Mum and back to me again. It might have been the way she said it. Although on its own, it was insulting enough. Or perhaps it was the tone. Disbelieving. A statement more than a question. Mum had stared at her, she'd told me. Looked right back at her without saying a word, to see if the silence would give the woman

175

a moment to reflect, to hear the echo of her rudeness, her prying nature. Her judgement. But the silence didn't have the desired effect.

'YOU SPEAK ENGLISH?' she shouted, giving my mum one last chance to engage in a conversation about the baby. Why it was so light when she was so dark. What she was doing with it. Where she really came from. But all she did was smile and push the pram away.

Bianca coated my hair and scalp in a conditioning treatment to try to inject some moisture before the wedding 'as a matter of urgency'. She also wanted me to come in for an extra treatment a few days before. She wouldn't take no for an answer when I said I didn't really have time, which was sweet of her in a way. How genuinely attentive she'd been in caring for my hair for the past ten years. More caring towards it and accepting of its natural state than I had ever been.

I charged my phone and tried not to stare too obviously at the other clients. As much as I hated having to tackle the question of what to do with my hair at these appointments and the anxiety they brought up, I found the environment itself a world away from everything else going on in my life. I liked Bianca. I liked that each of the hairdressers was renting a chair there and so the clientele as well as their hair and their stories were as varied as the people styling them. From the ladies of a certain age who attended at the same time every week without fail, who took pride in their appearance and wouldn't be caught dead looking less than their best going to the supermarket or to bingo, to the little girls who wanted twists with colourful bobbles at the ends and all the women in between. Being there, you had to surrender any concept of time because your stylist would likely be working on three clients simultaneously. Putting one under the steamer before going back to check on how the colour was taking under thousands of squares of tinfoil on another. I'd never been in there for less than three hours, no matter what I was having done, and I never minded.

A small girl of seven or so was having her hair plaited down into cane-rows in the chair next to me. The first time Sera had sat me on the floor in front of her while she wove my hair into the same formation, I had cried out in pain. She'd told me to stop being dramatic, said that it would loosen up in a couple of days. Until then, I'd had to walk around with raised eyebrows and a startled look on my face. Cane-row. Rows of cane. Rows and rows of sugar cane in the Caribbean. Sugar cane harvested by slaves. The sugar-cane sculpture in the City. I wondered what they were called before colonialism, these plaits. All these different thoughts were accumulating, piling one on top of the other like a stack of paperwork on a desk, building up. A stack which would surely soon topple onto the floor in a heap.

When my phone had enough power, I unplugged it and checked Instagram. I rolled through the feed, stopping occasionally to admire a cake creation at one of the Hackney bakeries I followed or the pregnancy bump of someone I went to sixth form with. I was scrolling so quickly, I almost missed it. A collection of photos in a single post from Caleb. One was a selfie of him looking pensive and wearing sunglasses. The next was an epic shot of the Marina Bay Sands Hotel in Singapore and the final one looked like it might be a view from the top, with the infinity pool in shot and the city sprawling below. There was a caption. 'To new beginnings in my new favourite city.' The first comment below it, from a user I didn't recognise, said: 'Asia aint ready for you, bruv.'

They'd broken up.

'No way,' I said, jolting forward to get my face closer to the screen, like seeing it close up would make it sink in.

'No way, what?' Bianca enquired, but I carried on reading and didn't answer. 'Go on. My life is drier than your hair at the moment. What's the goss?'

I carried on ignoring her, not rudely or purposefully or because I'd been offended by her comparing her life to my hair. Because I was dumbfounded. They'd broken up.

'Whatever it is sounds juicy. 'K, babe. See you in thirty minutes,' Bianca said, putting the steamer hood down over my head and patting me on the shoulders, before going off to find herself another client to gossip with instead.

Sera and Caleb were over. When? I needed to see her. This trumped everything else. I would show up on her doorstep as soon as my hair was moist again.

She answered the door. I'd rung the intercom downstairs and, despite an initial hesitation, she had buzzed me in. She was dressed up, like she was about to go out for the evening. High-waisted, wide-legged black trousers and a sheer dark green shirt with beading on the collar. Her hair was scraped back in a high bun and the baby hairs around her face had been neatly slicked down in tiny waves. It framed her face exquisitely. Not a hair in her eyebrows was out of place and the kohl eyeliner on her top lids had been applied with precision and confidence. I, on the other hand, looked awful. Bianca had finished the treatment with a blow-dry followed by straighteners, but almost as soon as I stepped outside the salon, it had begun to rain lightly and hadn't stopped. The route from there to Sera's had involved a long walk up Holloway Road and I didn't have an umbrella. The day had taken its toll on my make-up too. The bronzer and mascara I'd applied in haste nearly ten hours earlier now felt patchy and soggy. Sera put her earrings in as she leaned against the door frame and half apologised that there was no point in me coming in because she had to leave in a minute or she'd be late. She'd obviously decided that the best way to get over Caleb was to dust herself off and hit the town.

'I wanted to see how you were. I heard about Caleb.' I'd actually read about Caleb, technically, on social media, but that sounded like a weird thing to say.

'Never been better,' she said.

'Yeah, you look fine. Great, I mean. Where are you heading to?'

She fumbled with the earring back behind her earlobe. It slipped out of her hand and fell between our feet. We both crouched down to pick it up at the same time, banging heads in the process. Not hard, but it was enough to make me feel like a nuisance, more of a hindrance than a help.

'Sorry,' I said, regretting being there at all.

'Look, don't know what you've heard but it was his decision. There was an opportunity at work and he took it. Didn't ask me to go with him and that was that. Not that I would've gone. It needed to end and now it has. So, happy days. I've got to go. I'm already late. My mum's just left or I'm sure you coulda had a glass of wine with her or something. I don't know.'

It was clear from how she was acting that I needed her more than she needed me.

'I've been thinking about everything. Everything you said and the documentary. It's all I've been thinking about actually. I'm not sure if you were waiting for me to make a decision and, I don't know, inform you of it. You didn't really make that clear last time we – but, anyway . . .'

'Yeah, can we not, right now? Uber.'

'Sure. I just wanted you to know that I've been taking it seriously. And, yeah, you're right, it looks like there is a history of Andy's family owning a plantation in Jamaica. But I haven't found anything to say that my family, that it was where my family . . . that they were the ones they actually . . . and I think that's the point, isn't it? It's got to be, because otherwise – what would that mean? For us? For anyone?'

'Layla,' she said, not meeting my eyes.

'He's a good guy, Sera. The best.'

'If you say so,' Sera said. Then, finally, she was

180

looking at me. Her eyes were full of care and love. 'Look, you don't have to do anything, Layla. But I can't watch you marry him. It's too sad.'

She left me standing on her doorstep, without looking back at me once.

When I got home to my empty flat, I thought about pushing through the exhaustion I was feeling and starting on the wedding favours we'd decided on. Individually handwritten letters to each and every guest at the wedding. My commitment to following through with the idea instead of something less personal made me glad that we'd capped the guest list at fifty, but my heart wasn't in it. I would try again to make some headway with it tomorrow, while I waited for Andy to slope back home. He would be tired but excited to see me. I tried to think of something I could do to welcome him and soothe his inevitable hangover, but the whole idea of it felt hollow. We'd exchanged a few illegal texts because he wanted updates on what was happening with Grandad. He cared about him like he was his own grandparent, just wanted him to be okay. It was things like that which made it extremely hard to be angry with him or see in him what Sera wanted me to.

Instead, I opened my laptop and began to write an email to Gaia Dunn. I'd found her services listed in the 'Other Resources' section on one of the genealogy websites. Based in Kingston, at the Jamaica Archives and Records Department, she was a historian who also provided private genealogy services to individuals for a fee.

In the email, I explained that I was trying to piece together both my and my future husband's family trees as a wedding gift. I acknowledged the short notice but didn't apologise for it. I asked if she had any availability within the time frame to assist me. I wanted to trace my maternal grandfather's line, I said, and any 'overlap' between said line and my fiancé's family. I would be curious, I mentioned, to see if there were any 'correlations' anywhere along the way. If the branches of our trees had become twisted, grafted onto each other at any point. I listed in bullet points everything I knew, all the facts I thought she would ask for. I saved her the time, before she'd even agreed, so that nothing, on my part, would slow her process down. I tried a variety of knowing but self-conscious suffixes after writing down my and Andy's matching surnames: LOL – same name!; ☺; Weird, huh?; I know, right! Each was promptly deleted before finally being replaced with NO RELATION. It didn't quite express what I was trying to say but it was something, so I left it, desperate to hit send. I wanted to empty the newly amassed contents of my head out into that message and know that it was going to be read by someone impartial, knowledgeable about that kind of thing, experienced and non-judgemental. Someone who wasn't Andy, Sera or my mum. I ended the email confirming that the hourly rate listed on her website was fine, reasonable even, considering the time constraints. Told her to invoice me for a deposit which I would settle immediately.

I was asking Gaia to help me. Help me lay bare the truth. What I'd do with it, I still did not know.

14

12 days until the wedding

Kidney stones. Grandad had kidney stones. Minor. Treatable. Kidney stones. Mum had rung me practically screaming with joy that morning and despite everything I had reacted with uncontainable giddiness too. Dark prognoses like the C-word and numerous other miseries had been inching their way into my mind since the scan, and the relief that his pain would soon be gone without taking him with it was everything.

I was meeting Andy in the park opposite his office to catch up properly on his stag and now to celebrate Grandad's miraculous recovery. He'd been so exhausted when he got home from the airport that he'd fallen asleep on the sofa still clutching the half-drunk cup of tea I'd made him. I'd watched TV for a while on my own, listening to the sound of him snoring lightly in the background. I wanted to hear about his trip or at least the bits he was authorised by Dan to divulge, but I was also pleased that we didn't have to talk. If we'd never gotten engaged, would any of this have happened? Maybe that had been the tipping point for Sera. The documentary had made it easier for her to pin her misgivings onto something concrete. She'd said he was alright to practise on, not to stay with for years to come, grow old with, have babies with. But she was seeing it all wrong, seeing me marrying him as being in his possession, too close to what his ancestors had done. Perhaps she saw it as rewarding bad behaviour which, though in the past, had had repercussions for black people ever since. I agreed with that in part, but I didn't see why my relationship had to be the one made an example of, to prove that point to the world. *This* was our relationship. Us on the sofa, me watching him sleep, him making me laugh. Hundreds of these tiny moments. But I knew I had to face up to the knotty stuff too.

I still didn't feel ready to tell him what was going on, partly because I wasn't at all sure what exactly *was* going on, but the thought of talking about anything else felt disingenuous. I could see James and Lydia in my mind, their heads shaking, fingers wagging at me. This behaviour was against all of their teachings. 'Communicate, communicate, communicate, Layla,' they were shouting, like some kind of premarital warning klaxon.

I'd stroked his face lightly with the tips of my fingers as he slept but stopped when it made him stir. I had missed him but had also appreciated the time without him. Not feeling, for a couple of days at least, like I had to hide everything that was going on in my head. Breathing space. I'd turned the TV off and gently nudged him, whispered that he should head up to bed and that I'd be right up after locking the front door and putting the dishwasher on. We were both in bed, asleep, by 9 p.m.

*

I waved from the bench I'd commandeered when I saw him approaching with a paper bag in his hand. He put it down and took my face in both his hands before planting kisses on my forehead, then my nose, then my lips. The whole sequence made me feel bashful and I quickly scanned the area to see if anyone had clocked the overly effusive PDA. 'I'm so happy about Roy,' he said. 'But I've been googling kidney stones all morning and they sound like a real bitch.'

I laughed in spite of myself.

'Sandwich potluck?' he said, shaking the bag but not letting me see what was inside. I fished out an avocado wrap, leaving him the duck one.

He told me that the guys had loved Bucharest and there was already talk of a first anniversary re-stag with WAGs allowed this time. I listened to him laughing about all his mates and missed Sera so much it hurt.

'So, what did you get up to?' he said.

'Nothing much.' I took the final bite of my wrap and washed it down with the iced green tea from the bag.

'No brunch?' Andy said.

'Umm.' I hesitated. Hesitated because I was trying to decide whether to lie. Just say, yes, brunch went ahead as usual, like clockwork, and it was fantastic. But it would have felt like crossing a line. I would officially be a liar then, which would not only have been completely at odds with the way Andy was being, affectionate, making time for me when he was busy and still tired from the trip, but also at odds with the wife I wanted to be. 'Nope. Probably not this week either,' I said, knowing that my answer had only left me wide open to further questioning.

'What's going on with Sera lately?'

'She broke up with Caleb,' I said quickly, hoping it would be enough.

'Oh shit. That's not much fun,' he said, before pausing and adding reluctantly, 'It's just that, er, Alex said she thought you might have fallen out over something.'

Fuck. Alex. He literally only spoke to his sister once or twice a month, tops. I glossed over it with 'Nothing major'. I could feel myself welling up and worried that the lump forming in my throat might actually appear in my mouth followed by a gush of tears.

Andy immediately put his arm around me and drew me towards him. He kissed me on the head. I looked up at him as he stared out into the middle distance, his expression contorted with concern, trying to think of something to say to make me feel better.

'What can I do? I don't like seeing you like this,' he said.

'Nothing. Honestly. Look, don't worry. It's gone two, you should head back.'

I could tell he didn't want to go but he did, reluctantly. I was glad I hadn't actually cried but he was officially worried about me now, it was obvious. I would try to be jollier, make a concerted effort to be a bit lighter and more bride-like. Glowing, prone to giggling, walking on air. Things like that. What I really needed to do, urgently, was to get out of my own head, count my lucky fucking stars. Stars which included Grandad being on the mend and my dreamboat of a fiancé having the patience of a saint and an ability to remain unfazed by my melodrama, who I loved so much it was almost incomprehensible. But I couldn't shake the anxious uncertainty. I was no longer able to mentally visualise being in my dress, being at the church, saying any vows. My mind just didn't seem able to conjure up that particular daydream any more. I wondered for a second how it would sound if, when Andy got home after work, I were to say to him, without any kind of context: *Hey, you. How was the rest of your day? By the way, not really sure I can go through with the whole 'God joining us together' thing on the 21st. Yeah, I don't actually think I can marry you. Not you per se. Your name. I mean, I can't be your . . . yeah. Not to worry though – we can still go on our honeymoon!* But it could not be made light of. I was scared that by the end of the month I would be completely single, with no friends. And I was already being given a preview of what that kind of loneliness felt like. Grimly, it made me think of Joyce Carol Vincent. Her skeleton being found after three years on the sofa in her bedsit just down the road in Wood Green when I was fourteen. The TV set still flickering in the background and no one even noticing she was gone.

I pulled out my phone and reread Gaia's reply, which had come through in the dead of night when I'd woken up and couldn't get back to sleep. She was on board. I'd already settled her PayPal request. All I could do was wait. I sat there for a bit longer working through my phone. Listening to a voicemail from my mum. Cleaning up my inbox. Deleting emails I couldn't be bothered to open. One from a charity I had a direct debit set up with, another from Jack's Flights with the subject *direct* flights to Jamaica at £314 rtn. Then I checked to see if the weather forecast on my phone extended far enough in the future to cover 21 August. It didn't. Soon, two hours had passed. I'd mindlessly hopped from web page to web page, clicking on shiny things that caught my eye like restaurant reviews, horrifying news stories, new forms of physical exercise with made-up names like 'yoga-la-tees'. I would get halfway through one before getting bored and navigating to the next, leaving the previous page open, telling myself I'd come back to it later. All the while my mind raced ahead to the next thing, thoughts of going home, cleaning the whole flat in its entirety in the same cathartic way I'd cleaned my inbox, then having a twenty-six-minute power nap before going for a run and making dinner for Andy in the hope I might be able to be a little nicer that evening.

As I got up to get on with that plan, stretching out, casting my eye back over the bench to check I hadn't left anything behind, my phone beeped. I slowed down to see who it was before coming to a complete standstill. It was Sera. Screengrabs and a video from Sera. The Twitter landscape confused me. I had to adjust my brain to get into its language. Who had posted first, who the retweeter was, who was merely liking, who was commenting.

It looked like Sera had retweeted a video of a kid being arrested. I knew him, the kid. It was Harry Jackson, from our school. So many kids had slipped behind during the pandemic and we'd been offering tutoring to try and get them back on track. I had worked with Harry in his home in Homerton while his mother cooked food she regularly dished out to anyone in need at her local community centre. Sometimes she managed to convince Harry to go with her, do his bit, but that was becoming a rarer event the more teenaged he became. Harry was mixed-race too. He had golden-brown skin and brown curls on top of neatly cropped sides. He was shy with long, thin fingers which he always seemed to keep in his pockets. I'm not sure why that was something I noticed about him, but it gave me the impression that he was a nice young man. I hoped that if I ever had a son, he would both look and carry himself a bit like Harry Jackson. He'd made huge strides in his schooling during the course of our sessions.

I watched the video. The camera action was shaky. Occasionally the person recording would interject with his thoughts on what he was capturing. Saying, 'Harry. Harry Jackson, ya know! Even him, ya know. An athlete. Does shit for charity. Always got his head in a book, dis one, ya know! And look. Nah, no one's safe. No one. He looks shook, boy. Mad t'ing. Mad t'ing.'

As well as Harry, there were police officers in shot. One looked to be in his mid-thirties, male, white. Another was older, also male, also white. He had red hair, a narrow face. A towering body. The kind of man I'd feel uncomfortable walking behind me on a poorly lit street. Uniform or no uniform. Officer Redhead can be seen patting Harry down. He struggles, not making it easy for him. He's told to keep still and cooperate, to stop inhibiting a police search. Harry appears to disengage his upper body, letting the officer move him as he sees fit, not aiding him in any way but not stopping him either. He looks like he wants to ask a thousand questions but doesn't know where to start or how to articulate them, so acquiesces, wanting it to be over as quickly as possible. He answers their questions with 'No comment. No comment', like he's heard it from somewhere, from friends who've been stopped in the past who've said you're allowed to say that, as many times as you like. You don't have to answer nothing. Officer Redhead gestures to his partner. He steps up, asks Harry to remove his cap. When he is slow to do so he asks again. When he still does not, the younger officer seeks guidance from Officer Redhead with his eyes, like he is a rookie or having second thoughts about the whole thing. Like he realises they've made a mistake. Officer Redhead nods, as if to say, 'Go on. Make him.' The younger officer reluctantly but forcefully pushes Harry back towards the brick wall at the side of Caffè Nero. And the raid on Harry's person is executed in view of everyone. He is helpless to stop it. I can only imagine how humiliated he must have felt. How scared.

The video alone was enough to fill me with fury and dismay, but Sera was sharing it with me for another reason. Underneath it, she'd written the comment:

Sera @SeraphinaC   15:01
TREATING ALL BLACK MEN LIKE CRIMINALS IS NOT OKAY
#STOPSTOPANDSEARCH

And one of the first responders had been Andy, saying:

Andy @theAndyMcK   15:12
Well said @SeraphinaC. But worth pointing out –
stats show S&S effective at keeping us safe.
And don't forget, plenty of white people get stopped
too! (Not caught on camera as much obvs!)

And then Sera had commented on his comment with:

Sera @SeraphinaC   15:42
Don't think we really need your voice on this one.
Thanks anyway, D&I Dude!!

I didn't sit down on the nearest bench so much as collapse onto it in a heap. And it surprised me that the first emotion to rise into my chest was not shock or confusion but pure rage. *What the fuck?*

There was no way I was going to be able to sleep or clean or be nice now.

All I could think about was running. Throwing my phone in the nearest bin and running away from it, as fast as I could.

It took me twenty minutes to get from Russell Square back to Finsbury Park. The Tube ride did nothing to rationalise things in my mind; in fact, the racket of the train speeding down the tracks, the announcements, the doors beeping, everything about the journey only worked me up even more.

When I finally reached street level again my reaction was immediate and, admittedly, un-thought-out. I phoned him, my hand trembling slightly as I scrolled to his number in my favourites and put the phone to my ear.

'Hey, missing me already?' came his voice. It was hushed and I imagined him taking the call at his desk, the odd colleague somewhere in the vicinity.

'Yeah, something like that,' I said. I started to pace with my arms folded. I could feel the sternness of my expression.

'You okay?' he said. 'Look, I can't really talk right now. I've got a meeting starting in —'

'Busy? Really? You can't be that fucking busy if you've got time to comment on videos on Twitter.'

'What? God, yeah. You've seen it? You must be upset. Poor kid.'

For a moment, I began to veer off course slightly, talking about what Harry had been through, the video, how angry I was about it. 'He's the last kid they should be stopping. What were they even looking for? There are real criminals out there and they've got time to be roughing up a kid who wouldn't hurt a fly? It's shit like this that . . . well, that pisses these kids off to the point where they think they might as well be — I don't know — it gives them trust issues. It's all bullshit. Just racist bullshit.'

At that, I heard him get up from his desk, open a door, to a meeting room or somewhere, and close it behind him before his voice came through at normal volume.

'You sound really worked up,' he said, full of concern.

I was silent for a moment, took a deep breath as I tried to choose the words I needed to get across why I found the way he'd given his twopence worth pointless, unnecessary and, frankly, totally unacceptable.

'You *do* know it's racist, don't you? That's not news to you, right? The way the police profile black people, single them out. You do understand that, right? Because from your comments, I feel like – I don't know – like maybe you don't. And that's . . . problematic.'

'Well, yeah, I know that, but, I just – the stats are there. I didn't think there'd be any harm in mentioning that. I wasn't trying to diminish what Sera was saying. I can delete it straight away if –'

'That'd be a start. And, yeah, you are diminishing it, that's exactly what you're doing, in a public forum. Without thinking about what you're saying or how it sounds.'

'I'm sorry. I didn't think –' And then came the *but*. 'But Sera – is she – has she got it in for me or something?'

'That's not the point. There's no fucking excuse for the police and there's no excuse for you coming at it with that kind of commentary.'

He let out an exasperated sigh. 'Completely. You're right. I'm sorry. Look, Lay, I've got to go now. Please, let's just talk about this properly when I get home.'

'Fine. See you at home,' I said and I hung up even though he was in the middle of saying goodbye. I felt wretched for doing it. But I had nothing else to say to him. And besides. He wasn't the only one I needed to speak to.

She answered within a couple of rings.

'What are you trying to achieve by sending me that?' I began and then I barely came up for air. She didn't interrupt me or try to ask any questions. She just listened. I could feel her listening, waiting me out. But as I listened to myself, to what I was saying, like I was outside of myself, a spectator, I realised I was using virtually the same lines of defence as Andy had. I knew I was doing it and I wanted to stop, but I persisted. I was trying to protect him. Sera viewed social media as a means of bringing about real, meaningful change in the world. Deep down, that was where she was coming from with showing me Andy's comments to what she'd posted. But if I didn't at least try to make her see that he hadn't meant anything by it, what chance did I stand with everything else?

'He had no need to pipe up about what was going on with Harry,' came Sera's voice. 'He left himself wide open to this, showing what he really thinks. So, why are you defending him?'

'Why are you attacking him on, on everything?'

'I'm just looking out for my people.'

'Yeah, well, I used to think that included me too.'

We both went quiet. An awkwardness had set in which was no longer possible to ignore.

'He's sorry, okay? He really is,' I said. My tone was softer. I didn't want to fight any more. There was a sharp intake of breath at the other end of the line followed by a huff which told me that Sera had had enough of the conversation. Maybe even of me.

Then suddenly I was the one left listening to the three abrupt beeps that mean that the other person is gone and you are on your own. Completely.

15

Before

I had already been planning to move back in with Mum for a while as a stop gap until I could find a new place. One with fewer housemates – housemates who actually knew the meaning of the word clean. So, when the first lockdown hit, I was counting my lucky stars that our lease was at an end and I could go back to my old room.

Andy and I had only been together for a few weeks when people were told they had to stay at home. I was immediately anxious about whether we would be able to keep our spark alive in spite of what was going on around us. A strange new atmosphere had settled over London. A mixture of fear and uncertainty, punctuated with hope. Paintings of rainbows adorned window-panes. The sounds of applause drifted through the streets every Thursday evening. And sometimes, one of our neighbours would place a solitary chair in the centre of the courtyard below the flats and, unbidden, seren-ade us all with the sounds of her cello. There was a sense that, in spite of all the death and doom in the headlines, there was resilience out there too. Gradually, my fears over whether Andy and I would get through it faded.

Officially, physical contact was off the agenda; kissing,

holding hands, sex suddenly an offence between people from separate households. But unofficially – and as guilty as I felt about it, twitchy that we would be caught and fined or, worse, reprimanded at school – we didn't slow down. Andy would ride over on his bike on the weekends or, instead of heading straight home after my fortnightly supervision of the children of key workers and the vulnerable at school, I would take a detour to Andy's flat and stay the night. The rule-breaking aspect seemed to make everything more intense. The secrecy, the sneaking around, the justification of everything in my own mind. There was no option for my mum to work from home, so I figured there was as much risk of her bringing Covid back into the flat as there was of me. The thing neither of us wanted to risk, however, was passing it on to Grandad. So, from March until August, our Sunday visits were off. We would call him and ask him to put his records on in the background and talk to us like we were all in the same room. We even upgraded his house phone, getting a new one with a speaker feature delivered to him so that the calls could roll on without him having to keep the handset pressed to his ear. It wasn't the same but it got us through.

Andy and I started talking about moving in together as soon as lockdown began to ease but didn't actually find a place until the summer holidays. It was a split-level, two-bedroom flat and all my favourite places were within walking distance. Mum's, Sera's, Dotori for Korean food, Woodberry Wetlands for weekend walks.

Andy had been all too happy to relocate north of the river, having fallen for it over the months we'd been together. But his favourite feature about the flat seemed to be the pre-installed hooks on the wall in the hallway to hang his bike from, displaying it like a piece of artwork.

A slightly exasperated 'Cha! Finally!' had been Mum's reaction to the idea. I imagined she was keen to have her own space back. Sera, on the other hand, had raised her eyebrows. 'Bit nuts, moving in with someone you've been with for five months, but okay.'

'The world is a bit fucking nuts right now. Nuts is a good thing when you're in love, right?' I said. I left it at that, acutely aware of the lack of progress in her own living arrangements.

Going to the garden centre, as a pastime, wasn't something I'd ever heard of anyone doing before. In fact, I had never even been to a garden centre because Mum and I had never had a garden. But I was willing to see what it was all about, especially as it was the only place, apart from the park, anyone was allowed to go. It was Andy's parents' idea that we met at one they'd been going to for years just outside the M25. It had an open-air cafe, landscaped areas, things to spend money on and things to look at that weren't screens.

The estate agent had made a point of correcting us each and every time we'd referred to our garden as a garden. 'The outside space is a real bonus for what you're paying,' he'd said, and, 'The outside space can accommodate a bistro table and perhaps a chair, but only one.' The outside space was essentially a north-facing tessellation of half a dozen paving slabs with a few tufts of moss sticking out. But Andy was convinced we could turn it into a charming, urban oasis with the right plants, some weedkiller and a bit of advice from his parents who were avid gardeners. His mum had once designed a bronze-medal-winning garden at the Chelsea Flower Show and had even been approached by Sky to front her own gardening special to rival what the BBC had going with Charlie Dimmock. She fell out with the producers when they wanted her to wear camo and come up with a catchphrase.

I was, I knew, Andy's first 'girlfriend of colour' because his mother had told me so at our only other IRL meeting at Jessie's party. The phrase had irked me. It had made me crinkle my nose when she said it, which is how I looked when I cringed. I was hopeful she hadn't picked up on that response, though, because I'd pretended to sneeze immediately afterwards just in case. Sera had said it was pure rudeness. 'Like she wanted to let you know that all eyes are on you. You will henceforth be representative of all black people, and based on your performance they'll decide whether to let any more of your kind in.' But I wanted to give Andrea the benefit of the doubt. Perhaps she had simply been stating a fact. Besides, the concept of Andy having a serious girlfriend of any hue was relatively novel. Before me, he'd been single for two years and apart from that he had only introduced them to one previous girlfriend. I was keenly aware that things between Andy and me had moved fast. I found the speed of it all thrilling, owning it rather than blaming the pandemic for the way we'd gone from strangers to acquaintances to boyfriend and girlfriend and now cohabiters visiting the garden centre together in less than six months. I told myself it would have happened anyway because it felt right. It was meant to be. And if Covid had taught us anything, it was to recognise how short and precarious life was and to seize it. My mum thought it was romantic, she trusted Andy, watched how he cared for me. I told myself that Andy's parents must be buying into the intensity of our relationship too as they were now investing in our outside space. So, I put my positive pants on and tried to remember the Latin names of some of the plants I'd googled and planned to drop into the conversation the annual pass I'd just bought for Andy to Kew Gardens to impress them.

'You'll need something hardy out there. Three or four smallish pots with a few hostas, some Madagascar periwinkles with some lily turf and anemones. Oh and an acer.' I was glad she'd finally stopped there as I was seriously starting to worry that I'd accidentally turned the camera to face the neighbour's massive garden on the Zoom call when we'd given them a virtual tour of the flat.

'What do you think about a living wall?' she added.

'I don't think it will be living for very long if I'm left in charge of it,' I said with a chuckle. I realised Andrea was not the right crowd for plant-based humour when I turned round to see Andy and David stifling their own laughter. Andy stepped forward to rescue me, placing himself in between me and his mother and draping his arm over my shoulder.

After an initial sweep of the outdoor plants, we stopped for coffee and cake. We caught up on Andrea and David's plans for renovating their house. They were in a battle with the council about a tree they needed to remove. Andrea wanted to show me the drawings of what they were planning to do. But after a few panicked minutes spent digging in her bag she realised she couldn't find her phone and couldn't remember seeing it since she had used it to pay for the coffees. David checked his pockets too and scoured the area but couldn't find it either.

'Just check with the little coloured girl at the till,' he said. 'See if anything's been handed in.'

It wasn't a full cardiac arrest, but I suddenly began to feel my heart palpitate and my temples throb like I had forgotten to take a breath for a few seconds and my body was trying to tell me to do something about it. I did. I inhaled deeply and the sensations began to sub-side. But the echo of that word did not. I had seen a reaction to it in Andy too. The way he was suspended for a moment. As though he was annoyed at how close the trip had come to almost going perfectly, almost a clear run, without incident. Andrea on the other hand had not heard anything untoward, and duly approached the black girl at the till to ask her if anyone had found a phone. I guessed then that it was a word she probably used too. Perhaps it had been a word Sasha, Alex and Andy had heard growing up, used themselves for a time, maybe, without being aware of the vintage of it, the political charge it came with. The word had instantly transported me into the world of a John Grisham novel set in America's Deep South where black is pitted against white. Where black people aren't black at all but coloured. Coloured in. Not the standard, the archetypal, but added too, besmirched. And 'little'? Where the hell had that come from? Had it been to soften the blow of 'coloured', make the whole description more complimentary somehow? Because it was clear to see there was nothing little about the girl who'd served us. She had at least two inches on Andy's dad. Not to mention the fact that she was all curves – big and shapely from her lips to her waist. Before my mind had a chance to run away with itself, I came back into my body instead of floating a few feet above it, and joined in with Andy's sentiments of relief that the phone had been found in the folds of the lining of Andrea's handbag. Then he initiated our goodbyes.

'What a treat to see you both,' Andrea said. 'I just can't wait until this is all over and we can have a normal meal, in a restaurant, without any of this nonsense.' She shook the mask she'd removed after exiting the building.

'Enjoy the garden, you two. And well done for putting up with him, Layla,' David added. The accompanying smile was full of warmth. It was an in-joke he was trying to establish with me. I could feel how hard he was working to form a connection. To show how much he liked me. I wanted to like him back. I really wanted to.

*

On the drive home, I was quiet. Andy had put on an old Coldplay album. But then he turned the volume down with the controls on the steering wheel. Click, click, click, the music faded into the empty space of the car. I knew he was getting ready to say something. I was glad that I'd left it to him to make the first move. I needed to see if he'd noticed and what he thought of it.

'Sorry about my dad.'

'What about him?' I said, playing dumb.

'I've told them they should say black about a thousand times, but – well, yeah – sorry you had to hear that.'

I was glad I'd heard it. It meant I could do something about it, eradicate it from their vocabulary before they met my mum for the first time. I definitely wouldn't be telling her about the incident. Or Sera for that matter. I once read an agony aunt column which had advised a woman trying to patch things up with her cheating husband never to tell her family or friends or anyone close to her what he'd done. She'd advised speaking to a therapist or someone outside of her immediate circle. Because even if she thought she could one day forget the affair, her family, her best friend never would, and her husband would be hated and deemed untrustworthy for the rest of their marriage. I didn't want to leave an indelible mark on my mum's impression of Andy's parents when I knew or at least hoped they would become a permanent fixture in my life, because of how much I hoped Andy would.

'I know it's just a word, but I felt it go through me.' I

wasn't trying to make him feel bad. I just wanted him to understand.

'I know, I know. I saw you – I don't know – bristle when he said it. Which I completely get. It's not right. I'll tell them. It's just a term they grew up hearing, and I guess it's in there now. Stuck in their vocabularies. And they're getting on a bit now so . . .' he said, forcing a laugh.

'Uh-huh,' was all I could say in reply. I let some of the faintly clinking piano solo on 'Politik' float into the silence for a few seconds as I considered what he'd said. I stared out of the window. We passed by the Polish War Memorial, and I watched as a few walkers completed their ascents to the top with their kids on their shoulders.

'Have they always had iPhones?' I asked him, my gaze remaining fixed out of the passenger window.

'Huh?'

'Your parents, they both have iPhones, don't they?'

'Yeah. I don't know. They're usually pretty late to the party when it comes to technology. I think they hung on to their brick handsets for as long as they could.'

I waited for a moment and made sure what I was going to say would be sufficient, get to the nub of the point I was trying to make so that it would be all I ever needed to say about the matter.

'Well, if someone can learn how to use a smartphone, so late in life, I'd say they're probably capable of learning any number of new things. Including how not to use outdated racial terms that black people find offensive. I don't know. Maybe. Just a theory.'

We drove the rest of the way in silence. The only sound in the car was a confused insect buzzing among the flowers in one of the pot plants. I felt sorry for it finding itself trapped in our car. I hoped it wouldn't make its way to the front and sting me, but instead would continue to nestle into the dusty pollen of the lavender for as long as it could before it died of neglect in our garden that wasn't a garden.

16

(Still) 12 days until the wedding

I was in no mood to talk wedmin that evening. I was feeling calmer, but I was still pissed off. Pissed off at Andy for making that thoughtless, idiotic comment. I was doubly pissed off with Sera for telling him it wasn't his place to comment on the video. But even though Andy didn't get why she suddenly had it in for him, he didn't really have a leg to stand on. He had erred in the public domain so all he could do was lie down and take it.

I was also actually pissed because I had spent the last few hours in a bar on my own trying to avoid going home. As I let myself into the flat, I was already getting ready to explode if Andy so much as mentioned the words 'finger' and 'food' in the same sentence. He didn't seem to notice me come in. He had his AirPods in, listening to one of his podcasts, which he usually did while he cooked. He looked completely engrossed in the meal he was preparing, prodding at half-cooked lamb cutlets, all herb-encrusted and looking like something straight out of a fancy restaurant. He was even wearing an apron. I didn't know we owned an apron. I couldn't help but notice how serene he looked, just at that moment. It wasn't that he was smiling. He wasn't. It was in the way he moved, an unmissable air of contentment, blissful, privileged ignorance. It was how he used the kitchen utensils and adjusted the temperature on the oven. The sense of security he had in the assumption that I'd let the Twitter episode slide. He had everything in life that he could possibly need or want. Healthy, living parents. A stable career. A home he loved. Friends he could rely on. And me. This was all in stark contrast to my appearance. I looked weary and bedraggled, consumed. I knew I did because I caught my reflection in the large mirror we'd hung on the wall which ran from the living room to the open-plan kitchen back when we moved in, when we'd try to create zones, the feeling of more space. One of the many insignificant but also somehow tremendously important ways we were building a life together. I headed straight for the fridge and got myself a can of Coke from the emergency stash I turned to in times of extreme fatigue.

'Oh, hey, you're home. I didn't hear you come in,' he said, looking up at me from the oven door after placing the lamb back inside. He hurriedly began removing his earphones and made his way over to me.

'Hi,' I said, noticeably downbeat. I busied myself with the ring pull on the can instead of making myself available for the kiss I could tell he wanted to greet me with. I put the can to my lips. The first sip gave me the slap in the face I needed but what I actually wanted was more wine, so I put it down, bypassed Andy and crossed to the other side of the kitchen where I flicked the cork off the bottle breathing on the table and filled a glass in three heavy-handed glugs before gulping some down.

'You know how sorry I am about –'

'I know,' I said. I genuinely felt his regret about the whole thing. He had sounded mortified during our phone call. And now, as he was reiterating his apology, even the rhythm of his breathing seemed earnest somehow. I wanted him to be able to let it go. And besides, we had bigger fish to fry. The beginnings of the conversation had been bubbling up in my gut for days. Now they were somewhere in my chest. I wondered how long they would take to reach my mouth, and how many more times I would try to push them back down.

'I just want to get on with the wedding,' he announced suddenly, moving around the kitchen as he spoke, tidying up some mess from the cooking, getting cutlery out of the drawer and laying our places at the table. 'I'm ready for it,' he went on. Inside I was wishing he'd stop. 'I want to get married, get to Spain. You and me.' *Stop.* 'And you know what I've been thinking for days now?' *Please stop.* 'We need to make our minds up. We need to decide.' *Oh God.* 'Come on – what are we dancing to? Huh? Because I can't wait to dance to whatever it is, in front of our friends and family.' *Chest.* 'When you're my wife.' *Throat.* 'Mrs Andrew McKinnon.' That was it. Enough to tip me over the edge. I caught sight of my engagement ring then, glinting at me against my glass. It suddenly seemed ugly to me. Too small for my finger. Too green. Too shiny. Too metallic. I downed the rest of the wine and readied myself to tell him everything.

I knew it was the wine making me do it but I didn't care.

'Andy, I need to talk to you about the wedding. I've been doing some research. I found something and I don't know how to feel about it. How we deal with our past plays an important part in the way we live. Do you agree with that? I think I do. I mean, I do. That's what I think.'

'What are you talking about? What kind of research?' he said, clocking my expression, a combination of the world being about to end and deep-seated confusion.

'I've been looking into my family history. I've felt lately, more than ever, a need to do that. To be better informed about what I'm carrying with me.'

'And?'

'And, and, McKinnon and McKinnon. That's us.' I paused. 'But it's not. It's not just us. It's bigger than us.'

'Okay, I'm lost.' I couldn't blame him. I wasn't intentionally trying to dance around what I wanted to say, it was just happening. I tried to get my shit together.

'What exactly do you know about yours? Your family history? What about that big estate, huh? That must've cost a fair bit in its day. It's got a ha-ha, for goodness' sake.' The attempt at humour was misjudged. 'Sorry,' I said, looking down at my feet. I inhaled deeply, looked him in the eye and spoke again. 'The money for that house, that estate, came from slavery. And the people your family, um, er – engaged – to do the work that made the money to build that house were mine. My people. My actual family, in fact. Owned.' I corrected myself quickly, before it was too late and I bottled it. 'I meant, owned. Not engaged. Your family probably owned mine.'

The room went silent, until finally Andy uttered, 'Oh, Layla.' I had never seen him look like that before. It was like he was an apple and someone had reached inside him with a sharp instrument and violently removed the core of him. *Please don't cry*, I thought, *please don't fucking cry. You are absolutely not allowed to produce tears over this. Do not make this about you.*

'I don't know what to say. I'm – I'm – I don't know.' He spoke with shame and deep sincerity even though he wasn't really saying anything. 'So, is this why things have been so weird between us?'

'Kind of,' I said. 'The house, the old seat, where your parents are having the party, is named in compensation records from 1837. There was a D. McKinnon, he owned slaves – enslaved people – in Jamaica, traded sugar, and when it was abolished, when it was finally over, he got a payout. Duncan McKinnon? Your, I don't know, four times great-grandfather, I guess. He had overseers on the island but there are records of trips he made out to the plantation so he could manage things himself. So he could see the work being done. Make sure it was up to scratch, efficient. Productive. And that was in St Catherine where Grandad's from, where my family has always lived. The documentary talks about the way, even after slaves were emancipated – I mean, they say emancipated but really they were indentured, forced to carry on working in pretty much the same manner and conditions – but

anyway, sometimes they stayed near their former plantation, and it benefited them to keep their former slave
family's name, so they did and I think that – I'm trying
to work out if –'

'What documentary?'

'Sera sent this documentary to me –'

'Sera sent it to you?' There was something new in his
voice now. It made him sound croaky and creaky, like
the words were getting stuck. He was seething. His eyes
started flicking from side to side, darting around the
room and then trying to hold on to something, anything
that made more sense than me. The sound of the fan
oven was louder than ever. The smell of singed lamb
was beginning to fill the room. He took it out quickly.
Turned everything off. Stood with his arms folded across
his chest, looking incredulous. 'Why?'

'She just wanted me to know, thought it was important. She was looking out for me.' Once again I was able
to defend the person who wasn't in the room, but unable
to tell him the real reason she'd sent it to me. In the end
he didn't need me to.

'What, so you'd leave me?' he said. 'Layla, come on.
This is bullshit. This wasn't me. This is stuff from hundreds of years ago.'

And then the tears came. Mine.

'Sorry,' he said, grabbing my hand. 'I shouldn't have
said that. I'm sorry. I'm sorry about my family. Is that
what you want me to say?'

'I don't know. I don't know anything. It's just a fucking mess,' I said. 'But yes, I would like someone to be

sorry. Yes, I want that. Because it is incomprehensible to me that a human being should be kept in chains. Half of me has been wronged and the other half should be sorry.'

Then, in almost a whisper, I heard him say it and it made my heart beat twice as fast with relief that he still felt it.

'I love you.'

All I wanted to say was *Thank fuck! Let's forget I ever brought this up and just elope.* But, I couldn't. He was lucky I wasn't Sera. If Sera had been there telling him all this, there would have been raised voices, flaring tempers. It would have been like Prime Minister's Questions. She'd be grilling the shit out of him, talking to him about reparations, not letting him wriggle off the hook. Not just accepting it.

So, I said, 'I don't want to be your property.'

And then he came in close, he took my hand. The one with my engagement ring on. He played with it between his thumb and forefinger. He did that sometimes. Before, it had instantly made me feel safe. Now it made me feel sick. I released my hand from his, pulled the ring from my finger and placed it on the table.

'I can't wear this any more. Not knowing where it came from.'

'We don't know that. It's just a ring.'

'It's an heirloom. An ancestral asset. I can't parade around in it like it's an innocent thing.'

I allowed myself to lean into him, the closeness of his body saying it was alright to do so. It was all out in the open now. I felt lighter for it. We stayed there like that for a long time not saying anything. Until there was something I had to say, just in case he thought I didn't. Even though it might have been impossible in light of everything. Even though it probably didn't make as much sense as it had before.

'I love you too,' and over his left shoulder, where my face pressed into him and he couldn't see my eyes, I turned my gaze to the pink streaks filling the sky just beyond the kitchen window and allowed myself just one thought. How beautiful the world is sometimes, when it is silent and still and not doing anything to hurt us.

He could see that I needed to sleep. He led me upstairs to our room with a mug of camomile tea and put it on the bedside table. He switched on the lamp and closed the blinds so that the glow from the street light outside wouldn't disturb me. He pulled the door behind him and a few seconds later I heard the TV go on in the living room. He probably needed to decompress. I didn't have the energy to take a shower. I'd had so many showers lately, sometimes three or four times in a day because it often felt like the only way to reset myself. To wash away the dirt I kept accumulating in my research, the emails, my own thoughts. My skin felt dry, wicked by all the rinsing and the towel-drying.

The tea was welcome. I lay back and carefully pressed the base of the mug over my navel as I nestled my head into the pillow. The heat of it brought comfort and the scent of the camomile wafting towards my nose made my eyelids begin to feel heavy. But suddenly, I forced them open, remembering the email from the travel website and wanting to act before I had a chance to be rational. And then I texted my mum:

I'm booking flights to Jamaica. Cheap deal. 5 days. This week. Can you get the time off? PS I'm being serious. My hen party has fallen through. This is the replacement. I NEED this trip. Booking asap. Let me know.

It was impulsive but I didn't care. And that was something I got from my mother anyway, so I knew that if she was going to agree to come, it would be in the same spirit, knowing that the paperwork, the tests, all the details could be worked out over the next couple of days. There was no shoulda-woulda-coulda about my mum. Just as I began to wonder whether I would still want to go on my own if she said no or whether there was any way I could rope Poonam and Siobhan in at short notice, my phoned buzzed:

I'm coming and Dad wants to come too.

I smiled at the sight of it, followed all the links and booked three return flights to Kingston, only starting to believe I had actually done it when the confirmation email from BA landed in my inbox. I immediately sent a message to the 'Lay's Hen' group on WhatsApp explaining that they didn't need to save the date for it any more and I'd decided to spend a few days away with my family instead. The sense of relief in doing so made me wish I'd taken matters into my own hands sooner. It was unconventional, a hen trip away which included the grandfather of the bride, but it made sense. Of course

Grandad should be there. I realised there was only one person in the world who could tell me what to do about everything and that I shouldn't have left it so long to talk to him properly. Short of going back in time to speak to my great-grandmother's great-grandmother, I needed to hear Grandad's point of view. And I had to be there with him, back where it all started. Look him in the eyes. Creamy and golden from all the smoke-filled lives he'd lived.

I knew Andy would be scared when I told him. Scared that I was a confused, mixed-up bride running away from everything and never coming back. Taking a break which carried the danger of a break-up. It would also take a great deal of persuasion to talk him down from booking a flight for himself. But I knew he would eventually understand why I had to make the trip without him. With my family. He would be reassured to know that I wanted him to take me to the airport. To kiss me goodbye at security. To wait for me.

'Don't worry,' I would say. 'I'll be home in a few days. And if anyone asks, just tell them I'm on my hen do.'

17

Before

He was clutching his sister's hand when he stepped off the boat. It was 8 June 1954. His thin brown suit had felt oppressive when he'd boarded in that heat, but woefully insufficient in the early-morning temperature that greeted him at Southampton. The crossing had taken two weeks. Boredom and bouts of occasional seasickness had been punctuated with exploring the ship, roving the upper decks, eating boiled potatoes, overcooked runner beans and Spam, and above all, missing home.

As a twelve-year-old, he had had to travel on 21-year-old Cynthia's passport. She had taken it upon herself to raise him after their mother's breakdown had brought so much sorrow to the family. Their father had been a transient presence in their lives but gave his blessing for Cynthia to take Roy with her to England in search of a better life. Roy hadn't asked why or for how long. He simply followed where his sister led.

He hadn't known what to expect in the country he was bound for. Some had said the pavements were covered in gold, that everyone was rich and spoke like royalty. Others had said that their fathers, uncles, older brothers were sharing rooms, sharing bathrooms and there were certain places they couldn't go, certain shops that wouldn't serve them. That they had been spat at when they arrived. He had been scared. His sister had been resolute.

Disembarking, the cold air found gaps in the weft of his suit and pierced his skin like tiny needles. He wanted to get back on, set sail again. Another two weeks. He wanted to go home. But instead they travelled straight to Birmingham by train where Cynthia's boyfriend, Teddy, who had made the same journey a year earlier, had already found a shared flat and work as a bus driver. They got married as soon as they could and did their best to settle into their new lives, the three of them together. But Cynthia cried for weeks and weeks after arriving. It was supposedly summer but there was nothing of the tropical heat she had known on her island. She clung to the Baptist church – to the only kindness she recognised since she'd left Jamaica.

In early 1958, Cynthia declared to sixteen-year-old Roy that a miracle had happened. The miracle of life inside her. She had prayed for it and God had answered her, finally, after so many years. But she didn't want her child to be called the names she'd been called since setting foot in that country, when they were simply walking down the street minding their own business, or treated differently at school because of the colour of his skin. She wanted to go home with her husband and brother by her side, said she wished she had never brought him there and was sorry she had. But for Roy, gradually, home as he knew it had begun to lose clarity. It had been replaced by something else, a burgeoning relationship with another small island. By then, he had a job, friends, and he had learnt not to hear the N-word any more. Whenever it was shouted at him, he would imagine they were saying something else, something less hateful, that he had finally been accepted.

They argued about it, yelled at each other until they were hoarse. But in the end, she left without him. He'd gone on to work in construction and manufacturing. He'd been a hospital porter and a mechanic, a labourer and even a miner at Hamstead Colliery before it closed down in the late 1960s. He had bought his own house and lived his life quietly, modestly. With pride. His only regret being that their rift had never fully healed before Cynthia died.

England was where he'd grown up. It was where he'd learnt how to be a man, earn his own money, feed his own belly. Where he'd fallen in love and out of it again. Become a father. That's what made a homeland. Not passports and documents – pieces of paper that could be torn in two or burnt to ash. England was home now.

18

9 days until the wedding

My body was tired from the journey but my mind was alight, energised. Because I was finally, actually there. I'd texted Andy the moment I landed, just as I'd promised. But apart from that, we had agreed to stag rules. No contact. All I wanted for the next five days was to be fully present with my family, to soak up every second of Jamaica and for everything to somehow be okay when I got back.

I wound the window down and let the cab flood with noise, diesel fumes tinged with charcoal, the lilt and laughter of young girls in navy-blue skirts and pale blue shirts on their way to school. The colourful houses seemed to be expressions of the owner's individual style: purple brickwork with yellow window frames, or hot-pink doors and lime-green facades. Heat hung in the atmosphere, dripped from it like laundry which hadn't been spun before being put out on the line. Mum was scrambling through her handbag looking for bite cream after complaining of being stung by a mosquito almost as soon as she stepped off the plane. She had been quiet during the drive and I wondered if the culture shock we were experiencing from Kingston through the window alone was making her nervous. We'd both seen the shoeless, shirtless man begging with his hat, weaving through the stopped traffic after we'd come off the highway, and we'd both said nothing, not knowing what there was to say apart from how sad it was, how real it was, and maybe even how unwelcome it was in the middle of our dream trip.

Grandad held his hand out of his window so that he could feel the heat of the day outside. We were going to stay with his nephew. Mum's cousin. Cynthia's son, Damien. Mum had made all the arrangements. She had never met Damien in real life but had exchanged emails, and eventually, when technology caught up, video-called him a couple of times a year, usually in Grandad's company. But you don't need to meet someone to be family.

At the roadside I saw a sign for young, green coconuts and home-made punches so I asked the driver if we could stop. His name was Rocky and he sounded almost exactly like my grandad. Inflection, intonation, lilt and all. He had already regaled us for most of the journey with stories from his career as a cricketer playing against the likes of Brian Lara in the 1990s, how he'd travelled as far as Pakistan and England and to every island in the Caribbean before returning home and buying himself a taxi. His main jobs were airport pickups so that he could travel vicariously through his conversations with passengers landing at Norman Manley. He had invitations from people all over the world to go and stay with them, he said, to be their private chauffeur in their home country. He told me that he was a proud Jamaican and nothing would take him away from the island again. 'Not money. Not woman. Nuttin'.' Mum and Grandad waited in the car while I went to buy a drink. The girl selling the punches from under a tatty Red Stripe parasol was busy writing labels and sticking them to her bottles: peanut punch, mauby, sorrel, Guinness, carrot. She said hello but didn't stop writing to look up at me. I asked for whatever was chilled and waited. She bent down to retrieve a plastic bottle with a green lid and an orange liquid inside. Carrot. I was happy with that. It was the one I would've chosen. The one I always ordered from the roti shop near home. Finally, she looked up at me to complete the transaction. She smiled with warmth and recognition, like she knew me from somewhere.

'Oooohhh,' she said. 'You have a nice face. Where are you from?'

'Here,' I told her.

She looked at me again and held out the bottle for me to take.

'Well, welcome home, darlin. Welcome home.'

We arrived to find everyone out on the veranda. There were a dozen people, either sitting in chairs or standing on the cool tiles under the awning which spanned the width of the house. I thanked Rocky for the lift and accepted his business card, then I turned and faced the house. I was tentative about the big family reunion and hung back behind Grandad and Mum. I recognised Damien, his father Teddy – Grandad's brother-in-law – and Damien's daughter Ann from the photos I'd seen on

Grandad's sideboard for as long as I could remember. Others would be cousins or neighbours, all there to meet and greet relations from England. I couldn't keep up with who I was meeting, whose hand I was shaking, who I was being embraced by, questioned by, handed a drink by. My nerves weren't helped by a cousin – by blood, marriage or just as a term of endearment, I wasn't sure – forgetting to release my hand after shaking it vigorously and ogling me, marvelling at me, beholding me. 'Cha – shi lightie! Unu sure dis one your pikney, Val?' Val was my mum. Val was her house name. Like a pet name that was easier to say than her real name. Not that her real name was particularly difficult to say. Another term of endearment. I hoped I would have an adopted version of my own by the time I left. Grandad stepped in then, and said firmly, removing the man's hand from my own, 'Dat's right. Dat is her mother and dis is her grandaddy. And mi nah wan' fi hear nuttin' more bout it.'

19

8 days until the wedding

Grandad's plot of land was about forty minutes away from Damien's house on the outskirts of Spanish Town in St Catherine. During the drive, Grandad talked to Teddy about Cynthia. I had never heard him speak about his sister in such detail: the way she used to sing and dance with wild abandon around the house, how she could drink most people under the table at parties, and how she drove like a rally driver. She sounded like a hoot and I laughed along with their memories of her even though we had never met. There was a clear connection between Grandad and Teddy and no hint of any bad blood about his and Cynthia's decision to return to Jamaica all those years ago. Teddy told us all that he'd been a bus driver while he lived in England, but it had been hard, the first year especially, without any friends or relatives there.

'Unu arriving deh to join mi mek everyt'ing feel better. Mi neva bin so happy to si nobody! Mi tell you,' Teddy admitted.

'Cynthia, bwoy!' Grandad said. 'Strong and soft at the same time. Mi nah know how, but she mek it look easy.' Mum and Teddy both nodded their heads in recognition. And at that, I noticed Teddy's grip tightening on his knee, just a slight squeeze. The memory of soft, strong Cynthia passing through his mind like a ghost. I could tell he was trying to hold himself together, the big man that he was, keep himself focused and just as strong as his late wife had been.

We were greeted by the sweet scent of fruit trees when we arrived. The plot was smaller than I expected. I'd imagined it rolling out into the distance when Grandad told me about it at the hospital, secluded without another house for miles, with the sea on one side and mountains in the background. But in reality it was about an acre in size with a slightly ramshackle outbuilding. Still, the trickling sound of a small stream and the dappled shade the trees cast over the grasses springing up wildly managed to make the whole thing seem idyllic. All it needed on it was a colourful little bungalow, a rocking chair, a few chickens running around, maybe. Grandad's eyes shone as he inched his way around the parts of the land that were not too overgrown. Every so often, he would crouch down to the grass and feel it with his hands, push his fingertips into the soil, hold what was his. Mum linked his arm as they surveyed it together. I could see him pointing things out to her and smiling as they took everything in. I took a photo of the two of them, their backs to me, their arms still entwined. As caught up as I was in the excitement of being away, of meeting everyone and finally being there, my fingers were still itching for my phone and my mind still whirred relentlessly. Mum appeared at my side, having left Grandad and Teddy to wander by themselves.

'You look far away,' she said, waiting, it seemed, for me to tell her why I was staring into the middle distance instead of catching them up. I thought it best to throw her a bone of some kind to pre-empt any probing. Probing, I feared, might cause me to crack open and suddenly tell her everything. I had managed to dodge her questions about exactly why the hen party had fallen through, but on the plane I'd told her that Sera had a lot going on and I'd taken the responsibility of it off her shoulders, not wanting to add any more stress to what she was going through. But there was something about being so far from London now, on a trip we had always vowed to make, that made me want to open up to her. I knew it would help to let her in.

'Yeah, far away is how I feel I guess. I'm just a bit annoyed at Sera.'

'It's not easy going through a break-up. She probably isn't herself at the moment.'

And before I had even begun, I snapped myself shut like a clam. 'That was quick,' I said.

'What?'

'Taking her side before you've even asked why I'm annoyed. As if she might not have legitimately annoyed me and I'm just being a bitch about her break-up.'

'Has something happened?' she said.

'Yes,' I said and told her about Sera and Andy's Twitter showdown. I could feel a headache building. I reached into my bag for my hat and sunglasses so I could avoid Mum's search for eye contact.

'Oh. It sounds like it's Sera you're angry at for bringing it to your attention, not Andy for making those comments in the first place,' she said.

'I'm not angry,' I said. Mum let my lie hang in the air for a moment without saying anything, so that I could hear the echo of it and perhaps reconsider, be honest with her, or with myself at least. 'Well, yeah, I am. With both of them, I guess. Both of them.' My forehead tensed as I considered my feelings, now that I'd spoken them out loud. I was angry with the pair of them equally. With that, Mum drifted away, back to join Grandad. I saw her give him a bottle of water and his medication. She had been prompting him to take it every few hours. He had been moving better since we'd arrived in Jamaica and no longer grimaced when he walked or sat down. I liked to think it was being there, the shot of vitamin D he was getting, the reunion with so much that he'd once known. Whatever it was, I was just glad he was getting better and we were together.

Back at the house, Grandad went to sit by himself in the rocking chair looking out over the lush, green garden. I could see him from my bedroom window. He gathered up a couple of ripe mangoes which had fallen from the trees, got back into his chair and rocked back and forth with one in his lap, occasionally using a small, sharp knife to slice a piece off and pop it into his mouth. I watched him like that for a few minutes, knowing that he couldn't see me and that I was looking at him in his natural state. He looked peaceful, like his internal landscape was becoming more spacious, and I felt a little envious of that. It seemed like a good moment to catch him on his own to talk to him, but I wasn't sure how I'd begin and I didn't want to ruin the atmosphere and the still of the afternoon. So, I closed the shutters and lay down on the bed and closed my eyes . . .

I was woken up a little over two hours later by Ann, Damien's 28-year-old daughter, and Mum entering my room and nudging me until I opened my eyes again.

'What's wrong?' I said, surprised to see their faces hovering above mine and immediately assuming I should be worried.

'Nothing,' they said, almost in unison, grinning excitedly.

'It is time for you to go to the ball, Cinderella,' Ann piped up, duly handing me a beaker full of pink liquid. I sipped it, still adjusting my eyes to all the light now flooding in as Mum opened the shutters. It was supposed to be rum punch but it was more rum than any other ingredient, and I could almost feel it hitting my veins, jolting me awake. Ann ran through the plan at full speed. Tonight was my hen party. I had thirty minutes to get ready. Some of her girlfriends were on the way and we were going out for drinking, skanking and liming at Dub Club. The word lime was used like a verb and meant anything from relaxing, to dining out, to chilling, to socialising, to enjoying life. 'There's a curfew on, so we're starting early. Fashionably early.' I did as I was told, jumping off the bed and heading to my case to choose something to wear. Mum was more than up for the whole thing. She was beside herself, occasionally bobbing her head into my room to suggest which top might go with which skirt. In the end, I did away with them all and went for my best outfit – a burnt-orange playsuit which I paired with some statement resin hoops and a matching necklace. I borrowed some heels from Ann because I'd neglected to pack any, pretending not to notice too much that they were half a size too big which was a feat considering I was a size seven and a half. It was clearly a family trait.

'Those are what I call my fuck-me pumps,' she told me proudly. 'So watch out you don't mash up di heel or lose one, Cinderella. I need those back.' Before I could overthink what it meant that I had selected that pair out of a whole wardrobe-full, I heard honking and shouting from a car outside the window, so I grabbed my clutch bag and click-clacked my new fuck-me pumps all the way down the tiled corridor and out the front door.

If the music in any of the bars was anything like the bangers playing in the car on the way there, we were in for trouble. Mum and I would be shacking it out, shoeless, on the dance floor within a matter of minutes. The last time I had been on a night out was with Sera in the Easter holidays. Half of me wished Sera was there with us, it was going to be her kind of night. Her enthusiasm for a wild adventure in a new city would have given Ann and her crew a run for their money.

I leaned my chin on my forearms out of the open window of the SUV. The warm breeze passing over my eyelids combined with the jet lag and the excitement of actually being in Jamaica made me feel like I was in a parallel universe. The car was full. Ann had clearly put the word out that overseas relatives were in town and it had given Coral, our driver, and Deshane, who sat at the other rear window, sandwiching my mum against me, the perfect excuse to party. At stop lights, we'd wait side by side with other carfuls of people who were trying to get ahead of the curfew which had been in effect since the start of the pandemic to try to curb the spread of the virus. Windows down, tops down, speakers blaring, heading to their own sundowner spots. The various radio stations and playlists would blend together and the drivers of each car would peer into the next, assessing the other drivers' tastes, their hairstyle, their clothes, their wheels. As we pulled away from one set, Koffee began to sing of gratitude, thanking God for di journey, and Ann and her girls all joined in, losing themselves in the track and giving no fucks about who was watching or listening or whether they were in tune. They weren't but it didn't matter. They were giving thanks for their own journeys, at the top of their lungs.

A couple of flash cars overtook us on the inside in quick succession, thrilling Ann and Coral in the front and making them erupt with screams and laughter. It clearly rattled my mum. 'Are they allowed to do that?'

she said. Coral and Ann creased. Coral reached over to turn the music down for a millisecond while she said, 'Yes, Auntie. Dem c'yan do whatever dey wan. Dey livin' dem lives. Dem bes' lives. Just like we!' before cranking it up even louder than before. I loved the fact that my mum was not actually Coral's auntie, and yet, she was now. She had never met Ann in person before yesterday but there was clearly a bond, Mum suddenly becoming a mother-cum-grandmother figure since Ann had neither in her life. Cynthia was gone and, from what I had gleaned, Ann's mother had mentally checked out of motherhood while Ann was still a child, although she didn't physically leave until Ann's late teens when she moved to the US to be with someone new and become someone new too.

I could feel my mum's eyes on me then. Specifically, on my left hand, where it now rested, bare and conspicuous, upon my knee. *Shit*. Without looking at her, I tucked it under my thigh, making the leather seat squeak and the whole thing even more obvious.

'So, baby girl, you all ready for your big day?' Ann asked, full of excitement. The other girls began to coo and clap their hands. I could feel my face glowing with heat, a combination of the sun and the nauseating feeling of uncertainty I felt in the pit of my stomach.

'Just over a week away,' is what I went for out loud.

'Oooh. Not long. Not long. And what is he like? The lucky bwoy?' Ann said.

'Andy is one of the good ones,' Mum interjected. 'A good, good man.' This was met with a symphony of 'awwws'; meanwhile I was wondering how noticeable it would be to open the door of a moving vehicle and quietly roll out.

'Not many o' dem dese days, y'know,' said Deshane. 'Especially not online, mi tell you. If mi get one more aubergine emoji coming thru' my phone ...' and she kissed her teeth instead of finishing her sentence.

'But what is he *like* like?' Coral wanted to know, her eyes seeking me out in the rear-view mirror. 'Tall, short? Fat, t'in?' I knew that what she was asking really was 'Is he black or is he white?' but I played dumb. It just felt easier.

'Five eight. Dresses nice. Bluey-green eyes. A bit of a head-turner, I guess. Yeah, I can't complain.' It now felt like there might be actual flames coming from my face and the emergency services would soon be on their way. I took a sip from my water bottle, offering it to Mum afterwards.

Ann had already started following me on Instagram. Her iPhone was like a sixth finger, a permanent append-age on her right hand. So I should've guessed that she already knew what Andy looked like. At the next stop light she whipped it out, announcing that Deshane and Coral could see the groom for themselves, which they seemed to have an overly excited interest in doing con-sidering we'd only just met. They inspected the screen. I turned to look out of the window as if I didn't know what was going on. Mum seemed genuinely oblivious. There were muted mumblings between the girls as they looked at the photo. What had they expected to see?

Was he their idea of a good-looking white man? I didn't ask.

'Layla, unu didn't want fi marry a nice black man?' Ann and Deshane snickered lightly, highlighting that, while they'd thought it, only Coral had the balls to say it. Sera had said it too, of course, but I had greeted her with confusion, suspicion of some kind. As if, in the asking of the question, there was some suggestion that by not dating more black guys, I had done myself and them a disservice. That I had missed that the world is, in fact, full of good black men who know how to love well and sweeten the lives of anyone they choose to spend theirs with. I knew that to be absolutely true. And yet I still didn't have an answer. Perhaps I never would. Nevertheless, I opened my mouth to respond, hoping that something would leap into my mind, but before I could speak, Mum swooped in. 'The heart wants what it wants.' A chorus of 'true, true' rippled through the car and I smiled at Mum with my eyes and gave her a slight shove with my shoulder that nobody else could see to say thank you.

'Well, Miss Bridey. Whatever your heart want tonight, it all yours. Tonight, it all about you,' declared Ann.

For the rest of the journey, Ann and Coral talked among themselves while Deshane questioned my mum hungrily about life in London. I chose to look out of the window again, watching billboard after billboard roll by at the side of the highway, selling dreams to the people. And then I closed my eyes again so I could focus on what Spice was trying to tell me in the lyrics she was belting out about *frenz* like it was a private performance just for me.

It was my round. I got a whisky and ginger for myself and another Red Stripe for Mum. I'd lost count of how many I'd had. The sound system vibrated with bass and the air was still pleasantly warm.

To begin with, it had been disconcerting to see my mother being approached by various men, their faces close to hers as they attempted to conduct deep and meaningful conversations over the music. She would periodically come back to where I was standing to relay snippets of some of the gems they were coming out with in a bid to get her number and whatever else they had set their sights on. There was no denying that she was a desirable woman, at ease in her smooth, line-free 55-year-old skin. She carried herself confidently, effortlessly. She even enjoyed a couple of dances with one of the more mature gentleman suitors trying to woo her.

I needed a breather and found a spot to perch myself against a poseur table. It was ideal for people-watching. I could see Deshane not too far away. She was twerking against a topless guy and lip-syncing to the song 'Sweet Jamaica' by Mr Vegas which had been pulled up five or six times by the DJ at the request of the punters who couldn't get enough. Ann and Coral were dancing together nearby, Coral looking slightly worse for wear which was concerning considering she was supposed to be driving us back. Mum was still at the bar. She had obviously clicked with the bartender as they were talking rapidly about something. Relatives maybe. Everyone we were bumping into either seemed to know someone in our family or was a member of our family several hundred times removed. I left her to it and carried on looking around. It wasn't long before the inevitable happened. That wasn't vanity speaking. It was inevitable because the girls had given me a heads up about Jamaican men before we'd arrived.

'Dem t'usty,' Deshane had declared.

The look on my face told her I didn't know what that meant. 'Y'know – t'usty. T'USTY! Cha, man.' So, Ann, straightening her spine and waving her hand like she was Princess Kate, cleared her throat and said in her best British accent, 'She means thirsty, darling. And dey will want a full glass of you to quench demselves. Be careful, Bridey.'

One of these thirsty Jamaican men found me and began trying to talk to me about how beautiful I was, how smooth and light my skin was. He asked about me just enough to gather that I was visiting from London and on a girls' night out. I sipped my drink and did my best to look uninterested. But Mr T'usty was charming and not easily dissuaded. It didn't help that of all the men there that night, he was the most attractive. Forward and yet aloof somehow. He told me that he had his own business, he was a fashion buyer and a music producer and travelled all over, to the US mainly. Predictably, he knew people in north London, some of the haunts I knew. It did not alarm me that he rested his hand on my shoulder in a bid to close the gap between us, under the guise that he didn't want to miss anything I was saying or for what he was saying to me to be lost in the music and the darkness. His eyes were like pools of aquamarine gemstone and there was a minty note to his breath each time he leaned in. I tried not to laugh at his jokes or do or say anything which could be misconstrued as flirting. I tried not to look like I was enjoying the attention too much, not to him, not to my mum, who was keeping an eye on things from the bar and occasionally mouthing the words 'NEED RESCUING?' I signalled back to tell her I was fine, which made the guy look over his shoulder and wave at her too.

'Your sista?'

'Nice try,' I said. 'My mother.'

'I cyan see where you get your beauty from.'

'Sorry, I'm with someone.'

He pretended to look around ostentatiously. 'Where? Mi nuh si nobody.'

'He's in London. My fiancé. I'm engaged.'

I began to raise my left hand to prove it before remembering there was no evidence to back it up. T'usty would probably think I was bullshitting him, that I was still fair game. I wondered where it was, the ring. If Andy had moved it off the kitchen table, given it back to his father. Or reissued it to some white girl he had bumped into in the street who had no problem wearing it. Unlikely, maybe, but the thought still made me feel queasy.

'Engaged? Bwoy!'

'My cousin's single though.' I pointed to Ann who

was simultaneously winding her hips, smiling from cheek to cheek and waving at us. He considered her for a moment, but seemed to think better of it and turned his whole body back to face me again.

'Engaged not married. Mi still have a chance.'

I laughed. He was persistent and grandiose with it, which felt out of place in the sweat-soaked darkness. I tried not to make eyes at him, tried to come up with a new tactic to get rid of him without me having to be the one to walk away.

'Serious t'ing, marriage,' he said as he sipped, staring at me.

He paused for a moment, rocking his head back and forth to the music; he took in the room and swirled his glass in his hand lightly, the last dark drops of liquor splashing against disappearing ice cubes. But before long, his eyes were back on me. It wasn't the old cliché of being undressed with someone's eyes. He was studying me, trying to work me out.

'You ever been married?' I said. 'Assuming you're not married right now, that is.'

'Nah. Mi free. Free and easy. Dat's how I like it.'

'Good for you.'

The conversation was waning. I'd appreciated the mild flirtation. The way I'd felt desired for a few minutes by someone who wasn't Andy. It felt validating. Exciting. Just within the limits of what was acceptable behaviour. I downed my drink and gathered up my things. I smiled, looked at him, rocked my head back in a reverse greeting of some kind so that I could gaze along the bridge of my nose in his direction one last time. I wanted to leave him with the idea that he hadn't had a run-of-the-mill, nightclub pickup attempt with just some girl, but someone he'd find difficult to get off his mind for the following twenty-four hours.

As I began to move away, I felt him grab my left hand and almost boomerang me back round to face him. We locked eyes for a split second before I slowly, precisely, removed my hand from his and left him there, dumbfounded, in the shadowy corner of a Kingston nightclub, standing in my wake.

I realised then what Ann meant about her shoes. They were her 'fuck me . . . I'm fucked off my face' pumps. It was the only possible explanation for why I was throwing up on them in the street. In between lurches of alcoholic reflux, I hyperventilated and cried, Mum standing over me. Coral, Deshane and Ann were still inside.

It was surreal for me to have my mum holding my hair back at the age of twenty-nine. I doubted she was relishing it either. It was drawing the attention of other revellers and I felt embarrassed for her. Worrying about what other people thought of her was one of her favourite pastimes. The whole thing was unbecoming and made me look and feel as helpless as a small child. I apologised profusely whenever I came up for air.

'I'm sorry. I'm so sorry,' I said, tears and saliva streaming. I felt Mum wave one of the other girls away, ushering them back into the club in an attempt to claw back some privacy until the situation had played out.

'What's going on with you, Layla?' Mum said.

'Everyone – everything,' I spluttered.

'It's okay. Take deep breaths. Don't worry.'

'No, it's not. It's not okay. It's not okay. We were their slaves. McKinnon. Same ones. And . . . Sera called it . . . She won't be my – my – isn't my – my – if Andy and me – if we . . . And I can't, I don't know – which, what – how to . . . I want – want – need them . . . both. Need to keep everyone. Everything . . . it's not fair. It's not fair, Mum.'

She didn't say anything for a moment. She just let me bring it all up – the words, the worry, the poison I'd drunk – so I didn't have to feel the feeling of any of it as keenly any more. She rubbed my back. Just watched and listened and waited until I was done. And then suddenly it was over. Suddenly the fresh breeze passing through the street reached my nostrils and the sips of cold water began to settle my stomach. I stood up straight and tied back my hair.

'That's it. All of it. That's what's going on with me. My best friend thinks I'm a sell-out, thinks I'm being disloyal to my race, and the ancestors of your future son-in-law were the worst kind of people and I don't know what to do about it. It's all a fucking mess,' I summarised, even now never feeling entirely comfortable swearing in front of my mother.

She perched on a wall and patted the space next to her. I sat close enough so she could put her arm around me and draw me into her embrace.

'That's a lot. A lot to have going on up there,' she said,

sweeping a loose curl off my forehead and tucking it behind my ear. Minutes passed, the music coming from the club softened, the volume coming down slightly. It was probably nearing 10 p.m. when, just as the night was getting started, the place would have to close and after-parties would spring up in houses throughout Kingston. I felt like I might be the only person in the whole city ready to call it a night.

'Y'know, the day I found out I was pregnant with you was the same day someone called me the N-word in the street.'

I was suddenly, instantaneously sober. I was horrified at what she'd said and could feel my mouth gaping. It was like I had been slapped across the face.

'It was my lunch break. I was walking to a park to eat my sandwich – twenty-five, twenty-six at the time – and completely lost in thought about what I was going to do about – about everything.' She gestured to her tummy and then towards me and I knew exactly what she meant. 'There was a car going past. I noticed it slowing down alongside me,' she carried on. 'It was an old banger. I remember that. Rusty. Full of dents. Thick puffs of smoke coming out of the exhaust pipe like the engine was about to conk out. And the radio was blaring. But not quite loud enough to drown it out, what he said, the man leaning out of the window. I say man, he probably wasn't much more than a teenager really. It stopped me in my tracks, right there, in the middle of the pavement.'

I thought about my 25-year-old mum, not long having lost her own mother, still fairly new to London, and how alone she must have felt. It made me wish I could go back in time so I could befriend her, be there for her the way she was there for me at that moment, and always had been.

'Do you want to know the first thing I thought after it happened?'

'That he was a racist –' She stopped me, before she had to hear her daughter using any more profanities.

'The first thing I thought about was you.'

'Me?'

'Yes. You. Tiny, embryonic little you, in here. Whether you'd heard.' I looked at her. I could tell she was being utterly serious but I couldn't help but let out a little incredulous laugh.

'Okay, not heard,' she clarified, 'but picked up on it somehow. They say that, don't they? That babies in the womb can hear. They're receptive to so many things going on on the outside, and inside too. Inside the mother. Completely irrational, I know. But it was all I could think about.' She smiled sadly and clasped her hands together and rested them on her knees as if she was gathering up all her thoughts together into the palms of her hands before offering them up to me. It dawned on me how much of a struggle the past few weeks had been, without telling her what was going on.

'You young people. You're so funny. Taking it upon yourselves to fix the past. You can't do that. You have to move forward. But you can't blame Sera for reacting the way she has to this thing about you and Andy. The history of our families. It's complex. Sometimes, it's not easy to move through this world as a black person. It can be painful. And I think that's the place she's coming from. A place of pain.'

'What was it like for you and my dad?' I asked quickly, almost without realising I wanted to know, had never known.

'Well, when you told me that you were meeting Andy's family after only a few weeks, I did think – wow – that's further than I ever got with your father. Not that we were together for more than a few months. I didn't meet his family. Never even once. I met his friends but one day he told me, admitted, he could never take me home to his parents. He said even though his love was colour-blind, his family were not and that was just the way it was. He wasn't prepared to stand up for me or what we had, just kept it tucked away where no one important to him could see it.'

'And Grandad? Was he disappointed? I mean, when he saw me for the first time and –'

'What? Of course not. He's loved you from the first time you met. He said you reminded him of Mum. And actually he was the one who made me phone your father, to tell him about you, otherwise I probably never would have. I called him and said, "You have a child in the world. Just thought you should know." His first concern seemed to be about what it would do to his bank balance. But we didn't need anything from him. I didn't want anything more than what he'd already given me. "Thank you for my girl," I said and hung up. It was the last time we spoke.'

I didn't know what else to say. It was the longest we'd ever talked about my dad before and it felt strange, like I was hearing about someone else's life instead of my own. Apart from fleetingly brief daydreams in which I would hire a private investigator or use a DNA kit which shows all your long-lost relatives pinpointed on virtual maps, I had never had a strong enough urge to go searching for him. I didn't feel like there was a father-shaped hole in my life I needed to fill. I didn't need him.

I began to get up, smoothing down my playsuit, ready to grab the girls and head back to the house. Mum stood up too. Then she took my hands in hers and squeezed them, examining my face at the same time, her expression trying to assure me that everything would be okay.

'Look at what happens when we let go of all the crap. Just for a moment. Black versus white. The boxes we're put in. When we realise that we're all just people. And sometimes, together, we make beautiful things. You are a beautiful person, Layla. You are an amalgamation of so many different things and that is your strength. But it also puts you in a difficult position.'

I didn't know how much longer I could take being in that position. But luckily, before I had a chance to admit that to her, the girls bounded out of the club and the moment was gone. I straightened my spine, smiled back at Mum and let go of her hands. Then I turned round and walked a few steps ahead of everyone all the way back to the car.

20

I could still taste the bitterness of bile at the back of my throat the next morning. Grandad had raised his eyebrows and laughed to himself at my dishevelled appearance – eyes barely open, traces of mascara still visible, my hair slightly matted with tufts of it escaping my hairband. We'd both found ourselves in the kitchen, the only members of the household awake at 7 a.m. I was trying to work out how to use the coffee maker, the old-fashioned kind where you have to load filter papers with coffee dust and watch and wait painfully while it percolates drip by drip into a cone-shaped glass jug. I eventually gave up on it and accepted some ginger tea. Grandad had found some fresh roots growing in the garden. I could see soil under his fingernails as he chopped a thumb-sized piece into slices, placed it at the bottom of a chunky glass and covered it in boiling water from the tin kettle on the stove. I wondered if it had belonged to Cynthia. Just one of many things they hadn't been able to bring themselves to part with after she passed that probably brought comfort to Damien and Teddy to have around, even though it would have been easier to flick the switch of an electric kettle.

I wasn't sure what everyone else had in mind for the day, but before I had sobered up completely, I made a decision. I had to go and do the thing I could easily have left Jamaica without doing. The thing I thought I would only do over email from London because that way it remained at arm's length. I'd received Gaia's last email just before boarding the plane.

Dear Layla,

I am now ready to share my findings with you on what is a most interesting family tree. As previously mentioned, it would be best if we could set up a Zoom call to go through everything. It usually helps to have discussions of this nature face-to-face (or screen-to-screen), particularly as you may find some of the information difficult to digest. It can also feel a little overwhelming as findings often generate more questions than they answer. If you'd prefer a phone call, that would be fine too. I am conscious that your wedding is fast approaching.

Regards,
Gaia Dunn

Her email signature listed her phone numbers, her social media handles and the address of the archives building where her office was. I phoned but there was no answer. I left a voicemail saying I knew it was Saturday but was there any chance I could meet with her. Told her I'd be going home early on Monday and needed to hear what she had to say. I took my phone to the bathroom with me while I showered, brushed my teeth again and moisturised my face. Then I texted her repeating almost verbatim what I'd said in my voicemail. I would hold off emailing her for a few more minutes, I told myself. I went back to my room and got dressed. Then I sat at the edge of the bed, ready but with nowhere to go. Until finally, my screen lit up. *Come to my office. I can be there in 30 mins.* I copied the address into a message to Rocky the driver and waited outside for him to arrive.

The archives building had a strange atmosphere. It was cavernous and deathly quiet save for the few hushed voices of the skeleton admin staff working there on a Saturday. It was cool and had the feeling of a mausoleum. I shivered.

Gaia arrived behind me and found me staring into my phone, reading a text from Mum that said if I was out on my own, she wanted a message from me every hour to let her know I was okay. I didn't know what stories she'd heard about Kingston – the politics, the dangers, the crime – but instead of saying something sarcastic about being a fully grown woman she didn't need to look after (except for when I was emptying the contents of my stomach onto the corner of the street), I agreed to her motherly demands.

Gaia Dunn was an elegant Jamaican woman. She wore heels and a colourful shirt dress of red, green, orange and black which billowed loosely. A small, gold crucifix hung around her neck and her skin was immaculately smooth, entirely make-up-free save for a pop of red lipstick. She looked to be in her mid to late forties and had the kind of face that was always smiling even when her lips weren't. I instantly wanted to hug her like she was an old friend. An old friend who probably knew more about my life than I did, who might very soon become my worst enemy, depending on what she had to tell me.

She led me to a room at the end of a wide corridor which she had to unlock with two different keys. We sat down and I felt a wave of butterflies lurch in my stomach. I tried to play down the significance of the meeting, when really I could feel the weight of it, the way it felt like everything that had been going on had been building up to this moment.

'So. Layla,' Gaia said slowly and more forebodingly than I would have liked. She smiled a compassionate smile as she took her glasses off and inspected the lenses for lint or smudges before replacing them. 'Obviously you were able to give me quite a lot of information in the first instance, which was extremely helpful. Before I go through everything, I wondered, I wanted to ask – and I hope you don't think I'm being forward – this "gift",' she said making air quotes with her fingers, suggesting to me that she knew full well that this was more of a fact-finding mission for myself than the wedding gift I'd framed it as. It had been stupid to pretend. I realised then that I had spent so much time in denial one way or another. Denying that my friendship was in crisis, denying that Sera and I might be growing apart. Denying that there were valid reasons for interrogating my perfect relationship with Andy. 'The way you're laying out in black and white – for lack of a better expression – the lives of both sets of your ancestors. Have you considered how it might affect you?'

'It already is. Affecting me,' I said, surprised at myself, finally ready to start being honest.

'I can understand that. Some people do these searches and think that everything will be tied up neatly with a bow. But –'

She could see me tapping my fingers anxiously against my knee so she didn't waste another moment in getting started. 'I've followed your maternal grandfather's line, just as you requested, and of course your fiancé's paternal line too. Shall we begin with your side?' I nodded and took a deep breath.

She began handing me documents. First, she showed me entries in the baptismal registers in St Catherine for Grandad's mother and father, my great-grandparents. I'd seen photos of them before. I tried to bring them to mind as I traced my fingers along each of their names – Jocelyn Davies and Henry McKinnon. Then there were the names of my great-great-grandparents – Loretta Placey and Edward McKinnon – information I'd found out from one of the genealogy websites when I'd filled out my family tree as far as I could. But there was new information that I hadn't come across before, that Loretta had been a seamstress and Edward had been a labourer. I pictured her, needle in one hand, fabric in the other, as her children ran around her feet. Edward arriving home, sweat-soaked and exhausted. I tried to imagine them off the page, more than just the photocopied sheet of paper I held in my hands, living real lives.

'Can I keep this?' I said to Gaia, barely able to take my eyes away from it to look up at her.

'Of course. These copies, everything I show you today, are for you to keep. It will be a lot to process, so having the opportunity to look back over them, especially with family, is very important.'

Then came their marriage certificate which made my breath catch a little in my throat. I felt history in my hands in a way I never had before. Loretta and Edward were married on 16 June 1895. The thought of descendants of mine handling my and Andy's marriage certificate one day, decades from now, suddenly rushed into my mind and made me feel woozy. Gaia handed me another piece of paper. Her tone of voice changed as she told me it was Edward's death certificate. I was surprised at the sadness it filled me with. A man I had never known who, of course, was long dead, but there was a sense of regret that he wasn't around, somewhere in the world, getting on with his job or sitting down to eat with Loretta and his children. He had died of cancer. Mum had told me we didn't have a history of cancer in the family so I knew what to tick when it came up on medical forms. But it had claimed the life of her great-grandfather and she had never known. It was one of many unknowns we'd been so sure of. I wondered how many more there were.

Then came the generation before. Edward's parents – Georgina Taylor, a domestic, and Andrew McKinnon, a sailor.

'Andrew. No way,' I said quietly, smiling at the thought of whether Georgina ever called him Andy.

'Yes, another Andrew. That made me smile too.'

The penmanship of the certificates was becoming more ornate and trickier to read. I squinted and moved the paper closer to my face. Gaia guided me through it. Her tapered nail extensions were the perfect tool for pointing out where I should focus my eyes along the page. That Andrew was born in 1850 making him my three times great-grandfather.

I waited for the next one, for Solomon McKinnon, who was the man listed on Andrew's birth certificate as his father. I tried to do the maths, working out that Solomon would have been alive in the 1820s and 30s, and perhaps born into slavery. Just the thought of having that possibility proven by Gaia made me feel sombre, made me try to swallow down the lump forming in my throat. Then she handed me something else.

'Now I'd like to turn your attention to this document,' she said. 'You can read from here.' Her nail scraped lightly just below the bold but faded lettering at the top of the A4 piece of paper. I did as I was told, suddenly feeling like one of my students when I asked them to read aloud for the rest of the class to hear.

'"A Return of Slaves",' I read, only slightly louder than a whisper, noting how the beauty of the penmanship was in stark contrast to the brutality of what was written and why. '"In the parish of St Catherine in the possession of Boyd McKinnon as owner. 25th day of June 1825."'

'Between 1817 and 1833 it became mandatory for slave owners to register their slaves,' explained Gaia.

'Because even though the slave trade had been abolished, slavery had not and plantation owners were still allowed to transfer enslaved people between colonies. This is an example of one of those registers.'

It took me a moment to relate what I was holding to what I had already pieced together from the database. 'What? But I thought it was Duncan, the name of Andy's four times great-grandfather. The owner of Ballyoche House. That's what I found in the database.'

'Yes. And that is correct. I have birth certificates and a family tree here which work back from Andrew – your Andrew – right up to Duncan. But if you look here –' she pointed to the family tree diagram she had drawn up – 'you will see that Duncan had an older brother with no dependants. That is Boyd McKinnon. The owner of a small estate on one of the 814 sugar plantations on the island surveyed in the early nineteenth century. Duncan received the payment as next of kin following Boyd's death, which happened before the compensation was awarded. Duncan himself was not the owner of the estate. He had some association with it of course. But the owner was in fact the five times great-uncle of your fiancé.'

It felt like it should be a relief, a revelation. But I didn't know whether it felt better that it was a great-uncle rather than a great-grandfather. I stared at Boyd's name, carefully inked in curling letters on the page. Then I realised that it didn't. It was the same. It was still in Andy's bloodline, and it still sat heavily in my gut.

I held on to the return tightly, unable to lift my eyes away from it. I could see on the desk out of the corner of my eye that Gaia had already lined up the next document. A land deed for Boyd's estate – Providence Valley, St Catherine – something else I remembered from the database. It was the grandest of all the ones I'd seen so far. It was funny and yet not funny at all, the disparity even between the pieces of paper we had to show for all these long-dead ancestors. My family's records hadn't been much more than a few lines, while this land deed was large and resplendent complete with a ruby-red wax seal. There was something awe-inspiring about all these pieces of paper and yet I also couldn't help thinking how easy it would be to turn them into little aeroplanes and launch them out the window.

The Slave Return listed names like Cudjoe and Johnny and Othello, people who ranged in age from ten to fifty-two. Other names included Hannibal, Jamaica, Ben and Yaho. Under 'Remarks' were the names of their children. Like Betty, Elizabeth and Amey. The name Boyd appeared again, but in the column titled 'colour' to the right of it, *this* Boyd was listed as Negro and it dawned on me that he had been renamed in honour of his master. Sweeping my eyes down it, barely blinking, I was astounded by the sheer number of terms that had once been used to categorise people based on the colour of their skin. The colour of their ancestors' skin. Some I knew, like Sambo and mulatto. Quadroon and Negro. But mestee was unfamiliar to me and I had to ask Gaia what it meant.

'It was another gradation of blackness. Derogatory, of course. It means a person who is one-eighth black and, like all of these terms, it set the tone for racism and colourism today.' I was under no illusion dark skin was deemed less favourable than fair skin almost the world over. But somehow it took me aback that light-skinned slaves were worth more money, were more acceptable to society, in those days. How little had changed.

I scanned down the list of names but didn't see mention of anyone by the name of Solomon.

I looked at Gaia and asked, even though I was still afraid of the answer, 'Where is Solomon? Or does one of these names belong to another of my ancestors?'

She shifted uncomfortably in her seat. 'So, Layla, this is where, I'm afraid to tell you, we have reached an impasse. I haven't been able to locate a birth certificate or any records for Solomon. I can't find anything between Andrew's birth in 1850 and the Return of Slaves in 1825. The link is broken here.'

'So, does that mean Solomon wasn't owned by Andy's family?' I asked her point-blank, staring into her face.

'Not necessarily. Maybe he was known by a different name. We can't be sure. It's not always possible for people to trace back their enslaved ancestors every step of the way. Rarer still that one might discover the African origins of their bloodline. Records are often destroyed or lost or incomplete. I have exhausted the resources at my disposal. And I'm afraid that for your McKinnons, this is where the paper trail ends. I cannot say whether your ancestors were among the enslaved people your fiancé's family owned. It is possible, very possible. But we don't know.'

The words 'I'm afraid' filled me with both a crushing

sense of disappointment and instant relief. Who did I think I was, hiring a historian? I was nobody. I had confused matters. I didn't know any more whether it was about race or ancestry. The past or the present. Black or white. And I was angry that Andy's family could be traced back and back and back, but mine couldn't. Not even by a professional. It felt like another inequality, something being denied to black people. I wanted to say that to her but I didn't know how to word it, and I knew it wasn't fair to take my frustrations out on her. The person I really wanted to take it out on was Boyd, who would've ended up dead if he hadn't been dead already and just a name on a deed. I could feel myself sweating and I was breathing more audibly, my diaphragm rising and falling, flaring my ribs and inflating my lungs to maximum capacity just fantasising about how that fictional meeting might play out.

'So you've hit a brick wall. That's it?' I said.

'Instead of thinking of it as a brick wall, could you perhaps see it as a door? A closed door. The fact that this is as far as we have been able to go does not diminish what you've learnt so far. The journey you've been on. It doesn't discount the information you have in your possession or prevent you from moving forward. Can it be enough to ask the question without getting all the answers, Layla?'

'I don't want all the answers. I never have. I just want it to be okay for me to love who I love and to not feel like I'm taking for granted all the hardship people went through to get me here.'

'Layla, even if we had found a link, you wouldn't be able to go back and ask them what to do about it. You'd still have to make that decision for yourself.'

I reached out my hand, took Gaia's and shook it in an overly formal gesture of thanks and farewell. I left the building and stepped outside into the heat of the day, squinting as my eyes adjusted to the bright sunshine. I looked from left to right, left to right, several times while fixed to the same spot. I was trying to decide where to go and what to do. But I had no idea.

I sat on the steps of the building, plonking myself down in a heap. The main road in front of me was noisy – car horns beeping relentlessly, some out of frustration at the traffic and others trying to get the attention of passers-by. The chatter of talk radio blaring out of some and music out of others gave the whole atmosphere a discordant, jarring quality that mirrored exactly how I felt inside. Home suddenly seemed like a long way away and I wondered for the first time since I'd arrived what I was doing there. Why had I come all this way? I had a modern-day relationship in present-day London. Why the hell did all of this really matter? Who would care if I put the possibility of this horrible but distant connection to one side and just got on with being together? And then I remembered.

Sera.

2 1

Before

Sera hadn't wanted to go. I was the one who wanted to. We hadn't hung out with each other for nearly a week. Not since we'd partied hard after A levels and then gone into hibernation. It was a time when I knew the inside of Sera's head better than my own. I'd started to keep a few things at her house and she did at mine, so we could drift in and out of each other's homes and go straight to our Saturday jobs at TK Maxx and Sainsbury's without being caught short. We were two eighteen-year-olds wanting to feel more like they were twenty-five.

'I'm not feeling it. Let's go Zu Bar instead,' Sera had said as we'd crossed the main road onto the cobbled street in a pedestrianised part of Soho they'd tried to make quaint. It wasn't. It still smelt bad and had unsavoury characters huddled together in dark corners, but we ignored those details and tried not to get our heels caught between the cobblestones.

'We're going in, Sez, so quit your moaning. The others are probably already inside.' This was our last opportunity to get up to some antics as a group of five before everyone headed off to uni. I needed Sera to get on board.

'If it's shit,' I placated, 'we can go straight to the club, okay?'

'It is. Shit. But whatever.'

We clicked across the street, the pinch and smokiness of the evening air indicating that it was nearly that time of year when the leaves would begin to fall and the sky would darken before the day was through. I caught sight of a grand clock on top of one of the buildings across the square. 9 p.m. The place should have been kicking, but it seemed desperately in need of CPR or a fire drill, anything, to shake things up. It might have had something to do with the fact that there was a man urinating against the side of the building, quite close to the entrance, but I didn't want Sera to be right so, as we waited to go in, arms linked in our usual fashion, I assured her that we would be the ones to inject Cellar Bar with a pulse.

There were two bouncers on the door, a man and a woman, whom I barely paid any attention to now we didn't have to rely on fake IDs. The guy in the couple in front of us, who had unwittingly dressed in exactly the same colours as his girlfriend, seemed to know Bouncer Man and was reminiscing about how long it had been since they'd seen each other on the last day of college several years and hairline inches ago. While I tried to get Sera talking about Emma's new boyfriend and whether or not she'd realised he was gay and who should be the person to tell her that he definitely was, the guy reeled off all the film and TV sets he'd been working on and the names of all the actors he had in his phonebook. I hadn't heard of any of them, so I stopped listening. His lady friend was also tiring of the trip down memory lane, digging her nails into her boyfriend's hand to get him to wrap things up so they could go inside. I had begun to kill time by doing the bump against Sera's hip, nudging her along to an imaginary rhythm. She didn't reciprocate and left my behind to ricochet back without so much as a sway to help it on its way which only made me do it harder and laugh at my own jive-related high jinks. That's why I was only half listening when the bouncer stopped us, re-latching the hook at the end of the velvet rope to the opposite pole, barring us from the entrance.

'Sorry – here it is,' I blurted, assuming I'd been slow in holding up my passport because I was too busy grooving along to no music. I flicked to the photo page and began ushering Sera, who was lagging behind me and hadn't even taken hers out of her bag yet, to do the same so we could get our bare legs out of the cold.

'Layla, let's go,' Sera said.

'Huh?' I looked at my passport, double-checking I was on the right page. 'Bit official, I know, but it's all I've –'

'Lay. Come, we go.'

'Sera, chill.'

'Not tonight, ladies,' the bouncer informed us, without making any attempt to inspect my ID.

'Not tonight?'

'Laaay –' Sera pleaded in a whisper. I heard but chose to ignore.

'What's not tonight?'

I pushed my hand forward again and tapped under my date of birth in case it was his first day on the job and he didn't know what he was doing. I turned to Sera to make sure she was showing hers too but she just stood there, not moving. It was like she'd shrunk herself. She seemed shorter than me for the first time since we were eleven, her shoulders concertinaing inwards for reasons I didn't understand. So, I took a breath, looked from Sera to the doorman and tried to get back to square one and work out what I was missing and why we weren't being allowed into a bar which was open, barely busy, and especially when we'd dressed ourselves in a way that was both pleasing to the eye and pleasing to our mothers.

'He said, not tonight. Try somewhere else. There's plenty to choose from,' Bouncer Woman chimed into the confusion on the doorstep. I turned to her to explain that I didn't know what that meant. She seemed to know. Her colleague seemed to know, and as I turned to Sera with my face contorted in puzzlement, I suddenly realised that her bowed head and folded arms, the way she'd slunk away so it no longer looked as though she was trying to get into the bar in the first place and the whole thing was just some kind of misunderstanding, said that she knew what it meant too, because she'd heard it before, on a night out with friends from Sainsbury's or her cousin or someone else of colour. That's why she didn't want to go there. That's why she looked like she was about to cry even though she never ever cried. Again, I looked searchingly from the faces of the gatekeepers to my friend and down to my own shoes, my skirt, handbag, nails – acrylic-clad – before looking at my friend again and finally I saw the only explanation for why they wouldn't let us in. I'd never noticed it so clearly before. And for the first time, I couldn't just pretend it wasn't there.

I backed away from them, the velvet rope, tried to look like I wasn't bothered and mumbled something about how it was their loss because we'd probably have ended up spending all our wages in there buying copious amounts of vodka and cranberry juice. I began to go down the steps and grabbed Sera by the elbow, leaving the condescending stares, the blue-green eyes of the woman especially mocking, staring out from her face as smooth and pale as milk. I turned back to look at her and tried to lip-read whatever it was she was saying to the Bouncer Man, but I couldn't.

Sera didn't say anything. Nothing. Minutes went by and she didn't speak. She fumbled with her bag and picked at the skin around her nails like her life depended on it.

I decided to break the silence with the declaration, 'Stupid bitch.'

'Who?'

'Her. Obviously. Her.' It was vague of me and I felt embarrassed so I returned to being quiet again before piping up, 'What's their problem?' I don't know why I pretended not to know. I wish I hadn't. Sera looked vacant, like she couldn't even muster the energy to be angry about what had just happened.

'Their problem is they're racist. I told you the place was shit but you didn't listen. So can we go home now? My vibe's dead. The night's dead and I've got a shift tomorrow, so –'

'They can't do that,' came my tinny, innocent little voice. I was furious at the idea that there were people in the world, in my hometown no less, who thought the way we looked meant something. I wanted the way we looked to mean nothing, and the way they looked to mean even less so that everyone could get on with their lives in peace and we could get into the bar. Sera responded with the kind of laughter that is nothing more than breath passing through nostrils, making it sound sinister and the person who provoked it seem stupid, which is what I was.

'They can't be racist? Please.'

'I mean, they can't not let us in . . . for no reason.'

Sera's breathy nostril laugh came again, this time with a hint of pity at my naivety.

'Look, Lay, this has obviously never happened to you before and I'm happy for you, but they are the way they are. And there's nothing you can do about it.'

Before I had time to put my arm round her shoulders, which is what I should've done in the first place, I saw an opportunity to put everything right. Emma and the others were crossing the square heading for the bar and, possessed by the injustice of it all and a deep desire to put the whole thing behind us and get on with the night, I took Sera firmly by the hand and dragged her towards them. Abigail was at the end of the pack. I looped my arm through hers and leaned forward just enough to let the group know we were with them and ready to get fucked and forget all about our crappy minimum-wage retail jobs that we couldn't wait to quit or get fired from, but without allowing them to slow in order to do proper greetings. I didn't stop to listen to Sera's mumbles of protest, I just held her hand tight enough that she couldn't get away, so that we arrived back at the foot of the steps to the bar a conjoined gaggle of mainly white girls with a couple of friends. I enjoyed the expression of turmoil and utter disappointment on the faces of the two racist creeps on the door as they realised they had no choice but to pull back the rope and allow us all in. That, or individually ID us and contrive a reason about why we were all barred or single out two of us, admit to their racism and face the wrath of the normal, non-racist white people we were clearly friends with.

The mere seconds it took for the whole scene to play itself out were like elastic moments slowing in time. I couldn't stop thinking how sweet the whole thing felt, how much of a coup I'd pulled off, how much Sera and I would laugh once we were through the door, knocking back our drinks and victory dancing for having over-come the racists. But when we got in there none of those things actually happened. Instead, Sera and I barely spoke for the rest of the evening. I continued to fight the cause, not knowing when to give up, demand-ing to speak to the manager to tell him of the injustice perpetrated on us, assuming those two individuals to be anomalies in his otherwise upstanding workforce. I thought he'd offer us a couple of free drinks and repri-mand them immediately. And while I did notice him taking one of the accused away from his post on the door and observed him having what looked like strong words with him in the corner of the bar, I couldn't hear what was said because of the DJ and couldn't see his expression because of the swirling purple lights being refracted by the mirror ball. We ended up having to pay for all our own drinks at £7 each which meant I could only afford five of them. Sera proceeded to tell Emma that her boyfriend had been seen kissing Ryan Owens behind a tree at the park which made her burst into tears and lock herself in a toilet cubicle for forty-five minutes.

We all left together, just as we'd arrived, but with vodka coursing through our young bodies, barely adults but with the weight of the adult world pinning us down. And even though I could feel the warmth of it moving around my system like molten silver with the power to skew my thoughts and make me forget how to use my own legs, I was certain that it was the strategically placed foot of the racist bitch woman with the milky skin by the velvet rope that made me trip down the stairs to the cobbles below and not the alcohol.

22

(Still) 7 days until the wedding

I had no particular plan for the rest of the day. Mum and Grandad had gone out somewhere and the house was quiet. And then Ann appeared, looking fresh, happy to be alive and like she'd had a full eight hours' sleep after a stay at a health spa instead of the three or four hours she'd actually had after an evening of hard-core winding plus more drinking with Deshane and Coral on the veranda after Mum and I had gone to bed. I decided I would join her for the rest of the day in the hope that some of her energy and general has-her-shit-together-ness would rub off on me and I could experience Kingston exactly like she would on a typical Saturday. Ann was in the final year of a hospitality degree at the University of the West Indies, but to earn money on the side, she managed a number of Airbnb properties between the city and the coast. She'd already told me all about her plans to apply for hotel management roles on Antigua or St Lucia and I envied the way she seemed to have the next five years of her life all planned out. She had no intention of finding a significant other. Her friends were the loves of her life, she said. And it was clear that it was true, from the way her eyes lit up when she spoke of their exploits and the way they'd linked arms in the street after we left the club, leaning on each other in their drunken states. Holding each other up, never letting one another stumble. I missed having that. I still couldn't believe I didn't really have that any more. I wondered if I'd ever get it back or if Sera would be the first and last best friend I would ever have.

Ann took me to Coronation Market. Rainbows of produce lined the walkways. Vendors shouted and catcalled as we passed by. Fruit stalls were selling 'matrimony' which turned out to be fruit salad. Polystyrene bowls piled high with guava, pineapple, grapefruit and mango, condensed milk poured on top and sprinkled with nutmeg. Ann bought us a couple of bowls and we walked through the market scooping it into our mouths.

'So what happened with that guy at the club?' she said, finishing off her last piece of pineapple.

'What? Oh, nothing, he was just trying his luck,' I said.

'He was hot. I thought you might've wanted a little taste . . . a final fling before you're a married woman.' She laughed, cackled almost, with the audacity of her suggestion. I went quiet, didn't laugh along even though I knew she was joking. I seemed to have lost my sense of humour. If I was being honest with myself, I hadn't really been able to see the funny side of anything since that brunch with Sera.

Ann could well have detected a lustful glint in my eye as Mr T'usty and I spoke last night. His face flashed into my mind and I remembered how good he smelt. I'd definitely flirted. It was coming back to me now and I felt bad about it. I'd told myself she probably hadn't been able to see from her vantage point. The club was dark and the conversation had barely lasted five minutes, ten at most. Besides, there was nothing wrong with the feeling of being wanted, and liking that feeling. Not to mention the comfort I took from the thought that if I decided to stay in Jamaica instead of walking up the aisle next week, I probably wouldn't end up a lonely spinster. I could find someone new. Someone who wouldn't cost me my best friend.

We walked some more and Ann stopped to buy a brightly coloured head-tie from a woman who was making them in the chair by her stall. All the while she continued to speak at the rate of knots, almost without stopping. She talked about fashion, celebrity gossip, guys she had been on Tinder dates with, her father's business, her grandfather's penchant for gambling. Everything. Anything. She had an infectious energy I wanted to soak up and she made me feel totally relaxed. So, when she got round to asking me where I'd snuck off to in a taxi so early on a Saturday morning, having waited long enough for me to volunteer the information on my own, I felt compelled to be completely open, telling her all about Sera, Andy, the database, my wedding day hanging in the balance, Gaia, how shit I'd been feeling, how I'd run away to Jamaica to escape everything going on in London while at the same time heading straight into the eye of the storm. It was the first time she'd been quiet in over an hour. Her mouth fell open, like she was watching a particularly juicy reality show. But suddenly the corners of her lips curled up into a wicked grin and her eyes seemed to widen as though she were having a eureka moment.

'Deh is someone you need to meet,' she said, practically pushing me back to her car. On the way she described to me a great-great-aunt of ours. Aunt to Grandad and Cynthia on their mother's side. A 98-year-old font of family knowledge who lived on the outskirts of the city. She knew things about our family no one else knew. Nuggets and gems you couldn't buy or google or archive. Then the penny dropped. She was the same old aunt Grandad had once told me about. I was sure he thought he'd outlived her.

'Wait, Auntie Queenie is still alive?' I said.

'Alive?' Ann kissed her teeth and laughed. 'Yes, baby girl. She alive. You will see. Death too scared to come for Auntie Queenie.'

The woman who answered the door had my nose. Or rather, I had hers. It was the same nose I'd recognised in all the family members I'd met over the last couple of days. She recognised it in me too, or I felt she must have, given the strength of the embrace she gave me on the doorstep. It took me a moment to realise that she was probably not the 98-year-old aunt I had come to meet, but her daughter. A woman who looked to be in her late sixties, slightly shorter than me, dressed in a long, loose skirt and a fitted white top with a scooping neckline and short sleeves. The house smelt faintly of Dettol tinged with spices. I noticed that she had a small, dark scar in the centre of her chin, the only imperfection in an otherwise perfectly symmetrical face which seemed to radiate good vibes.

'Annie, lang time mi nuh si yuh,' she said.

I saw Ann roll her eyes and seek me out with an *I told you so* expression. Her being told off like she was a kid, even though she was a grown woman, was way too funny and I had to stifle a laugh. No doubt Ann would one day find herself chastising the younger generations coming up behind her for spending too much time staring at their phones instead of visiting her of an afternoon too.

'Yes, Auntie. Sorry bout dat. But I'm here now.' She turned and gestured in my direction. 'This is my cousin Layla. Her grandfather is Roy.'

'Roy? Roy! Lawd, Jesus! Mi nuh see 'im since, cha, mi nuh kno – since Cynthia fun'ral. But mi hear dat him did coming back fi a likkle visit. An dis a him pikney? Lawd!' Her voice was full of excitement. Her calling of the Lord's name was genuine and pious and without vanity. She took one of my hands and squeezed it between both of hers, not letting it go. Then she reached out and touched my cheek, knowing implicitly that I would not mind. I smiled at her, letting her guide me into the house, closing the door behind us, still gripping my hand, keeping the connection we'd made.

'Yes, he's back home now, Auntie Faye. Back in Jamaica,' Ann continued the introduction as she finished off sending a text. She moved around the room with a sense of familiarity.

267

'Lawd! All dis time him bin inna Hingland.' She dabbed at her glistening face with a handkerchief she'd pulled out from her sleeve like a magician.

'Where's Auntie Queenie?' Ann asked. 'She sleepin'?'

'Mada here, yes. Shi dozin' right now. But I'm sure shi wake soon an ago bi happy tuh si yuh pretty, young faces.'

'Layla wants to meet her. Wants to ask her some t'ings. Family t'ings.'

'Mi sure shi wud luv tuh meet yuh, Layla. Mi mada ninety-eight years old. Yuh kno that? Shi a amazin' uhman.'

'She sounds it, Auntie Faye,' I said respectfully. It felt natural adding the prefix of Auntie, Uncle, Cousin, etc., as willingly as I had been since I arrived. How easily bonds were being forged, family ties accepted instantly. I felt proud to be one of them. To have found them, had the chance to be in their company. That feeling became more apparent, meeting Faye. Waiting for Queen Queenie to rise from her slumber was like I was about to meet royalty. Like she was the central, innermost ring in the trunk of our tree. My mum had never even met her, and yet there I was.

'Yuh know what dem sey. Dem sey dat wen yuh old like her, yuh inna yuh second childhood, needin' help wid everyt'ing, relearning t'ings yuh used to know, t'ings you cyan't remember no more. Life movin' more slowly and everyt'ing. But Mada nuh forget nuttin'. Shi might need yuh tuh speak a likkle louda, but shi nuh go nowhere. Shi strong. Shi sharp. Shi 'ave a mind like shi twenty-five. Lawd! Mark it down ten, yuh will si fi yuhself.'

Faye excused herself to go into the kitchen to make us some tea. In the middle of the wall, above a TV set that time had forgotten, a large framed painting caught my eye. It looked like it had once been vibrantly colourful but had faded over time. Behind the dusty glass, a black woman craned over a free-standing wooden mortar. In her hands, a pestle. I could imagine it moving up and down, her back straining, her arms aching as she pounded. A shoeless girl in a pink dress was clutching at the woman's long skirt, demanding comfort, or acknowledgement, or for the food to be ready immediately. Behind them both, a scene of humble domesticity. A kitchen or maybe a corner of the room which served as their entire home. A lit stove with a pot boiling in its flames. Flagstone floor beneath her bare feet. A ginger cat slept in a heap, curled up around the table leg in the foreground and, further back, a small dog prowled underneath the table looking for morsels dropped by the young boy seated above who looked to be trying to get his mother's attention by calling out to her. It looked like what I imagined to be a basic Jamaican household of Auntie Queenie's childhood. The mother's expression was haunting. Her eyes glazed, her mind somewhere far away, somewhere things were easier, I thought to myself. Somewhere fingers were never worked to the bone. She looked like she was dreaming of that place. I felt sorry for her. I wanted to paint another version of it where she finally arrived there. Her utopia. I took a photo of it, stared at it on my phone for a while and made it my wallpaper.

When Faye returned, the aroma of the room changed. She placed a tray down onto the glass coffee table in the middle of the sitting room bearing four mugs and a steaming saucepan much like the one in the painting.

'Tea?' she said. I nodded. Ann shook her head, almost violently, which seemed an extreme reaction. She went on to pull out a half-finished bottle of Ting and drank from it demonstratively as if to prove that the tea was unnecessary as well as unwanted. Faye tutted and ladled a scoop into a mug and passed it to me, before serving herself. Despite the smell wafting through the room and beneath my nostrils as the cup reached my lips, I was unprepared for the taste of it.

'Yuh like gyarlic tea, Layla? Or dis di first time yuh try it? Drink it off. It gud for yuh. A lickle gyarlic, lickle ginger. Boil it up so, every day, an yuh never bi sick.' Ann started snickering like a naughty little sister watching my face contort at the taste. So, like a goody two-shoes older sister, I knocked it back, drank every last drop. Then I asked for a refill.

The smell of the tea must have roused Auntie Queenie because she joined us soon afterwards. She was delicate-looking and petite. Again, she had the nose I'd seen so many times lately, but there was also a hint of something else. I looked at her in disbelief, trying to work out to what degree I was part Asian. It was like sending off for a home DNA kit and getting the results, live. She looked frail with age lines gathering her skin together across her forehead and beneath her eyes. Her frailty worked in tandem with her grace, the economy of her movements.

Faye turned off the TV which had been on mute in

the background and Ann sat up straight and slid her phone into the pocket of her jeans. Faye closed the distance between herself and her mother, going over to meet her and support her for the final few steps to her chair. Faye reclined her mother in the seat which automatically propped up her feet. Queenie stared at me for several minutes without saying hello. Ann and Faye explained who I was – a family member from London, England. Roy's granddaughter. She seemed to take it in and understand but the silence made me feel bad for showing up there unannounced. I didn't know if it was normal for her to be so quiet, so I waited. Eventually she patted the stool next to her footrest, gesturing for me to come closer. I did so, collecting her tea on my way and transferring it carefully into her open hands.

'Tank yuh, dear,' she said. Her patois was soft.

Faye dashed out of the room and returned brandishing a pile of photo albums, as if she knew that her mother would be requesting them soon, like they'd been waiting for an occasion just like this one, an opportunity to look at them again with someone new. They would have the chance to talk about the photos, the people they loved and missed, the places they hadn't been to for years or the ones that had since been knocked down and only existed within those pages. We pored over them for what felt like hours, passing them around the circle, pointing out little details, refixing loose photos that were slipping out. I snapped some with my phone that I knew Mum would want to see if she didn't get the chance to pay Faye and Queenie a visit of her own.

'My mada's grandmada born in slavery. Shi a child in slavery,' Queenie told us all, though I'm sure it was mostly for my benefit and that Ann and Faye knew this detail well.

'Mi helped luk afta her wen mi a lickle girl. Shi did live to be one hundred an' four. Fi true! Shi wud tell me dat shi used to pick beans. Dat was all. Every day, 'er job was to pick di beans. I wud aks questions like: yuh ever try fi run away? Wen yuh guh to school? But shi neva did.'

They were the kinds of questions I would have asked as a child too. Perhaps even as an adult. I was fascinated by the fact that she had met, spoken to, cared for someone who had been enslaved, let alone the fact that she – we, all of us – were related to her. I was in the presence of a living, breathing time capsule.

'Mi wanted fi know how shi experience it,' Queenie continued. 'Whulla it.'

'All of it,' Ann quietly translated in my ear as Queenie continued.

'Wha her life did like inna slavery. Yuh cyan't tek dat away from anyone, cyan you? Dat kinda life.' The room fell quiet for a moment and I wondered if everyone was thinking the same as me. How they would have fared if it had been them. How grateful they were to be born later. To be free.

'Layla a get marry, Mommy. Soon soon. Shi 'ave a man waitin' fi her at home,' Faye said, changing the subject suddenly.

'Well, mi wish yaah lang an happy marriage, Bab.'

I could see Ann getting fidgety. She cleared her throat

demonstratively and stared in my direction, trying to catch my eye. She could tell that I was avoiding raising the subject of why we were really there but she was all too happy to jump right in and see what else Queenie knew.

'So, Auntie Queenie, it your big sister who married Roy's dad?'

'Yes, Henry. Dat was mi bredda-in-law. Henry McKinnon. God bless dem souls,' she said, making the sign of the cross and looking up to the ceiling, clutching the rosary beads around her neck.

I suddenly wished I had a piece of paper to hand so I could plot out exactly how everyone fitted together. I was hoping the fact that her being all that remained of that generation of the family, she knew things that perhaps Grandad didn't. That no one knew.

'You remember much bout his family? Mi always want to aks you, at what point, on dat side, was there a Scotsman? Him ever talk about where di name come from at all?' Ann was asking all the questions I wanted the answers to, but tactfully, thoughtfully. I was grateful she was trying so hard for me, trying to help me join all the dots. I wished she'd been there at Gaia's office to ask the questions too.

'Him name? McKinnon?' She paused and considered it. I could feel myself inching forward in my seat, willing her to tap into something in her memory. But then she kissed her teeth and shook her head from side to side. 'Mi nuh kno nuttin' bout dat,' she said, and I felt myself sink back and finally release the breath I hadn't realised I'd been holding. 'Wha is der to kno?' she continued. 'It is wha it is. It was wha it was. It nuh matta how eh cum tuh wi family. Wen mi great-grandfada did ha fi give up him – him – yuh kno – dey not even have surnames, so dem sey.'

'Give up? Give up his what?' I said.

'Him – yuh kno. Di two men him did 'ave at di time, di two men he get a likkle money for when manumission happen. Manumission? Nuh manumission. Cha! Wha it call?'

It was the first time that Queenie's memory had tripped her up, that she struggled to find the words she needed. I willed her on to strive for them, so I could be sure of what she was trying to say.

'What, Mommy? Yuh talk bout emancipation? Di end of it all?' Faye tried to help as I held my breath again.

'Emanci—yess!' Queenie slapped her palm onto her leg victoriously. 'Dat a wah mi a talk bout.'

'Wollan, wollan,' Faye said, trying to get Queenie to pause. Rewind. Clarify.

'Yes, slow down, Auntie.' Ann leaned forward in her chair then tried to get to the nub of it. 'Your great-granddaddy – he had him own slaves?'

'A black man?' added Faye. 'Yuh nebba did tell mi dat, Mommy. Lawd Jesus Christ!'

'Afta him masta free him, he did 'ave a likkle bit a freckles save up, an bought him own.' There was less and less English interspersed with Queenie's patois the more she spoke, the deeper we fell into conversation. I sought translation from Faye with shock-filled eyes as what had been buried came to the surface.

274

'Shi sey, after him master let him go free, he used the money he save up to buy some slaves of his own. Di slave become di master. So, on one side, we were di slaves and on di odda, we di owners. Bwoy! You learn sumt'ing new every day, mi tell yuh.'

Faye stood up, sighed deeply and then shuffled off towards the kitchen with our empty cups, chuckling to herself as she went while Ann got up and headed towards the bathroom. We'd all heard what Queenie had said and yet for some reason it felt as though I was the only one who had really listened. Why weren't they firing off questions one after another like I wanted to? I wished that I could be like them. That I could shake it off with a stretch and a sigh and get on with the rest of my life. I could hear birdsong coming through an open window. I tried to focus on it, lock into it in some way to distract myself from what I had just learnt, but I couldn't. And Queenie noticed. She reached for my hand and patted it with her own. Looking at me kindly, she said, 'T'ings nuh simple, Bab. Finga 'tink, you cyan cut it t'row 'way.'

I didn't know what she meant, but she was trying to make me feel better. She knew I was troubled and wanted to comfort me.

'Thank you, Auntie,' I said, forcing a smile to my lips without letting her hand leave mine.

After more tea and some salt fish fritters Faye insisted on making before we left, Queenie drifted back off to sleep where she sat. She looked peaceful. I kissed her forehead without waking her. Mum had called to say that they were in a taxi on their way back to Damien's house. They'd been to see the plot of land again. It was Grandad's idea. He was chuckling at whatever the driver was saying. That's good, I thought, glad that he seemed to be enjoying the trip and wanting to get out and make the most of it.

At the front door, Faye hugged me as tightly as when I arrived and then took Ann's face between her hands, pulling her in for a kiss on each cheek. She admonished her playfully again for leaving it so long and warned her not to do it again.

'Enjoy di rest of yuh time in Kingston, niecey,' Faye shouted from the threshold. But before I headed to the car, I turned back and asked, 'What does "Finga stink, you cyan cut it t'row 'way" mean?' Faye laughed and shook her head lightly.

'Mommy! She always has a little proverb or some such to share. I'm glad she had some for you. It mean, you should not cast off a member of your family who gets into trouble, or sumt'ing like dat. Dat mek sense to you?'

'I think so. Bye, Faye.'

'Goodbye, Layla. Unu be good.'

'I'll tr—I will. I will.'

I clicked my seat belt in as Ann pulled away, watching Faye and Queenie's house get smaller in the distance before finally disappearing behind a bend in the road.

'That was fun,' Ann said without a hint of sarcasm. 'I'm glad we did that together, Cuz.'

'Yeah, me too.'

'You ready to lime now?'

'Actually, do you mind if we just drive for a while? Get out of Kingston for a couple of hours?'

'Okay,' she said cheerily, seeming to enjoy the idea of another impromptu road trip further afield. 'But only if we play carpool karaoke on the way.'

'Deal,' I said, smiling at her silliness.

After a few minutes more, when I had failed to get the tunes going and hadn't been able to stop staring off somewhere beyond the passenger window, I wanted Ann's take. Needed to see if it might help.

'What should I do, Ann? Do you think I should be marrying him?'

She paused for a moment, then she said, 'I think it easy to look for the bad in t'ings. In people. Like everyt'ing with my mom. It would be easy for me to hate her for leavin'. Say dat she abandoned me or dat she wudda stayed if she really love me. But you know what is even easier than that?'

'What?'

'Seeing di good. Is he a good man, Layla?'

'Yes.'

'Then maybe that is enough.'

I sat with that idea, wanted to sit with it for the whole drive. How uncomplicated it could all be.

So, I loaded my first track, leaned back in my seat and sang along with Alicia Keys seconding what Ann had said. Making it all sound so good. So harmonious. So simple. The whole damn thing.

23

6 days until the wedding

Soft reggae floated from the speaker in the front room. It cascaded through the windows, seeped out through open doors and flooded the veranda. It was soft. Lovers' rock. The bass line blunted so as to take any harshness away. It made me feel like I was gently bobbing on a small wooden boat in the middle of a placid sea with the warm sun beating down on me. I passed by Mum's room; the door was ajar. I could see the shape of her body beneath the cover on her bed, still, but for each silent inhalation and exhalation. I left her to sleep, closing the door shut as quietly as I could.

Grandad was sitting in the rocking chair again. He tapped his fingernails against the wooden armrest in time with the music. He hummed along, clicked his tongue against the roof of his mouth to mimic the plucking of the guitar. He had spent very little time out of that chair since we'd arrived. It was as though he had found a safe space within its arms, within its motion. I left him to rock for a few more minutes, undisturbed. I halved and squeezed six oranges and two limes and added some water, pouring the liquid into a bulbous glass jug with red and blue flowers around its widest part. The light caught each one and somehow remained trapped inside, glinting beautifully. I added a tablespoonful of honey from a jar I'd bought at the market. I held the sticky spoon in my mouth until the sweetness had gone, replaced by the metallic tinge of the spoon. I mixed the contents with a wooden spoon which I left in the jug before putting it on a tray with two glasses. I cut two slices of the rum cake Auntie Faye had sent me back with, put them on two small plates and placed them beside the jug. I carried everything outside and smiled as cool, dappled sunlight and morning freshness touched my skin.

'Breakfast, Grandad.'

He had stopped rocking and was attending to turning dominoes over one by one. I'd noticed the burgundy box on the coffee table out there the day before. Cursory patches of yellowing Sellotape tried in vain to hold the corners together. The word 'Dominoes' remained readable, emblazoned across the lid. The decorative patterns on the back of the pieces had been rubbed away while the paint marking the spots on the other side looked patchy and pale. They were black with white spots as opposed to white with black spots. I placed the tray at the far end of the table at first, but quickly moved it to the ground. The table was liable to shake depending on what kind of mood Grandad was in, how hard he was going to play. I sat down on the non-rocking chair opposite with the table and the game between us.

'Y'alright, Bab?' Grandad said.

'I've only got six. I need another one.'

I looked out across the garden and, at that very moment, a mango fell from a tree and rolled towards the trunk. The air already hung heavy with the scent of jasmine and a delicate, fruity aroma I hoped to be able to recall when I was back in London and wanted to feel close to this place and all who live here – lived here – again.

"Ow your husband is? Him miss you, don't he?' He was trying to coax me out of my shell, trying to get me to shoot the breeze, to play like we would on a normal Sunday.

'He's not. My husband. Not yet.' I paused, but he didn't say anything. 'Have you shuffled them?' I added quickly, pointing down to the table, trying to get his head back in the game.

'Yes, Bab. A' my play?'

'No, me first. I've got the double six.'

A beat passed between us then. Sometimes I felt like my mind was so busy with thoughts, so loud with the voice of my worries that I wondered if other people could hear it. I wanted him to hear some of it then. I wanted his wisdom, his soothsaying. I needed it. I put the double six down in the middle. I enjoyed the clicking sound it made as it contacted the cool faux marble of the table.

'Grandad, our name – McKinnon –'

'De slave man name?' he said, laying a 6/3, click, scanning the other pieces in his hand, already planning his next move.

'Yes. That one,' I said. Click. 'Why did you keep it?'

Click. 'B'cos my fadda did give it to me. An' his daddy did give it to him, and him did get it from his fadda.'

I looked at my dominoes. I tapped at the table with my empty hand to signify I couldn't go, didn't have the five or two needed.

'But when you realised where it all started, that it was a slave name, I mean. Why didn't you change it then?'

'Fi why?' Click.

'To show that things have changed. That you don't belong to anyone any more.' Tap.

He looked at my face, into and around my eyes, the shape of me, his granddaughter, and I saw the corners of his lips rise in a knowing smile. I couldn't tell if he found what I was saying amusing or nonsensical or whether he hadn't heard me properly, or hadn't understood, maybe. But his eyes were full of sympathy, like he felt sorry for whatever had led me to having to ask such questions of ownership and belonging. I resisted the urge to repeat myself or to prompt him. I just waited.

'When-a dat?' he said finally. 'I always been my own.' Another beat, clunk, a shift of gear in the air. 'Touch 'im!' he boomed, and slammed down the winning domino. 'I always been my own.'

Those five words landed like beats on a drum, vibrating in the air. The only person Roy McKinnon had ever belonged to was Roy McKinnon. He'd always been his own. His own man. His own subject. His own keeper. It was profound and yet completely obvious. He was the master of his own destiny. 'I define me' was what he was saying with his words. Go and define yourself, with his eyes.

'Andy's family used to own slaves, Grandad,' I said, anxiously turning one of my dominoes over in my hand again and again under the table. 'In St Catherine.' I didn't take my eyes off him. I wanted to see if the expression on his face would give me any insight into what he was thinking, what he was about to say.

'Him know dat?'

'Yes. He does now.'

'And unu did tell him? Fi di first time?'

'Yes.'

'It mek you stop loving him?'

'No,' I said quickly.

'But unu don't know if unu should marry him? Dat it?'

'Yes. I think so. I've been . . . confused – I guess – about what to do. It's disrespectful, I think – isn't it? I don't know.'

'Unity,' he said and stopped, leaving me on a cliff edge for seconds before he finally put me out of my misery. 'Me just t'inking. Marriage. It is a kind of union. And dat di trouble wid di worl' right now. Der not enough *unity*. Mi think dis prob'ly as hard for him as it is for unu. But if you t'inking it disrespectful to our ancestors to marry, what about di disrespect you showing dem if you call di whole thing off? What about dat?'

I didn't know what to say, what he meant. I shook my head.

'All anybody ever want in life is dem freedom. Dat is

what dey neva had. Di slave dem. With freedom, nobody can tell you what fi do, who fi love. With freedom der not one race better dan any odda. Bab, you free. Go live, free. Go love, free. Dat is di most important t'ing you can both do to honour our ancestors.'

We played again and again. Each game interspersed with chairs rocking, heads bopping, the warmth of the rum in the cake warming our bellies. After half a dozen games, or maybe a whole dozen, I'd lost count, I won. I won one. I sat back in my chair and looked at the snaking pieces joined together in front of us. My winning double blank the tail to Grandad's double six head. My mouth fell open and I couldn't help but look from Grandad to the dominoes, to Grandad again in disbelief. He had tapped his knuckles on the table instead of taking his final turn, giving me two goes in a row, and it was that move that clinched it for me. I had never been victorious in a one-on-one match against him before. Never. And then I realised he had let me. To soften the blow of what was coming.

'You go win, Bab!' he said, slapping his knee. I smiled but didn't speak. I felt bad smiling a fake smile when he was beaming with pride, but it was all I could do to keep from crying.

'Mi did wan' fi tell you sumt'ing, Bab . . . Mi already tell your mum . . . Mi want to build a house on mi land, Bab. To live in,' he said. 'I am one of di lucky ones. Mi know dat. Di police nah cum try tek mi away, lock mi up like dem do a Kenneth. Nonna dat nonsense. But dem nah want me back der. No. Dem nah want mi, so why would I want to be der? Cha!'

He was only really half talking to me. He was taking the opportunity to speak his truth out loud. And his truth was that he didn't want someone, something – a country, a homeland – that didn't want him. Not any more. He had gone through that before, in the very beginning. I knew he had been battered and bruised by the move to England and the repeated rejections. Each time, he had recovered, he had picked himself up, strengthened himself and called wherever he stood home and he had done so proudly. But he didn't want to do it again. Not because he no longer felt British – because he still did, always would – but because he was tired.

'Mi lucky to recover from di illness. Mi lucky to have Teddy, Damien, all o' dem here, and to have another life right here, back where it all start. Mi jus lucky. Mi sorry, Bab –'

At that, I practically leapt into his lap so that I could hug him tightly. I hoped it was all I needed to do to show that there was nothing he needed to apologise for. He had my blessing entirely, instantly and unreservedly before he'd even said the words.

24

5 days until the wedding

I didn't use the word goodbye when the time came. I refused to think it let alone say it. Damien, Teddy and Ann came out onto the veranda as our taxi pulled up. Mum and I were exhausted. Grandad on the other hand seemed rejuvenated, rested and invigorated by the whole trip, happy in the knowledge that the next time he came back, he would not have to leave again.

I wanted to use the flight to sleep and reset but I already knew that I would spend most of it talking to Mum about everything we'd done in Jamaica. Everything Gaia and Queenie had told me. How important the trip had been to me and how grateful I was that we'd experienced it together. It had been emotional – there was so much love for me, us, in Jamaica. But I also knew that some of the journey would be spent crying silently behind my eyeshades and my mask. I couldn't avoid the fact that I still had to face up to what everything meant in real terms for Sera and Andy. And me.

Ann bear hugged me from behind, practically mounting me in the process. It was full of love and silliness and excitement. All the things I had come to associate with her in the short time I'd been there. I told her to come and visit and she in turn invited me to join her in St Lucia sometime.

'We'll be seeing you again very soon, Uncle Roy,' I heard Damien say to Grandad before Teddy joined them, stretched out his right arm and rested it over Grandad's shoulders. They looked liked brothers. The decades had done little to diminish their bond.

I could see the reality of Grandad's decision hitting Mum just at that moment, in the midst of all the good-byes. Even though he was coming back with us to sort out his affairs in Birmingham, it felt like a preview of his departure from us. There would be no more Sundays spent in Erdington. No more looking out onto the street from the bay window. The thumping bass of his record player would be silenced and he would be an ocean away. Grandad must have noticed the sadness in her too. I spotted him pinch her arm like he always did whenever we left his house, gathering up an inch of her fleshy bicep and bringing it together in an affectionate squeeze. It said *I love you. I'll miss you. Thank you*, without the need of words.

'Before you go, we have sumt'ing for you, to celebrate yuh forthcoming nuptials, Layla,' Teddy announced.

I tried to insist that it wasn't necessary, I didn't need any gifts, they had already done so much for us, but it was shut down with a chorus of kissed teeth and 'Cha, man!'

'This belonged to Cynthia.'

I took the threadbare velvet presentation box Teddy was handing me, looking at Grandad as I did so, and opened it to find a watch. The strap and clasp were gold and the clock face was small and plain, the glass tarnished and slightly scratched. It was simple and beautiful. I didn't wear a watch. Mum had bought me one for my eighteenth birthday but it had been committed to a box somewhere and left in a drawer.

'Ann, you should have this. It was your grandma's. I can't,' I said in one last attempt at polite refusal.

'Layla, dat kind of thing is fit for a bride, and I told you already, di only person me a-go marry is myself!' she said, creasing at her own joke, waving her hand around in the air in my direction to say she didn't want it and wouldn't be taking it back.

'We want you to have it,' Damien announced.

It went quiet for a moment. It was an awkward silence no one knew how to break until Grandad finally did.

'She kept looking pon it, over and over, so we didn't miss di ship, di day wi a-go.'

'To where?' I asked.

'To Hingland, man!'

At that, I lifted the watch out of the box to inspect it more closely. It was suddenly more precious. My first family heirloom. It felt like it had found its way to me, that it had always been written somewhere that I was to be the recipient, one day.

'We mek it aboard with plenty o' time,' he said. 'Plenty. To have time, all you ha fi do is mek it, she would se.'

I placed it on my wrist and locked the clasp, turned my wrist over again so I could see its face. It was slightly tight. I imagined it on Cynthia's petite, elegant wrist. How it would have capped off an exquisite outfit for her journey across the sea. Her best skirt and matching blouse, a tailored coat, the smartest suitcase she could afford and, of course, a hat. All English ladies wore a hat, she'd heard. She would have wanted to look her best for the British people, to present herself as a dutiful and respectable British subject.

On some unknown day, in some long-forgotten month of a year I'll never know, Cynthia's watch had stopped a few minutes shy of two o'clock. I looked into the eyes of every member of my family standing there in turn and once more at the watch.

That was a good goodbye, I thought to myself, smiling. One of the best.

'Time waits for no bride,' I said to them all, and set off, back to Hingland.

Grandad sat up front with Rocky. He didn't waste much time before he started telling him his plans for the little bungalow he wanted to build on his plot. Rocky said he had some contacts in construction he could put him in touch with and their conversation rolled on like that for the whole drive back to Norman Manley. Mum and I would occasionally smile at each other across the back seat, hearing Grandad's excitement, the possibilities he was imagining for himself. I was happy for him and I knew, deep down, she was too.

'Mum, all that stuff the other night. About Sera and, and everything. I should have told you sooner, what was going on,' I said quietly, even though I knew her motherly instinct had probably let her know long before Jamaica.

'Layla, you have to own who you are. Friendships change and go through things because people do. Instead of having expectations of other people, all you can do is take responsibility for yourself. If you and Andy want to build a life together, if you want to be together in spite of everything, or maybe even because of everything, then that is what you should do. You have to do what you think is right, not what anybody else tells you to do. If I hadn't, you wouldn't be here right now.'

'I just wanted to say – I need to tell you that I'm glad we did this and – and – I'm really proud to be your daughter.'

She squeezed my hand and placed it back onto my lap, carefully and gently, and turned to look out the window so I couldn't see her eyes.

25

4 days until the wedding

I'd often seen those people but had never been one myself. The people whose loved ones met them at the airport, as close as they can possibly get to the plane, because they can barely wait another minute to see them.

I was so surprised that Andy was standing there, I was almost embarrassed. I could feel my bottom lip trembling as I got closer to him. He was standing near a grandfather and grandmother, who were waving frantically at a mother and toddler in a buggy just ahead of me, and an Addison Lee driver with a grumpy expression and a placard that said 'Ian Scott'. We'd waited forever to retrieve our luggage. I wished I'd used the time to freshen up in the toilets. Brush my teeth, wash my hands and face, put some deodorant on to remove some of that feeling – the not being quite sure what day or time it is or where you are – that comes with a long journey. Then I might not have felt so self-conscious when Andy spotted me. He looked so handsome standing there in his sweatshirt and grey trousers, his stubble just long enough to make him look sexy and not like he'd fallen into a pit of despair in my absence. I felt bad that I hadn't taken note on a daily basis of how attracted I still was to him, and how happy I should be that he had chosen me over any other woman in the world.

Once we'd rounded the barrier and I finally reached him, the four of us stood for a second without speaking. Grandad slapped Andy on the back and Mum hugged him before announcing she couldn't go another minute without caffeine and that she and Grandad could be found at Costa whenever we were ready. I watched them go, pushing the trolley and leaving me with empty hands I could think of only one purpose for. I turned back to Andy and took his face between them, my two palms on his cheeks, and brought it forward to meet mine. We had one of those kisses where you can tell, even with your eyes closed, that the other person is smiling, where you can feel the shape and motion of it. His arms reached around to the small of my back and he pulled me as close to him as I could go.

'Missed you,' he said quietly, pressing his forehead up against mine before he broke away and reached into his pocket for something. It was a small black box with silver detailing around the lid and the clasp. He looked at me as he opened it and said, 'Will you marry me? Again.'

The box was empty. I stared into it. Stared at the ring-less space inside, the empty slit in the cushion which lined it, wondering for a moment if there was a punch-line coming. But then I understood that it wasn't a joke and that he was making perhaps the only gesture he could in a bid to make everything better again.

'I realised that you need a new one. Something without any history. We can go tomorrow if you're not too tired. Choose it together.'

How a proxy proposal could be even better than the original, I didn't know. But it was. It was somehow more perfect than the one in my favourite park with all the zen in the air. I couldn't speak.

'About Sera, I –' he started up.

'You don't have to –' I said.

'No, but I –'

'It was never your battle.'

'But what if she doesn't come to the wedding?'

My only reply was a sad sort of smile to show that I didn't really have the answer to that. I could easily have put it all back on to Sera in that moment, apologised on her behalf, blamed her again for all the Twitter drama, blamed her for all the trouble. But it didn't feel right, it didn't even feel true any more.

Andy didn't have to worry about trying to make anything better. He was there. I was there. And that was enough.

26

(Still) 4 days until the wedding

It took us nearly an hour and a half to get home on the Piccadilly line and somewhere between Acton Town and Hammersmith I dozed off with my head on Andy's shoulder. Already, Jamaica was beginning to feel like some kind of dream. Mum took Grandad back to Birmingham and said she would stay the night and pick up his suit for the wedding before coming back to London. Andy couldn't believe it when I told him that Grandad wanted to go back to Jamaica for good as soon as possible.

'The thought didn't cross your mind, did it?'

I shrugged and let out a non-committal kind of laugh without giving him a proper answer. Now that we were home, I was ready to talk and it felt like he was too. Both of us, ready to talk and ready to listen. I sat down at the kitchen table and Andy joined me. The smell of coffee floating from the cafetière gave my senses a delicious jolt and I was more than happy to throw away my arbitrary, self-imposed caffeine ban for good. I pushed the plunger down and poured.

'So, what did I miss?' I said, bringing the cup to my chin and pausing there for a moment.

'Well, it was pretty much the longest five days ever,' he said jokily but I knew there was some truth in it. 'Worked from home Thursday and Friday. Then I spent a night at Mum and Dad's. Had lunch with Alex and ended up staying there for a night too. Then chilled at home and FaceTimed Sasha and the gang yesterday. Remind me that toddlers and video calls don't mix next time I suggest doing that by the way. Absolute chaos.'

'Wow. Busy. Sounds like you did a whistlestop tour of the whole family.' I immediately began to feel self-conscious. What if all they had been speaking about was me, what was going on with us, how selfish I'd been to take off at a moment's notice and the way I'd started to dredge up their family history? I waited. I wanted to see if he'd offer up any details about what had been said. But then I couldn't wait any longer.

'Do they hate me?'

'Hate you? Of course they don't hate you. They asked after you, obviously. Wanted to know if you were okay, if we were okay. But we talked about lots of things. I guess you weren't the only one who needed to do a bit of a deep dive when it comes to family. Alex and I started trading memories about stuff from when we were kids. Moments – I don't know – throwaway remarks, fucking ignorant, half-remembered shit – that just wasn't right. Yeah, we just . . .' He sipped. 'And I watched the documentary too.'

'Oh.'

'As soon as I got back from dropping you at the airport actually. I'm glad I did. I kind of wished we'd watched it together, y'know, in the first place.' Another sip, avoiding my eyes. I knew what he was getting at. If I had let him in from the get-go, perhaps the journey would have been smoother, easier to manage, shared. I might even have realised sooner that it wasn't actually something to solve on my own but something for the two of us to work through.

'Then I watched it again. With Mum and Dad.'

'Oh. Right,' I said, not doing a great job of hiding my surprise. 'And?'

'They didn't really know what to say. I asked them how much they knew already, about the compensation, about the origins of the Scottish estate. Dad was a bit sheepish about it all at first. Bit defensive, I guess. He started off by telling me it didn't have any bearing on anything. Mum was a bit more open, weirdly apologetic, even though she didn't really know what she was apologising for – which part of it – but sorry about it all. About how it was affecting us.' He paused and took a deep breath. 'I've realised that we've all got work to do and that's going to take time.'

'I know. I know that.'

'Us being together, getting married, if that's still what you want to do – which I fucking hope you do, Layla – I really – I fucking love you and, and –' I could feel his emotion building and becoming harder for him to contain – 'us being together has brought my family into something completely new – a new phase – new realm – way of being – I don't really know what I'm trying to say – I, I –'

'Keep going,' I said, putting my cup down, shuffling my chair around the corner of the table so there was no longer anything getting in the way. We sat, knees touching, face-to-face, nothing between us.

'I don't want there to be anything superficial about what this relationship means for everyone. I want us to be a family that is growing and changing and accepting of that.'

'What if that's not what they want to do?' I said. I realised I was putting him on the spot. Forcing him to look into the future, speak on behalf of his family.

'Then I'll make sure they know. How important this is. Make sure that we – that this is a source of pride. There's no other –'

Tears were pooling, threatening to roll down his cheek. And then I realised that I had already started crying. I didn't know when. He had opened the floodgates for both of us but there was still more to be said. I was willing him on to let it all out.

'Our kids are going to be a beautiful mixture of all that is good about the world. And we'll tell them where they came from, all of it, both sides of the story. All of it, Layla. Our history is their history and I want them to know. And I want them to go out there and live the lives they want to live in the full knowledge of it.'

He sat back in his chair all of a sudden, like he had been taken by surprise by everything that had been waiting to come out. Self-consciousness was creeping back in and he turned his head. I wanted to wipe his tears away, but I didn't think he'd thank me for drawing attention to them. It was my go to tell him where I was with everything.

'In Jamaica, I went to see a genealogist. She showed me these documents, Slave Returns from the sugar estate of your five times great-uncle. It showed the first names of all the slaves he owned at the time. The ones who hadn't run away, or died, and the new ones who'd been born. It was just a piece of paper but it made me so angry. She didn't know if those people were my ancestors. She said it was possible, but she didn't know for sure. And that made me angry too. Then I met my 98-year-old great-great-aunt who told me that she had actually met, cared for, one of our relatives who'd been born into slavery. It blew my mind. To think of her living that reality. Then she told me about another ancestor of ours who had had slaves of his own. A black man. A freed black man. Someone whose blood I have in my veins owned slaves. And that made me even angrier. And then I realised how many other things I've been angry at. At my dad for not caring that I was born. At Sera for saying I had to choose, at you for not speaking up at times with your aunt, your parents. And angry at nobodies hurling racist insults at my mum in the street. I don't want to be angry. Action is more important than anger. More useful. Ann told me I should try to see the good in things. Well, not one of the things I've just mentioned can stop me from seeing the good in us.'

Finally, he sniffed back his tears and his running nose and turned to look at me as I continued.

'If someone were to ask me what I would change

about my life so far – and even before that, the past, my family's past – if someone asked me if I wished I had my dad's surname instead, and none of this had ever come to light, I'd say no. Do I miss my friend? Yes. So, so much. And I'm going to miss her like hell if we don't manage to find a way through this, but nothing makes more sense than us getting married. So . . .'

'So,' he sniffed.

'So, let's get married.'

27

The day before the wedding

I went to see Erica to collect my dress. It was wrapped and beautifully packaged in a bag with ribbons for handles. She came out from behind the counter and hugged me. Neither of us mentioned Sera's dress. I was heading over to Mum's where Andy would be joining us for an early dinner before meeting his groomsmen at our flat. He'd assured me he'd be getting an early night and the guys being there was for convenience, to keep tabs on them, make sure they were geared up for their duties and not so they could play Fortnite right up until they were supposed to be at the altar. It was their job to decorate the restaurant before they headed to the church. All the hand-made touches had been boxed up, labelled and placed in our hallway and in the boot of the car along with a hand-drawn diagram of where everything should go. The guestbook, the individually framed photos of every single married couple in attendance on their own wedding day – which had proved so challenging to source I'd almost given up on the whole idea – the foil balloons awaiting helium on site, the place names. The bridesmaids were also prepped and ready to go. Missing Sera and spending time with Ann and her friends had made me value the ones I had and I felt I owed them an explanation about why I'd seemed distant or erratic or both since the end of term. So I'd Zoomed Siobhan and Poonam to tell them everything. How despite the hen party feeling like a casualty, it really hadn't been, in the grand scheme of things, considering the fact that the wedding itself had almost hung in the balance. They'd both stared back at me for a moment, unsure what to say. Just about anything could have set me off, my emotions running as high as they were. But finally, Siobhan, true to form, broke the silence with 'Fuck me, Layla. Trust you to go and turn your bloody wedding into an episode of *Who Do You Think You Are?*' leaving us to piss ourselves laughing.

Saying goodbye to Andy on the doorstep of my mum's flat made me feel like a sixteen-year-old who'd been returned home safely after a first date. I leaned on the door frame, head tilted, my hand holding his as he stepped away before I pulled him back towards me, his face slotting into the nook between my shoulder and cheek where he planted a thousand kisses in quick succession. His breath was warm as it coiled up along the nape of my neck and mingled with the cool evening air.

'Der da-da der, der da-da der,' he sang, to the tune of 'Here Comes the Bride'.

'You can't remember how it goes, can you? Our actual entrance procession?'

'Of course I can . . . Der da-da der da-da dooo . . . no, no it's completely gone.'

I gave him a shove. I began to hum 'I Was Glad' by Hubert Parry, and could almost feel myself walking down the aisle. Over his shoulder I saw the moon hovering high in a clear sky without any clouds or stars. We didn't ask each other any questions. There were all the obvious ones. Are you nervous? Have we forgotten anything? Do you think we'll feel different this time tomorrow? We didn't need to know anything more about anything. It felt, in that moment, that we didn't need any answers. I couldn't put the lightness I felt into words, didn't want to try. Only wanted to feel. Since I'd come back from Jamaica, we hadn't stopped talking. We talked like we'd only just met, like we'd never see each other again. About everything. We promised to try to be honest with each other, even when the things we needed to say might be hard to hear.

'Goodnight, Layla.'

'Goodnight, Andrew,' I said and closed the door on one part of my existence. I would open it on another in the morning.

Mum and Grandad were in the kitchen together. I kissed them both on the cheek and told them I was going to bed.

'Make sure you sleep,' Mum said.

'I'll try.'

I didn't notice Grandad had followed me until I reached my room and turned round to see him standing there. 'You okay, Grandad? Is your room okay? I can get you some more pillows?'

'Mi comfortable. Everyt'ing fine. Mi did want fi sey — mi love you, Bab. Mi love you tuh mi heart.'

I couldn't remember if he'd ever told me he loved me before. If he had, I'd been too small to remember. I nodded and went into my room before my heart broke a little at the thought of him one day not being there to say it again.

I was bloated from dinner and should have been thinking of sleep, but instead I undid the zip at the back of my wedding dress, took it down from its quilted hanger on the front of the wardrobe door and pooled it on the floor in a heap of sequins and silk. Holding it by the barely there spaghetti straps, I stepped over its threshold and climbed inside. I couldn't reach the zip on my own but it was enough to have it wrapped around my body and feel it against me. I looked at myself in the mirror. I was make-up-free, hair piled high on top of my head. I felt young and beautiful. Flawed and finite. I wasn't thinking about Andy, or about what the weather would be like when I opened my eyes the next day. I wasn't even thinking about whether everyone would have a good time or not. I was thinking about Sera. I wondered if she ever thought back to that night at Cellar Bar or if she'd had so many other racist interludes that it paled into insignificance. I wondered if she hated me for making her go back. In all the years since, I had never brought the incident up with her. I had simply buried it. I had spent a great deal of my life indulging in a wilful, self-serving kind of ignorance about my heritage. Shrinking myself.

It takes guts for your friends to tell you you're wrong.

And, when you finally figure it out, it takes the same amount of guts to tell them they were right. I grabbed my phone from the bedside table and opened Whats-App. I held down the mic symbol to start recording. I watched the seconds tick by before I knew what to say, before I started to speak:

Remember our first day at school? When you said I was your sister, and the other kids laughed, because you were one colour and I was another, but it didn't matter? I really want to go back to that. I understand why if you still feel you can't, but you know where to find me tomorrow. I'll be the one sporting excessive lace, wearing a pair of shoes I can't walk in, marrying a man I can't live without, hoping that you've changed your mind. But yeah, I . . . I love you and I'm sorry. Bye. Bye.

I kept my thumb pressed on the record button. Just held it there, holding the message in my phone, in my hand, ready to let go and send or swipe and erase. I didn't know if it made any sense. I didn't know if she'd even listen to it. But I knew I didn't want to hold on to it any more. I wanted to be brave and honest and hoped I was speaking beautiful words that meant important things.

Then I let go.

28

Before

'Ooo, oooh, what about this one? It's supposed to be really good and the woman who wrote it used to be a stripper.'

I stood in the new release aisle of Blockbusters thrusting the film *Juno* towards my best friend. We had been in there trying to decide on a film for over forty-five minutes. By suggesting *Juno*, I was introducing a wildcard, trying to solve the stalemate going on between her choice of *Slumdog Millionaire* and mine, *The Secret Life of Bees*. We were, at least, able to agree that whatever we watched would be accompanied by a bag of toffee popcorn and a bucket of KFC.

'I think I'm feeling something old school,' she called back over her shoulder. 'An oldie but a goodie.'

'Okay, this is good. We're getting somewhere now. You thinking action, horror, musical or coming-of-age? Or gross-out?'

'Okay, okay, slow your roll, *Film 2008*. Something funny. I just wanna kotch. Switch my brain off for a couple of hours.'

'Got it,' I squealed, before running around the store like a maniac and returning with *Fame*, *Save the Last Dance*, *Flashdance* and both *Step Up* films.

'It's gotta be one of these. All old. All good. All with moves.' She smiled and I knew she was on board.

The Dance Film. My mum had introduced me to musicals which were heavy on the dance aspect at the tender age of two with *Singin' in the Rain*. Swiftly followed by *An American in Paris* and *West Side Story*. By nine I had already graduated to *Dirty Dancing* and *Lambada*. That was because my mum would basically allow me to watch any film with dancing in it, no matter the rating. If it contained a dance sequence, it was therefore a dance film and dance had no age recommendation. For Mum, the message was always: We can move. We are alive. Life is full of joy. Nothing else mattered, including the occasional sex scene.

'*Save the Last Dance*,' Sera said, taking the case from me. The one I hoped she'd pick. I dumped the others on a shelf marked 'ACTION FILMS', which made the sales assistant nearby, who wasn't much older than us, tut demonstratively and walk over in a huff to put them all back where they belonged.

'Why do you love this film so much?' Sera asked. We had watched it together at least half a dozen times. I knew entire monologues. I regularly played the soundtrack on repeat. 'All or Nothing' was my unofficial, personal anthem.

'Because the lead character has the same name as my bestie.'

'No, seriously. Is that what you want to do one day? Dance?'

'Nuh-uh. I am nowhere near good enough. I don't know. My mum told me the other day that I'd make a good nurse. She's so random sometimes.' I picked up *Twilight* and swooned over Robert Pattinson for a second despite the unnatural paleness of his vampiric skin. 'What about you? What do you want to do?' I asked her. There was a pause before she replied, but when she did, it was in an uncensored way. As if she had spent that pause drilling down into the heart of the question of what it meant to do something with your life, not just the job you do every day.

'Make a difference,' she said.

'Okaaaaay. Big t'ings,' I teased with a laugh.

'Forget it. I just realised how wank that sounds,' she countered quickly.

'I'm just playing. It doesn't sound wank. It sounds like you've actually thought about it, which is more than I've done. Maybe you could go, like, work for the UN or something. Or get into politics.'

'Prime Minister Seraphina Caplin? Yeah, sure. You give me jokes, Lay.'

'You'd be sick. I'd vote for you. And my mum. She's basically said she'll vote for anyone who isn't Gordon Brown because he's flopped, so yeah.'

'I'm thinking, like, social worker or lawyer or something.'

'Maybe we should take Sociology together for A level? Do you think they'll offer it? Depends how many people want to do it, I guess,' I said, answering my own question. But I could feel her brooding. Trying to find the words for something. She fiddled with some CDs for a moment before turning to face me.

'Lay. I'm gonna leave.'

'Yeah, let's go. Are we going back to mine or yours?'

'No, I mean, I'm gonna leave school, not stay on for sixth form. I've got an unconditional place at college after exams.'

I had to swallow at least three times to make sure that I wouldn't suddenly burst into tears. Eventually, I was ready to speak again.

'Cool,' I said. 'But why didn't you tell me?'

'I wanted to make my mind up. If I'd chatted to you first, I wouldn't even have gone to the open day. You would've tried to talk me out of it.'

'No I wouldn't. I would have –'

'Lay, you would, because I probably would've done the same if it was you. It's fine. We'll still see each other loads.'

'Will we? Sure you won't find a new Layla your first week there? I bet you do. And she'll instantly be better than me in every way because she'll be in her own garms and not in the same navy-blue get-up we have to wear every day. That's why you're leaving, innit? It's this ugly-arse uniform.'

'No,' she said, laughing at the same time. 'I just want a change. More subjects to choose from. Not being taught by the same uninspiring teachers in the same uninspiring building, day in day out.'

I got my mum's Blockbuster card out and handed it to the cashier to swipe. I had made light of it but the thought of not seeing Sera at school after the summer made me feel all at sea, like I was suddenly drifting and couldn't see land for miles around.

'You'll make a difference whatever you do, by the way. Already have,' I said. Sera was swinging our full carrier bag of Friday-night goodies by her legs in the pop socks she'd brought back into fashion on behalf of the entire year group.

'Shall we have a big night out at Canvas after exams?' she asked me, already knowing the answer would be a resounding:

'Hell to the yes. You know my mum used to go there?'

'No fucking way. How old *is* that place?'

'I know, right. When she first moved to London. It was called Bagley's or something back then. I can't believe we go clubbing at the same place my mum did.'

'Imagine your mum, shacking it out in Canvas. Lipsin' bare manz.' We issued a collective 'ewwwww' and broke down into laughter.

'What if our kids end up in there one day?' she said wistfully.

Just as we were about to reach the door, make our way out into the fading light of the day, she added, 'About college. I haven't told my mum yet. What if she thinks I'm making a mistake?' she said. 'Do you think I should go?'

I thought about it for a moment. What I really wanted to say was, *No. Don't. Please don't. Stay. Keep everything the same, just the way it's always been. I like things just the way they are.* But I surprised myself by doing the exact opposite. It had blown our minds to find out at our first parents' evening in Year 7 that our mums remembered meeting each other at a mother and baby class when we were only a few months old. They lost touch. Sera and I went to different

308

primary schools and then found each other again at the age of eleven. I told myself that her going to college didn't have to change anything. Didn't have to make me want to cry because we were taking different paths. I thought of our lives as two long wavy lines marked out on a piece of paper. The lines ran parallel to each other but every so often they curved in to meet one another, and then they curved away again. And so they would go. Our lifelines would run alongside each other, meeting, touching, overlapping many times before our time on earth was up. They had to. I would make sure they did.

So, giving her my best Sean Patrick Thomas circa 2001 impression, I grabbed her arm dramatically, turned to her and said: 'What do you want? Do you want to do it, Sera? I mean you? Do you want Juilliard?'

'Joker,' she said, laughing at me. And after a moment's thought, instead of worrying about who was around and what they might think, she faced me and said in her best Julia Stiles: 'Fuck it. Yes. I want it. I want Juilliard.'

Then she dropped the bag on the ground, and in perfect unison our voices rang out: 'Lesson one! Left. Right. Left. Right,' as we two-stepped from side to side with our hands in the air while trying to sing the intro to 'U Know What's Up' by Donell Jones with wild abandon, as though we were already in my living room with the DVD playing.

When our fits of giggles finally subsided, she rehooked the bag over one arm, put the other around me and squeezed me towards her in an affectionate side hug so that her cheek pressed up against mine.

29

#MeetTheMcKinnons

We danced to Ella Fitzgerald and Louis Armstrong. He put his hands on my hips and we did our best to remember our YouTube dance lessons while he did that thing with his eyebrows. The smile I flashed back let him know I felt the same and couldn't say it any other way. In fact, I had barely stopped smiling since I'd opened my eyes sometime around 6.15 a.m., unable to sleep for another minute knowing that today was finally the day.

I'd decided to wear my hair au naturel. Bianca had been there bright and early to make it look its best, adding just the right amount of the right kind of product to my curls in the makeshift salon she'd set up in Mum's bedroom. Then Siobhan, Alex and Poonam had arrived and turned the kitchen into something resembling a hotel breakfast buffet. They'd laid on a spread of fresh fruit, smoked salmon bagels, coffee and mimosas, and even though I'd had a few butterflies in my stomach, I'd still had an appetite, so I indulged with Mum, Bianca, the girls and Grandad until I was full. There'd been tunes playing and occasionally there'd be a knock at the front door with deliveries of bouquets and buttonholes, or the photographer arriving. It was like getting dressed up for a big night out with my girlfriends as a teenager and I was all the more at ease for being at my childhood home. Grandad seemed happy enough to let all the giggling and the selfies happen around him while catching up on the highlights of India beating England in the cricket.

My dress felt more luxuriantly weighty than it had at any of my fittings after the girls zipped me in – Poonam crouching down to bring the two sides of the dress together at the base of the zip and Siobhan guiding it up through the mid-section to where Alex had hooked the clasp together at the top. The ivory fabric swept down to a V just under my shoulder blades and there wasn't a sequin out of place. The girls wore matching dresses in different colours. I had little keepsakes for them all to thank them for being there for me, not just then but ever since each of them had come into my life. I could definitely feel them rallying around to fill the best-friend-shaped void in proceedings. I found a moment to take Alex to one side to thank her for being there for Andy while I'd been away too.

'I think I'm the one who should be thanking you, Layla,' she'd said. 'For a long time Andy was just treading water. Then he met you and it was like, finally, my big brother was back. And not everyone gets to count their sister-in-law as their friend. So, yeah. I haven't done too badly out of the whole thing either.'

My mum looked fabulous in a sleek, navy Bardot dress with white orchids embroidered around the bodice. Her gold heels matched her nail varnish and her make-up accentuated the beauty of her brown skin. She reached out to squeeze my right hand from where she sat in her pew as I walked past her on my way towards the altar. But I wasn't walking alone. On my left was Andy, holding my hand, looking out over his side of the congregation in the same way I was, thanking people with his eyes for being there. Neither one of us being given away after all, but advancing, like equals, towards our future together.

Andy put his lips to my ear at least a dozen times during the course of the day to say how incredible I looked and each and every time it made me feel bashful and girlish. If I looked that way, it was partly down to Erica, but even more so, it was down to the fact that I was preposterously happy. Plus, Andy hadn't scrubbed up too badly himself. He'd gone for a navy-black suit with a velvet collar and brown polished Burberry shoes with a tie I'd left at home for him as a gift to open that morning.

When it was time to take family photos, there was one particular shot I had already mentally framed and which would eventually take pride of place on the console table in our hallway. Andy and I were in the middle, and on my side were my mum and Andrea, and on Andy's, Grandad stood shoulder to shoulder with David. After that, the rest of Andy's immediate family had piled in for one more, Alex, Sasha, her husband and the twins dividing themselves equally on either side of Andy and me. It was the first time we had gathered and the union of us, all together, a new family, radiated warmth and goodwill and togetherness in a way I would never forget. Then, when the photographer wanted to take Andy and me off on our own, I saw Andrea seek out Grandad and say, 'Roy, we're all heading to the pub while Andy and Layla finish up the photos. Can I buy you a drink?' And off they went together, Andrea's voice trailing off into the distance telling him that Andy didn't stop talking about his cooking and Grandad's laughter in response fading the further away they got. Andy and I looked on after them and I felt him squeeze my hand. Then we smiled at each other and I knew we were both thinking the same thing. That that was a big moment, a heart-warming thing for us to see happening on our wedding day. But also that it had taken me, his own granddaughter, fifteen years to properly understand what Grandad was saying, so we hoped to hell that Mum would be somewhere nearby to translate.

Best Man Dan's speech was like a scene from *The Greatest Showman*. It included a brief but highly comical re-enactment of the first time Andy told his friends he'd met 'the one', featuring an usher in the role of Andy and Dan playing himself. He'd even roped in some glamorous assistants (all three bridesmaids) to wield signs instructing the audience when to Cheer, Applaud or Boo. It could have missed the mark abysmally, but Dan had the room in hysterics before rounding the whole thing off with heartfelt genuine sentiment about how honoured he was to be Andy's wingman for the wedding and for life. I was glad of all the laughter because Andy's speech, with talk of how we were going to soften the sharp edges of life for each other and live out the rest of our days together, had brought me to my knees.

Mum made a speech too. She'd written it down on index cards and wore her glasses to deliver it. Halfway through, she signalled to Poonam for help. Poonam duly inserted a USB drive into a projector I hadn't organised or even noticed. I could already feel myself blushing. And then a video began to play. I felt the room fade around me as a carefully curated, roughly edited montage of my early years unfurled – grainy, aged footage which could have formed part of an installation at an art gallery. First as a babe in arms, my mother in that beautiful state of exhaustion only a new mother knows. As a toddler running away from Mum then crashing onto the grass in fits of giggles. Grandad made an appearance, waving his hand towards the camera, disapproving of being filmed but smiling nonetheless. Onstage taking a bow at the end of my number in *Oliver!* – after I'd shared the role of Nancy with two other girls. Mum and me on a beach in southern Italy when I was fourteen. I'd been bad-tempered and hormonal for most of the trip, but in that clip I was smiling, eating Pringles from the tube and listening to my long-forgotten MP3 player, those headphones a permanent appendage that year. An outing to Piccadilly Circus and 'Happy Birthday' being sung to me by all the waiters at TGI Fridays, helium balloons attached to my wrists and ponytail. And then there was Sera's cameo. We were eleven or twelve. Dancing, or trying to, copying moves from an old Aaliyah video in my front room. And then another clip of the two of us fast asleep in the middle of a half-completed doll's house we had to build together for a DT project, the sound of my mum giggling off camera while it zooms in on the patches of paint dotted across our young, slumbering faces. From my twenties, there were photos from 10k charity runs I'd done and festivals I'd partied at. Clips from my and Mum's day trip to Venice which the video made look fun and impulsive rather than the exhausting and logistically challenging reality. And then there was me, Mum and Grandad at his house. Andy must have been filming. It was the afternoon I'd invented our own domino-based version of Jenga, stacking the whole set to form a tower before we each took turns to remove them one by one without it falling down. Grandad could be seen, beaming, beside himself to have successfully cleared one from the tower, but also stamping his foot so hard with excitement that the tower had started to wobble which made us all shout and laugh. The final frame of the film was a close-up of me, holding my breath, face full of concentration as I slid a domino out – time itself suspended, everything silent and still. The wedding guests held their breath too as they watched. Eventually the entire tower came crashing down and I looked into the lens, smiling at my husband-to-be on the other side of the camera, and stood up and took a bow. Mum had been documenting my life in all its excitement, mundanity, heartache, happiness, pain, success, triumph and failure quietly, sometimes in front of my very eyes, but mainly in the background, and there it was. It didn't feel embarrassing that everyone had seen it. Mostly it was nice to watch Andy watching it, the way he seemed to be both recognising the parts of me he knew and getting to know me again.

Everyone had eaten and people looked merry and full. The playlist I'd carefully curated was beginning to shift into evening mode and people were starting to mill around the room so I was hopeful that, despite the limited space in the restaurant, there would soon be dancing. I bumped into Andy's mum at a display table we'd managed to squeeze into the bar area. She picked up the picture of her and Andy's father on their wedding day. An ornate glass frame held the photo of his dad in a kilt and her in a satin puffball dress with small yellow flowers adorning the neckline.

'I don't look very happy there.'

'Andy said something about a run-in with a bumblebee?'

'God, that's right. We'd just come out of the church, and somehow it flew under my dress and got caught in one of the skirts, stinging me all the way up my leg. David had to practically rip the whole thing off me behind a bush until we saw it drop out. Couldn't fly any more, poor little thing. An auspicious start.'

'That's what they say, the worst weddings make the best marriages.'

'And how is your day going? Enjoying it?'

'Oh, I'm having a terrible time. Awful.'

'Yes, the best worst wedding I've been to,' she agreed. We both laughed and I felt a new closeness, one we hadn't striven for during the wedding preparations. I knew that Andy had continued talking to his family about what had been going on in the lead-up to the day. That he'd explained everything as he understood it when he returned the ring to his dad while I was in Jamaica. But Andrea, David and I hadn't spoken about it. Eventually the time would come when we'd have to, when it could no longer be avoided. But for now, it was enough that they'd changed the venue for their anniversary. And I knew that it wouldn't always be easy, but they were my family now and they were trying. It felt like the kind of moment we should end on a hug. But neither of us made the first move. Still, we smiled warmly at one another, acknowledging our new relationship. Mother-in-law and daughter-in-law, come what may. And off we drifted, back to our husbands.

It was the first time I'd been on my own all day. I'd clocked Andy dancing like a man possessed with his tie knotted around his head like a bandana, oblivious to where I was. I could see my mum dancing with Andy's dad and thought there was no better sight. I hoped someone somewhere was catching it on camera. I quietly slipped out into the gardens at the back of the restaurant. I hitched my dress up past my ankles and removed my heels one by one before tiptoeing through the grass to the bottom of the gentle slope which ran from the restaurant to a solitary tree. I only wanted to be away from the festivities for five minutes. I wanted to look back at the building and take it in, be outside of it all for a moment.

I rubbed the skin under the strap of Cynthia's watch on my left wrist and then reached into one of the pockets I'd told Erica my dress must have, so that I could hide my hands whenever I felt shy or overcome by the gaze of so many people. I felt around and found it, grateful that it was still there and hadn't fallen out when Andy had spun me round to that Stevie Wonder song. One of Grandad's dominoes. I sought out its paint-filled nooks with my thumb. It had two of them. One at each end. I imagined a long line of them, a whole set snaking across a table. The creation of a long line from individual parts. Like a family, and this, the next piece. Us.

30

The first day of teaching at the beginning of a new term always filled me with nervous excitement. It was impossible to deny how much I was like one of my students when it came to going back to school in the first week of September. I would treat myself to new stationery, a new outfit. I'd get up an hour earlier so that I would have time to ease myself into the day. That day, the first thing I did after opening my eyes was turn over and put my arm around Andy. His body rocked gently as he inhaled and exhaled, still deeply asleep. I kissed the skin between his shoulders and climbed out of bed without waking him.

On the Tube, I scrolled through my phone. I kept finding photos I hadn't seen from our wedding day which had automatically saved to my camera roll from all the messages I'd received after the big day. I liked that it had been captured from so many angles, the way it looked different through each lens. Mum's had all been of family, Andy's parents, the children who were there. I especially liked the paparazzi, fly-on-the-wall shot of Poonam and Best Man Dan lost in conversation, almost nose to nose, talking as though the rest of the room wasn't there. The caption read, 'Always a bridesmaid???? I think not!' I got off the Tube and walked along the high street towards school. I had my 'Get up and Go' playlist ringing loud in my ears and my mind was already several strides ahead of me wondering what the year had in store, not just for me but for my kids. How the faculty would change, and whether it was time for me to take the leap and move to a different school, take on more responsibility. It was a clear day but the wind was strong, I pushed against it as I walked and I thought about doing that thing I used to do when I would see if the wind could keep me from falling over if I leaned into it. Then I took a deep breath, walked through the school gates and headed for the staffroom.

She was there. Even though I had played over in my mind how I would react to seeing her again, how I'd handle it and what I'd say, I found myself inert, nervous, wanting to leave the room, to try to avoid her. She looked up as I entered but carried on talking to someone I didn't recognise. I put my bag down on a nearby chair without looking at her too obviously and went back across the room to boil the kettle. I stood, facing it, watching the steam rise, burying my attention deeply in the rumble of the boiling water. The sound of it melded with the ambient chatter of the other teachers regaling each other with how they had spent their summers, their pleas for another six weeks off. I became so lost in it that when I felt her hand on my shoulder, I jumped in surprise.

'Hi,' she said.

'Hi.' I breathed out and waited for the kettle to click off. 'I'm making tea – do you want one?'

'Your hair's looking blonde.'

'That Spanish sun,' I said, 'I wasn't ready for it.' She laughed and it felt genuine. It was a familiar sound I had missed.

'No tea, thanks. I've got a meeting before my first lesson, so . . .'

I poured the water over a mint tea bag in my cup and watched the colour seep out.

'But you're good, yeah?' she said.

'Yeah. I'm good.'

'Happy new year.'

'Happy new year.'

It was an in-joke. The day before school restarted was our very own, unofficial New Year's Eve. A bigger occasion than the real one in December. It would usually be spent at her place. Music blaring, we'd sit on the balcony, looking out over Holloway, the peripheries of Highbury and up towards Highgate. We'd arrange our wine glasses on her little bistro table, and try to keep in mind that the next day wouldn't be a bank holiday but a real working one we'd need to be bright-eyed and bushy-tailed for.

She turned to leave. I prodded at the tea bag with a spoon until I was satisfied it had imparted enough flavour.

'Oh and it wasn't excessive – the lace. You pulled it off.'

I wondered which photo had made her say that. If it was one in particular, one which had encouraged her to end the stalemate, inch back towards me, reach out her hand. But then she said, 'At least from where I was standing.' And whatever I'd planned to say next caught

321

in my throat and stayed there. I knew then she had seen me with her own eyes, that day, even if I hadn't been able to see her with mine.

A wall of sound hit me as I entered the classroom. Excited chatter, laughter, the occasional 'Shut up', 'Don't lie!' 'Did she?' and 'Aw, missed you too, babe'.

My arrival went undetected for several moments. I put my bag down, then my file. I went round the room placing a term planner in front of each pupil along with a smile or a brief 'Hello, Celeste' or 'Hi, Mahad' or 'Nice to be back, Amelia?' if they happened to pause their conversations to look up and acknowledge me.

Gradually, as I stood at the board ready to begin, the swell of noise subsided, eyes turned in my direction and the room fell silent.

'Good morning. Welcome back.'

'Good morning, Miss McKinnon,' rang out in near unison.

'Let's try something, just for fun. A slightly unconventional start to the term. Everyone up for that?' I asked rhetorically. 'There won't be any marks for this. You don't even have to hand it in if you choose not to, but let's try it, as a way to set the tone for the year ahead. A hugely important one for you all.'

The silence persisted and I could tell I had them intrigued.

'You won't need your textbooks. No notes, no handouts. Nothing. For the next ten minutes I'd like you to free-write, in English, about . . . well, you. We can work on translating them and, who knows, they could even form the basis of your mock orals next term.'

Thirty-two faces stared at me blankly. There was a smattering of bemused laughter but I carried on.

'Today, I'm interested in the history of you and so should you be. Where do you come from? What's brought you to where you are? How do you define yourself? And why does it matter?'

I paused for a moment, seeing their minds begin to start up and turn over like engines beginning to rev.

'You might already know exactly what you're going to write, or you might have more questions than you do answers about little old you. Write those down too.' I was holding the room, holding my breath, waiting for their buy-in. I almost had it, I was sure of it. 'You won't make the ten o'clock news. The world might never know your name. And that's okay. All that matters is that you do.'

At that, some of the kids picked up their pens, lowered their heads and began writing hurriedly. Others stared out of the window or down at their fingernails, trying to generate some feelings on the matter or to disregard the assignment entirely, happy to let the ten minutes pass by without writing a single word. Some looked like they wanted to know how to get the right answer, how to approach the task so that it would please me. But I wanted it to please them. Generally, though, the room was quiet. I took something from that, knowing that I had at least sparked a thought process.

'And, class. One more thing. It's not Miss any more. It's Mrs. Mrs McKinnon.'

I sat down behind my desk, leaned back in my chair and drew my hands together. Thirty-two pairs of eyes looked back at me. Took me in and seemed to accept me – me and my definition of myself. This was my offering to them and their definition of themselves. It was an exchange. Like everything in life, I supposed, a process of giving and receiving between people simply trying to work out how to be alive without hurting too many others along the way.

'Shouldn't throw you too much,' I added. 'Same spelling. Different person.'

Acknowledgements

To Amy St Johnston – our conversations over Zoom during those early stages and tentative first pages gave me the confidence to believe that I had the ability to finish this book and that, when I did, it would be something to be proud of. Thank you for your exuberance for the story and for all your support, editorial and otherwise. I got lucky when the first 5,000 words found its way into your inbox.

To Becky Hardie, editor extraordinaire! I remember our first meeting when you asked me if I was ready – *really ready* – for the work that was to come. I said 'yes' without fully knowing what it meant! But I think I knew then that, whatever happened, both *Dominoes* and I were in safe hands. The story within these pages is, quite simply, better for every question, idea, provocation and suggestion you put to me during the edit. I have been so lucky to have your expertise and guidance. Thanks, too, to early Vintage readers Nicole Jashapara and Ruby Fatimilehin, and to Asia Choudhry at Chatto.

Andrea Walker, thank you for connecting with the story so strongly, for championing it Stateside and for all of your encouragement and support.

Beth Coates, if you hadn't told me to keep going, there's every chance I wouldn't have! Thank you for telling me there was something there and that it could be something more.

To Jane Kirby and the rest of the team at Chatto and Vintage, thank you, thank you for all your hard work. I am ever grateful.

Tamasha and Hachette, thank you for planting the seed that playwrights could also be novelists and for seeking to diversify the publishing landscape.

Thank you to everyone who supported *Dominoes* when it was a one-woman show and I was just a crazy person parading around in my real-life wedding dress in rehearsal rooms from Poole to Edinburgh. Ann Akinjirin, Stephen Wrentmore, Jonathan Kennedy, Evie Holdcroft, Joseph Ed Thomas, Anne Mulleners, Craig Griffith, Richard Webb. That was how it started. This is how it's going. Thank you for being there in the very beginning.

Thank you to Courtney Plank at Six in the City and Oliver Wainwright at the *Guardian* for the tour and the article 'A slavery tour of London: the guided walk laying bare atrocities of the past' respectively. These were both great sources of inspiration for my (and Layla's) research.

Nik Maclean, you may not know this, but you are a source of inspiration for me. As a teacher, as a mother and as a friend. Thank you for reading an early draft. Thank you for saying that one of the chapters would make a great lesson for your English class. Thank you for educating me that there is no way in hell any actual teaching would take place on the final day of term before the summer holidays, no matter how much I wanted it to for my story, and thank you for every other insight you've given me to your profession.

To Leo at Apple 69, La Fortuna, Costa Rica. Thank you for evicting the ants from the little nest they'd made for themselves in the motherboard of my laptop during our trip just before my deadline. It still freaks me out to think that was the problem. *Pura Vida!*

To all my friends. My sincerest gratitude for every encouraging message, every supportive word and for every time you asked me how the book was going. And for the distractions whenever I needed one.

To the Taylors. Laurence, Carol, Lauren, William, Jenny. I am very lucky to have you all in my life. Thank you for welcoming me into your family.

Ashanti, Taja and Greg, Joe, I couldn't have asked for better. Thank you for cheering me on, for pepping me up and for all the laughs along the way. You're my best friends.

Mum, I don't think you know how amazing you are. So, here it is. Me, telling you, in a book with *our* family name on the front cover. Because of you, I can confidently tell my daughter that chasing her dreams is as essential as breathing. I will be there for her every day, the way you've been there for me. I will tell her that anything is possible, even when you have to take a sidestep or two along the way to stay in the game. I love you, so much.

Grandma, heroine. Windrush immigrant. Fighter. Thank you for all your sacrifices.

Grandad, soothsayer. Windrush immigrant. Legend. I know you're still smashing dominoes and knocking back whisky. Thank you for the sanctuary of that house.

And to my Ed and Etta-Spaghetta. One word ... Guuuyyysssss!

Phoebe McIntosh is an actor and playwright from London. She wrote and performed in a sell-out run of her first play, *The Tea Diaries*, at the Edinburgh Fringe Festival in 2013, followed by her solo show, *Dominoes*, which toured the South East and London in 2018. She has completed the Soho Theatre Writers' Lab programme, and her most recent full-length play, *The Soon Life*, was shortlisted and highly commended for the Tony Craze Award as well as being longlisted for the Alfred Fagon Award. Phoebe won a place on the inaugural Tamasha x Hachette creative writing programme in 2018 and was also selected for the Penguin Random House WriteNow programme in 2020. *Dominoes* was longlisted for the Bath Novel Award 2021.